What others are saying . . .

"If you're looking for a holiday-themed read that will warm your heart but also make you think, *A Very Bavarian Christmas* is the perfect pick! The storyline and characters draw you in from the get-go and you'll find yourself relating to their struggles, cheering for their victories, and being reminded that everyone needs grace and kindness, because we never know what it's been like to walk in their shoes."

~CRYSTAL PAINE, New York Times bestselling author, podcaster, and founder of MoneySavingMom.com

"Just in time to remind us all of the hope still waiting at the end of a hard year, comes Katie Reid's *A Very Bavarian Christmas*. Let her reluctant ornament decorator, Holly, remind you why home is a beacon, healing a gift, and how love, like hot chocolate and the meaning of Christmas, can warm you from the inside."

~LISA-JO BAKER, bestselling author of *Never Unfriended* and podcast co-host of Out of the Ordinary

"Bavarian Falls is the capital city of Christmas, and Holly Noel is its most reluctant citizen. Sparkling with humor and radiating with warmth, *A Very Bavarian Christmas* is a heartwarming tale in which Christmas spirit is abundant, but not without strings attached. Fans of Hallmark's Countdown to Christmas will be swept away by this powerful journey of healing, reconciliation, and the second chances we must allow ourselves to take."

~BETHANY TURNER, award-winning author of *The Secret Life of Sarah Hollenbeck* and *Hadley Beckett's Next Dish*

"Author Katie Reid shares an honest, true-to-life story of love and loss, acceptance and forgiveness. As heartwarming as a cup of hot cocoa and filled with authentic, memorable characters, *A Very Bavarian Christmas* will transport you to a world where romance and real life, heartache and promise converge, all generously sprinkled with Christmas magic."

~KATE BATTISTELLI, author of *The God Dare*

"I am not exaggerating when I tell you I literally could not put this book down. I read it in one sitting. The plot took me right into the holiday-loving town. I could picture the scenes as if they were my favorite Hallmark Movie. Happy holiday feels filled my heart as the plot and excellent character development drew me right in."

~JENNIFER HAND, Executive Director of Coming Alive Ministries, author of *My Yes is on the Table*

"*A Very Bavarian Christmas* is the perfect cozy read. As a perfectionist who fears failure and the dreaded 'not living up to my potential' more than anything, I identified so much with the main character of this book. And as a self-proclaimed holiday movie superfan, I adored the setting of a Christmas store in a Christmas town during the Christmas season! For anyone who struggles with a life that doesn't meet her hopes and expectations or anyone who loves sweet romantic comedies with a holiday twist, this book is a gift for every season!"

~MARY CARVER, host of The Couch podcast and co-author of *Fake Snow & Real Faith*

"*A Very Bavarian Christmas* is everything you want in a story to delight you over the holidays! I hope this is the first of many novels from Katie Reid!"

~AMBER LIA, bestselling co-author of *Triggers* and *Marriage Triggers*

A Very BAVARIAN Christmas

A Very BAVARIAN Christmas

by KATIE M. REID

A Very Bavarian Christmas
Published by Mountain Brook Ink
White Salmon, WA U.S.A.

All rights reserved. Except for brief excerpts for review purposes, no part of this book may be reproduced or used in any form without written permission from the publisher.

The website addresses shown in this book are not intended in any way to be or imply an endorsement on the part of Mountain Brook Ink, nor do we vouch for their content.

This story is a work of fiction. All characters and events are the product of the author's imagination. Any resemblance to any person, living or dead, is coincidental.

Scripture quotations are taken from the King James Version of the Bible. Public domain.
ISBN 9781953957-47-4
© 2024 Katie M. Reid

The Team: Miralee Ferrell, Tim Pietz, Kristen Johnson, Cindy Jackson
Cover Design: Indie Cover Design, Lynnette Bonner Designer

Mountain Brook Ink is an inspirational publisher offering fiction you can believe in.
Printed in the United States of America

Dedication

To the real Holly Noel:
You are the Christmas Queen, my friend.
Grateful for you and your Holly-day cheer.
To Bethany Turner, Robin Jones Gunn, and Annie F. Downs:
You played a big part in inspiring me to write this.
To the thirty-something who can relate:
I see you, and He does, too.

Contents

Chapter One: Annoying Music
Chapter Two: Bittersweet Traditions
Chapter Three: The Single Jingle
Chapter Four: Unmet Expectations
Chapter Five: Ribbon Curling Standards
Chapter Six: Risky Gift-Giving
Chapter Seven: Fainting Spells
Chapter Eight: Big Crowds
Chapter Nine: Frank Conversations
Chapter Ten: Crossing Boundaries
Chapter Eleven: Frenzied and Fanatic Shoppers
Chapter Twelve: Heart-Breakery
Chapter Thirteen: Winter Blues
Chapter Fourteen: Unsolicited Advice
Chapter Fifteen: Scavenger Hunt
Chapter Sixteen: Extra Weight
Chapter Seventeen: No Guarantee
Chapter Eighteen: The Yes of Christmas
Chapter Nineteen: Ice Fest
Chapter Twenty: Heart Turn

Author Note
Sneak Peek of Book Two
Book Club Questions for A Very Bavarian Christmas
Acknowledgments

CHAPTER ONE
Annoying Music

HOLLY COULDN'T BELIEVE THIS WAS HER actual life. She begrudgingly tied on her red apron and plastered on a forced, albeit festive, smile as she pushed through the swinging doors that led from the break room to the sprawling showroom of Neumann's, otherwise known as the mile-long Christmas store. Every hour, on the hour, a message rang throughout the store: "*Willkommen* to Neumann's—a mile of Christmas joy for every girl and boy. Whether you're one or a hundred and two, we've got something special just for you. Happy shopping!"

As she made her way to her workstation, Holly wondered why on earth she had let her mother talk her into working at Neumann's. "It's the Most Wonderful Time of the Year" swelled from the rafters, but a "Bah humbug" anthem retorted in Holly's heart.

This was never the plan.

Holly sighed and tightened her brunette messy bun before taking her position behind the ornament personalization counter. Moving back to her hometown of Bavarian Falls to regroup as a thirty-year-old had not been part of Holly's life goals. But here she was, on her fifth day of work, applying her art degree to fragile ornaments.

"Hey, Holly. Ready to make someone's holiday brighter?" her co-worker Andy playfully nudged her shoulder.

"I'll do my darnedest, but truthfully, Christmas and I aren't the best pairing. Reason #1? The music of the season drives me crazy."

"How could you not adore this soundtrack of yuletide

bliss?" Andy swayed his head to the rhythm of the music.

Holly counted the reasons on each finger of her left hand, starting with her thumb. "It's cheesy, predictable, lacks depth, won't get out of your head, and assumes everyone is happy during the holidays."

"Tell me how you really feel," Andy tipped his head to one side, eyebrows raised.

Although they hadn't known each other long, Andy reminded Holly of her older brother, Gabe, particularly because teasing was his preferred method of communication.

"Don't worry. Your secret's safe with me, Holly-girl," Andy placed his hand over his heart.

Holly flashed him a genuine smile as she picked up her clipboard with the printed spreadsheet of custom orders. "I don't understand why we can't use a computer instead of this clipboard."

"But that would be out of place now, wouldn't it?" Andy chuckled, gesturing to the time capsule of Christmas nostalgia that surrounded them.

"Hullllooo! Holly! I've got good news to deliver." The singsong voice of the store manager, Ms. Betty Jo Wilson, reverberated through the store.

If ever there was a woman who embodied Christmas cheer, she was it. With her rosy cheeks, blinking necklace that lit up brighter than Rudolph's nose and had a setting that could induce a seizure, and obnoxious socks that jingled as she walked, Betty Jo was one-of-a-kind.

"Special delivery for Miss Holly Noel! Your beloved nametag has arrived, and now you are…official. An official member of the Neumann family," the store manager cooed.

"Um…thanks, Betty Jo. Wow, my first *and* middle names, huh? I haven't been called by both names since…"

"I couldn't resist. I mean…is there a more perfect name for a Neumann's employee than Holly Noel? It made my day."

"Why…um, thank you."

"Now there's one thing left to do before I'm off to straighten up Station 10," Betty Jo explained in a loud whisper. "The angel ornaments end up in such disarray after the preschool groups visit. Those little cherubs act like little devils sometimes."

At this heretical admission, Betty Jo snort-laughed. "I digress. The matter at hand, or should I say, in my hand, is to present you with this nametag, Neumann's style."

Andy tried to muffle his laughter as Holly fought to maintain her composure.

"We have a tradition here, Miss Holly Noel, that you probably aren't aware of. When a new employee has been here for a week with satisfactory results, I pin on their nametag. Disclaimer, I've only poked two employees to the point of shedding blood."

Holly's eyes widened as Betty Jo repeated her snort-laugh.

"It was only a dab of blood, dear, that's all. I promise. I had you a tad worried, didn't I?" She offered one last snort-laugh for good measure.

"As I was saying, I will pin this nametag on your cute self as our theme music plays. Any employee within reasonable walking distance will join in singing, as we *willkommen* you to the Neumann's family."

Andy's knowing smile met Holly's you-knew-about-this glare as Betty Jo busted out her walkie-talkie to let the higher-up know it was time to cue the music.

N is for Nativity…that celebrates the Savior's birth.
E is for Emmanuel…Christmas is with us every day.
U is for the Unique ways…we spread this yuletide cheer.
M is for…"

Betty Jo, Andy, and a handful of employees—who'd hustled over from their stations as soon as they heard the opening notes of the theme song—jubilantly sang their hearts out. Andy was loudest of all. After N-E-U-M-A-N-N-S was spelled out and the final chord resounded, Holly's official nametag was pinned on her apron by Betty Jo.

Spoiler alert: no blood shed.

After the loyal entourage dispersed, Holly and Andy turned their attention back to the custom orders. Holly bit the right side of her lip as she concentrated on her first ornament of the day. As she rotated the silver ornament to add a flourish, the reflection of her nametag caught her eye and led her down memory lane.

"And behold, she shall be called, Holly Noel Brigham."

Holly wasn't there when her name was first declared, but every December 24, when a birthday candle was added to her cake, Holly's beloved Grandpa Dale recounted the moment.

"Your mama was big as a barn that Thanksgiving Day—ready to pop like a turkey." Grandpa paused the infamous account to briefly brush Holly's cheek with his weathered hand.

"Now, where was I?"

"The turkey," Holly wiggled in her chair.

"Ah, yes. The turkey. You see, your mama and dad could not agree on a name for you. They tossed around names like Wynter, Mary, Jeannette, and Isabella, but they couldn't come to a consensus for their second born, who was due around Jesus' birthday. Dinner was getting cold, and I had a hankering for cornbread stuffing, so I interrupted their debate with my own idea for a name that would be worthy of my granddaughter."

Holly joined in, as she and Grandpa Dale repeated his well-worn words, first spoken over her mom's bulging belly circa 1993: "And behold, she shall be called, Holly Noel Brigham."

And the rest is history.

"Holly…Holly…" Andy waved his hands in front of her as she stared off in the direction of the Precious Moments display.

"Earth to Holly."

"Gosh, so sorry. What do you need? I mean, how can I help you?"

"Just because you have your official nametag now, Holly-girl, doesn't mean you are entitled to head off to La La Land. Look, here comes our favorite customer."

Holly tried to focus on the task before her—pleasing Mrs. Rasmussen. It was going to be a long day for sure.

"Are all four ornaments ready this time? I'm late for a lunch date with Dr. Rasmussen, but I dashed over here after my hair appointment to make sure they are ready and perfecto for my little darlings."

Holly swallowed hard, unable to think of anything nice to say. Donna Rasmussen was one of Neumann's most frequent customers, but she was not the easiest to get along with. This much Holly knew, after only a week on the job.

Mrs. Rasmussen's bright white teeth were contrasted by her out-of-season tan—the result of a recent Caribbean cruise with her husband. She flashed a wide smile in Andy's direction. "You know, Henry doesn't understand why I get my darlings new ornaments every year."

"These are definitely collectibles. They're imported from Italy. You have great taste, ma'am."

"Oh, Andy, always the charmer. Thanks for being on my side."

Holly carefully retrieved the delicate ornaments from behind the counter for Mrs. Rasmussen to inspect, *again*. Earlier in the week, Holly had been tasked with her first ornament personalization order. In the process, she had accidentally misspelled a few of Mrs. Rasmussen's grandchildren's names. The blunder had not been well received. As badly as Holly felt, she couldn't help but wonder what the adult children of Dr. and Mrs. Rasmussen were like, since they'd given their kids such unusual names.

"Let me take a closer look." Mrs. Rasmussen relied on her turquoise-rimmed bifocals to bring clarity to her thorough inspection. "Hmm, okay. Let's see…" She inspected each stroke of Holly's hand lettering on the fancy ornaments. The seconds seemed to crawl through molasses as she continued to evaluate Holly's handiwork.

Holly's jaw clenched. She was sure she had gotten it right this time. In fact, it had taken her a whole hour to redo Hildebrandt. Try hand lettering that on a glass ornament that was only four inches in diameter.

"Okay. And, we're done!"

Holly tightened her lips and filled her cheeks with air.

"I am sorry to report that you two won't see me again until next week because, Holly, you've passed the test. I won't need you to redo any of them—these are just right for my little darlings."

Holly hadn't realized she was holding her breath until an exhale of relief emerged sharply.

Mrs. Rasmussen was satisfied. It was a Christmas miracle. Technically, it was a November 6th miracle, according to the life-sized Countdown-to-Christmas calendar adjacent to Station 8.

"I promised Henry I wouldn't buy any more decorations—well, this week, anyway. I'll pay for these gems today, but I promise I'll be back on Monday for the new additions to my Christmas village. Can't wait to add to my collection. Henry turned his pool table over to me because my Christmas village keeps growing. I told him we might have to buy another pool table so my village can continue to expand."

Suddenly a distorted version of Robert Palmer's "Bad Case of Loving You" blared over the holiday carols, interrupting Mrs. Rasmussen's pool-table-turned-Christmas-village narrative. She fumbled to retrieve her phone before the ringtone reached the chorus.

"It's Henry," she hurriedly explained. "Gotta run to the checkout. I'm late." She turned on a sugary greeting for her husband. "Hi, Hunky. I'm on my way! Sorry, but I had to make a quick stop." She flashed her pearly whites as she whispered, "Can one of you carry the ornaments to the checkout while I finish this call?"

"Sure thing." Andy volunteered, much to Holly's relief. He carefully put the lid on the box of fragile ornaments and made his way to the nearest cashier with Mrs. Rasmussen in tow.

"Yes, of course, Henry, I'll be there in ten…mwah!" The dentist's wife pursed her bright pink lips toward her phone and let them smack like an exclamation point. Then she called over her shoulder to Holly, "You know what, I'll take a picture of my darlings' faces when I present these beauties to them. Then you'll understand why I can't resist spoiling them."

"Sounds good," Holly said with an obligatory wave. She added the German greeting for "bye" for good measure. "*Auf Wiedersehen*, Mrs. Rasmussen."

Whew. Holly was glad that was over. Now, back to the custom orders on her clipboard.

Ten minutes passed, and Andy had not returned. Holly assumed Mrs. R. had convinced him to load her custom ornaments into her BMW and maybe even serve as chauffeur to her lunch date with Hunky—err, Dr. Rasmussen.

Crash.

Jingle.

Clank.

Jingle.

Thud.

"Ugh."

Had the "ugh" been an octave higher, Holly might have suspected that Betty Jo had tripped over the wedding ornament display, due to the jingles and all. But no, it wasn't the manager that ruined Holly's concentration, causing her to turn a "J" into a "U" on her ornament. The "ugh" originated from someone else.

He was lean and towering, with a boyish face and trendy-rimmed glasses that had one hundred percent been ordered from a popular eyeglass website. Holly estimated he was in his mid-twenties. He was quite a spectacle, all legs and wedding ornaments tangled in a clumsy contortion. He quickly stood, his blushing cheeks matching his red Neumann's vest as he tried to reassemble the disrupted display.

Holly's frustration dissipated as she realized how embarrassed this guy was. She set down her now-ruined ornament and hurried over to help.

"Oh man, I'm—I'm really sorry about the racket..." he stammered as his baby blues met Holly's brown eyes.

Holly diverted her attention to a stray ornament that had rolled out of reach—a result of the crash between the lanky human and the wedding display. She moved to retrieve it when the tall glass of water himself grabbed her forearm.

"No, wait, please. You don't have to do that. I mean, I appreciate it and all. But you shouldn't have to clean up my mess."

Holly met his eager gaze again.

"I'm Frank." He untangled himself and stood to shake her hand.

"Frank from the Falls? That's unfortunate." Holly sucked in a breath, wishing she could pull the idiotic words back into her mouth that floated in the air between them. It wasn't the first time she found herself saying out loud what she should have kept to herself.

"I know, right?" Frank laughed freely at Holly's teasing comment. "I'm surprised we haven't met before. You must be new here?"

"Not new to Bavarian Falls—but new to Frank from the Falls."

Insert foot in mouth.

Frank crossed his arms in apparent amusement as if settling into a front row seat to Holly's awkwardness.

"And new to working here. It's my first week, so, yeah, I got pinned today…I mean, uh, you know, got my official nametag." She didn't want to be rude, so she quickly shook his waiting hand.

"Holly Noel. Wow, look who's talking—that's quite the perfect name for this place, now, isn't it?

"So I've been told." Holly glanced back at her workstation.

Where is Andy?

"It's a pleasure to meet you," Frank, bowed in a gesture of welcome.

"Uh, thanks. Hey, if you have this under control, I need to get back to work. I don't think the customer who was expecting 'Jeremiah' on an ornament will appreciate 'Ueremiah' instead."

"Huh?"

"Never mind. Nice to meet you, Frank." Holly turned on her heels faster than she could spell *Ueremiah*.

She darted behind the counter and spotted Andy heading her way.

"What took you so long?" Holly planted her fists on her hips.

"Don't ask."

"Ugh."

It was Frank again, giving a sheepish expression and shrug in Holly's and Andy's direction after hearing a final *crunch* beneath his feet.

Holly blew a stray hair from her forehead as she began another ornament for J-e-r-e-m-i-a-h. The aptness and annoyingness of "Christmas in a Small Town" playing over the speakers was not lost on her.

No further run-ins with Betty Jo, Mrs. Rasmussen, or flailing Frank allowed Holly to complete sixteen hand-painted ornaments before five o'clock chimed inside the store. Finally, she was free from the arena of holiday hubbub…at least until Monday morning.

CHAPTER TWO
Bittersweet Traditions

A HARSH GUST OF WIND GREETED Holly as the automatic doors opened to the parking lot. She pulled her fur-lined collar around her neck to ward off the November air. The gray Midwestern sky matched her mood. She pulled out her car keys and walked swiftly to her blue Prius. The dent in its front bumper mirrored the dent in her bank account and her heart.

Once in the driver's seat, Holly rubbed her ice-cold hands together, willing the circulation to improve as she waited for her car to warm up. She decided against turning on the radio. Her ears needed a reprieve from the constant stream of Christmas music played at N-E-U-M-A-N-N-S.

In the biting silence, Holly let out a sigh, taking stock of her present situation.

She'd moved back to her hometown, taken a seasonal job all about the holiday that hurt her the most, and to top it off, she was living at home again—at the ripe old age of thirty—like a cliché Christmas movie.

Yep. That about summed it up.

Holly could almost picture it: heartbroken single girl moves home to sort out her disappointing life. She and the most eligible bachelor in town—who resembles a modern Mr. Darcy—run into each other in the baking section of the local grocery store.

Holly took creative liberties with the fictional storyline, to protect the innocent...

Within a week, heartbroken girl in cliché Christmas movie decides her hometown isn't so bad after all.

But there is one dilemma. How will she ever fund her dream

of opening a bakery?

Holly's imagination filled in the solution. After a few minutes of mental anguish, a homing pigeon lands on said girl's windowsill with a tiny scroll affixed to its neck, tied with a scarlet thread and a sprig of holly for good measure. Girl unrolls the scroll—making sure the animal is not harmed in the process—and finds a familiar address written on it in tiny calligraphy. Girl throws on her down coat but doesn't waste time zipping it. She arrives at her destination, lungs burning from the winter chill.

Could it be true?

Yes, of course! The charming movie bachelor has secretly funded her childhood dream of opening a bakery downtown in the brick building she had her eye on—because he's loaded, naturally.

Fast forward to the grand opening of the gifted bakery, aptly named Heart-Breakery—a nod to the owner's once bitter heart turned sweet.

Her most popular item on the menu? Bottomless break-up fro-yo—half the calories to ensure you don't have two things to cry about. If that's not sugary enough, the couple finally kisses outside the bakery seconds before the closing credits roll. Cue the idyllic snowflakes that appear as a magical backdrop for their newfound, delicious, and predictable love.

Bzzzt. Bzzzt.

An incoming text snapped Holly from her glucose-saturated holiday cynicism.

Have u escaped the snow globe yet?

Holly smiled, responding to her childhood friend, Elaine.

Almost! Weird day. When are you done at the inn?

In an hour. C U at 7, right?

Holly confirmed with a thumbs up before she began the drive home.

Exiting the parking lot, she sped past the *Stille Nacht* Sanctuary, trying to avoid eye contact with the gleaming monument.

Holly added a voice memo to the Notes app on her phone, "Reason #2: Bittersweet Traditions."

She had decided to keep an official tally of the reasons why she was not a fan of Christmas. She wasn't sure what she would do with the list, but for the time being, it satisfied her angst.

Driving past the sanctuary had fueled the second reason. Often "Silent Night" was the last carol sung at Christmas Eve services, while drippy candle wax burned hands and the wonder of the season warmed hearts. But what were once anticipated traditions, like attending the Christmas Eve service, now sparked painful memories for the beloved daughter of Carl Brigham.

For the first seven years of her life, Holly loved the fact that her birthday was on Christmas Eve. Her parents made a point of picking out an extra special birthday gift for her to open after the Christmas Eve service. Grandpa Dale and Grandma Bea, her mother's parents, came over to help celebrate as they all enjoyed a lavish spread of appetizers ranging from German cheeses with crackers to Buckeye cookies to shrimp cocktail.

Holly's older brother by three years teased her endlessly about her name and the date on which her birthday fell.

"You should have been born on October 31, li'l sis. Then you would've been guaranteed as much candy as you wanted instead of only candy canes. And then we could call you Hollyween, instead of Holly Noel." Gabe guffawed.

"Ha, ha! Maybe you should have been born on Christmas,

Gabe-riel, since you announced Jesus's birth to Mary all those years ago."

"Hardy har har." Gabe rolled his eyes as he walked out of the living room.

While Grandma Bea helped Holly's mom put the finishing touches on her birthday cake and Grandpa Dale went to locate Gabe, Holly and her dad were left in the living room, accompanied by the colored lights on the piney-fresh tree. Dad insisted on getting a real Christmas tree each year, much to the protest of mom's allergies. Only a Balsam fir would do.

"It's quite a special night, isn't it, Holly Noel?"

"Yeah, I guess. But I'm not sure I like my birthday being so close to Christmas anymore. Maybe Gabe is right. It'd be nice to have my birthday at a different time of year. Gabe gets presents in June, and a pool party, and he gets to go to Sugar Shock for ice cream, and…"

"Oh, sweet girl. *You* are the lucky one. Your birthday is closest to Jesus's birth. And He must have known you'd be exceptional at spreading Holly-day cheer, too." He chuckled at his corny pun.

"Oh, Dad." Holly's lip started quivering.

"What is it, honey? Did I upset you with my teasing?"

"It's not that. It's just, well, this year is different because you'll be gone soon. Y'know?"

"Yes, I know."

A salty tear escaped from her brown eyes, paired with an involuntary sniffle. Holly fiddled with the hem of her velvety dress, avoiding eye contact with her dad. She didn't know why she was crying. It wasn't as though her father hadn't been deployed before, but this time felt different. He moved closer to her on the sofa, placing his hand on hers.

"I know it's hard that I'm leaving soon. But I'm asking you to be brave. Braver than ever before. It reminds me of something I read once: 'We each carry our own brand of courage…yours in the letting go, mine in the holding on.'"

Holly crinkled her nose. "Huh? Can you say that in English, please?"

Dad tried again. "Let's see. How about this? When you're brave, it helps me be strong."

"But I don't *feel* brave, Daddy. What if you don't come back?" More tears fell, temporarily staining her velvet dress.

Dad reached into his pocket to retrieve his white handkerchief.

Holly wadded the cloth in her hands, the softness as familiar and comfortable as her father's soothing voice. She didn't know anybody else who used a handkerchief, except for the fancy one edged with scallops and dainty yellow flowers that Grandma Bea displayed in a shadow box in her guest room.

"There, there, sweet girl. You know what? It's no accident that you live on Kühn's Way. *Kühn* is a German word for brave. So, the place where you live is the way of the brave."

"Okay, Dad. I'll try to remember that."

"That's my girl." He squeezed her shoulder. "This time next year, your dear old dad should be back. Let's count on it, shall we?"

"How high do we have to count?" Holly blinked and wiped her sniffles with the back of her hand instead of on Dad's handkerchief that was still in her lap.

She never did get an answer as to how high she should count. An operatic version of "Happy Birthday" filled the room as Grandma Bea and Mother rounded the corner with a cake shaped like her favorite Beanie Baby, Chilly the Polar Bear.

Her reluctant brother entered the room followed by Grandpa Dale with camera in hand.

"Chilly!" Holly clasped her hands together.

"Should I turn up the heat?" Dad asked.

Mother shook her head, pointing to the cake. Dad gave her a knowing smile. He added his rich baritone voice to the mix, "Happy birthday, dear Holly No-el. Happy birthday to you."

Holly's tears were temporarily forgotten at the sight of her cake.

The vibrato of Grandma Bea's last note lingered in the air as Holly prepared to blow out all seven candles at once.

She inhaled deeply, puffing her chest with determination, before releasing a big puff of air, and a bit of accidental spit, on the glowing candles. Her birthday wish in 2000—besides wanting a June birthday like Gabe's—was to be brave, so that Daddy would be strong.

A lot of good being brave had done for that seven-year-old girl. The thirty-year-old version of her was back home shopping at Greta's Grocery for her mother as she had in high school. Of course, this time, she carefully avoided the baking aisle in case a Mr. Darcy look-alike was lurking nearby. She waited extra long to get the thick-cut salami, even though she preferred the thin, in an effort to honor her mom's specifications. Holly's car stuttered to a stop in the driveway of 725 Kühn's Way, Bavarian Falls. Zip code 12253 if anyone planned to send their annual "my family is better than yours" Christmas card.

Holly threw her keys on the counter and shoved her mom's very precise "check the list twice before you leave" grocery items into the fridge.

"Oh, there you are." Mom, outfitted in coordinating workout gear, entered the kitchen with a stack of clean kitchen towels in hand. She smiled at Holly as she snuggled the pile into a basket in the cupboard, squaring the corner of the top towel before patting the stack as if the towels were obedient children. A characteristic Holly did not seem to embody. "Did you—"

"Yep. I got what you wanted—Roy's famous rye bread, a pound of thick-cut salami, and a slab of *Spundekäs* cheese. It's all there."

Mom opened the fridge to discreetly inspect the contents of the grocery bag.

"You could at least wait to check the bag until I leave the room...I'm not twelve anymore, you know. I think I can—"

"Oh dear," Mom interrupted. "I did say *Rauchkäse* cheese, not *Spundekäs* cheese. There is a big difference between the two. Do you think you could go ba—"

"You know what? I've had a looonnng day at the most Christmas-y place on Earth and don't feel like going back out."

"If you're not going to do something right..."

That had been the mantra throughout Holly's entire childhood. She couldn't do anything right.

"It's cheese, Mom. Cheese."

"Holly, don't you think you're overreacting a bit?"

"Overreacting? Don't you think it's humiliating enough to be sleeping in my old bedroom with my Beanie Babies hanging precariously in a hammock over my head, and now my mom is voice-mailing me a grocery list—instead of texting like a normal person—to pick up her precious items, and *then* she reminds me how incompetent I am for not getting her darn list right?"

"Oh dear. I'm sorry." Holly's mom swiped at an imaginary

stain on the countertop. "I don't want this to come across the wrong way, but is it your special time of the month? You know, I have some dark chocolate hidden away. You're welcome to it."

Holly spun without a word and stormed out of the room, not willing to give the one and only Anna Brigham the satisfaction of being right.

Holly slammed her bedroom door and slid down to the cornflower-blue carpet. The carpet her dad had splurged on because it reminded his daughter of the color of Anne of Green Gables' puff-sleeved dress in her favorite movie. Like when Anne—with an "e"—cracked her slate over Gilbert's head, Holly had acted like a child about the groceries. She let her head rest against the wall. Being home brought out her once-angsty teenage self.

The least she should have done was let her mom share her secret chocolate stash. Then she could go back to it the next time she and her mom fought—which seemed to happen all too often.

Holly shouldn't let it get the best of her, but it was as if her mom was holding a victory flag above her own daughter's defeat. Not that her mom had wanted her to fail, but she was the one who had made it clear to Holly that her dreams of a community art space in the city needed a reality check—that they were "all wings and no roots" and "pie-in-the-sky instead of money in the bank."

As much as it pained her to admit it, her mom had been right. Holly's depleted bank account and deflated spirit were proof. Her temporary detour home felt more like a dead end.

Holly traced her finger on the carpet, wondering where to find joy again, like the joy she had when she first moved to Chicago and everything felt like Christmas Eve used to—full of expectant hope and endless possibilities.

The booming chorus of "Rolling in the Deep" jolted Holly from her melancholy musing, reminding her she had plans for the evening.

Holly grabbed her phone from her back pocket. It was time to pull herself together and go live a little, even within the parameters of her hometown.

Thank goodness for Elaine. The reconnection with her childhood friend had been a silver lining over the last month. Elaine also proved to be a reputable karaoke companion, so Holly could keep up her weekend tradition of singing her heart out to Whitney, Carrie, or Adele…whichever powerhouse fit her mood.

Holly untied her red work apron and hung it on the back of her door, leaving her nametag safely pinned to it. She touched up her makeup, refreshed her messy bun, and headed for the door.

As she passed the den, she slowed, spotting her dad sitting in his recliner, watching a game show.

"Hi, Dad." Holly rested her hand on his shoulder.

He muted the TV and turned slowly toward her.

"Huh-hi. How was your day?" His once soothing voice had been exchanged for a stuttering, more laborious version after he returned from overseas.

"It was interesting, that's for sure. I'll have to tell you about it later. I'm headed over to meet Elaine at the inn."

Later. That word was like a broken-in backpack for Holly, used in an effort to stuff down and transport her pain away from the present moment. *Later* was a diversion to avoid the unpacking of her big feelings.

Gone were the days when she and her dad conversed with ease. Now, lengthy conversations were too taxing on him. Holly kept things more surface level to be gentler on them both. In actuality, the short, simplified exchanges felt like an abrasion of steel wool upon the heart of a daughter who missed her dad's relational availability.

One of her favorite traditions they used to do when Dad's body and mind were still strong and sound was Saturday Workshop. Her mom packed them a sack lunch to enjoy while they tinkered in the garage. Dad blasted big band music from the stereo as he tackled fix-it projects at his work bench. Holly sat at her makeshift art station nearby, painting in time to the music. Carefree chatter and laughter splattered onto the drop cloth between them as father and daughter attended to their hobbies.

Presently, from the confines of his recliner, Holly's dad searched her eyes, as if trying to read her at a deeper level but not able to break through.

The familiar ache burned in Holly's throat. Her dad's words surfaced again from the past: "Be brave, child. I need you to be brave."

She swallowed hard.

"I love you, Holl-y-ee."

Holly brushed a quick kiss against his cheek. "I love you too, Dad. More than you know."

Holly turned toward the door before the rebel tear escaped down her freshly done face and made itself known to her father. Even though she was the child and he was the parent, she resolved to be strong for him as they once again repeated their bittersweet dance of letting go and holding on.

CHAPTER THREE
Single Mingle

THE EDELWEISS INN PARKING LOT WAS almost full. Unlike the Canada geese that flew south in winter, gaggles of tourists flocked to Bavarian Falls when the weather turned colder. Holly was grateful to find a parking spot, even though it was near the back of the restaurant.

The *beep beep* of her car doors locking was followed by an audible stomach rumble. Holly was ready for the inn's famous club sandwich.

She could have entered through the staff entrance like she had the Friday before, but Holly opted for the longer, more frigid walk around so she could take in the ornate beauty of the impressive front entrance. It was quite a sight with its snow-white pillars crowned with pine garland. Like a Thomas Kinkade painting, the golden glow from the chandeliers beckoned onlookers to come closer. But the showstopper was the tantalizing aroma of home-cooked cuisine wafting from the iconic restaurant.

So much history represented. So many meals served and guests welcomed. It was kind of like stepping into a different time and place, reminding Holly of her family's vacation to Mackinac Island when she was in middle school.

When the Brigham family had disembarked the ferry, Holly felt transported to another era as horses and carriages replaced horse-power engines on the island. The porch of the Grand Hotel was flooded with 1912 period attire as tourists gathered for a Titanic-themed weekend.

Grandpa Dale and Grandma Bea were still living then, but Dad seemed an ocean away. Mom did her best to plan the perfect getaway, trying to schedule every minute of the trip from the ferry arrival to the old-fashioned photos to lunch on the lawn in front of the hotel. But she stressed herself and her kids with her tendency to micromanage fun.

Thankfully, Grandpa Dale served as a needed diversion. He made room for his fifteen-year-old grandson and twelve-year-old granddaughter to get into a healthy dose of mischief and experience the vacation of a lifetime. Gabe and Holly ate their weight in fudge samples as they mooched from store to store.

The enchanting kaleidoscope of yesteryear afforded a temporary reprieve from the claustrophobic environment of home. Navigating puberty under the watchful eye of her overbearing mother while experiencing the emotional distance of her disabled dad was no picnic. The wind off the lake blew Holly's hair out of place as she jumped into the whimsical landscape with both sneakered feet. It was a needed escape from Holly's fractured childhood—from the tear that had taken place five years prior when dad came home broken.

The memory of the Mackinac Island vacation ushered in the familiar yet unsettling blend of pain and joy so intermixed they couldn't be readily or neatly separated.

God had certainly blessed Holly with big emotions, as her Grandma Bea used to say. But right now, she could use a break from all the feelings. Was that too much to ask?

Determined to keep the heartache at bay, Holly steadied herself on the handrail as she made her way up the steps to the grand entrance of the Edelweiss Inn.

Couples were everywhere, cuddling in the brisk night as they waited for their names to be called. Holly felt invisible as she meandered through the crowd. The cozy displays of affection surrounding her were a stark contrast to her dateless reality. Her hometown continually reminded her of what she didn't have. No dashing man on her arm, no ring on her naked finger, no future plans for a destination wedding. These hard facts clanged louder during the holidays as she showed up to parties, family gatherings, and downtown hot spots without a date.

One of the silhouetted figures in front of Holly, who had recently been involved in a marathon lip lock with his significant other, got down on one knee. Holly couldn't make out all he was saying, which was just as well. But she couldn't help but overhear the last part, "Danielle, you are a rare treasure. Not like any other girl I know. You are the only one for me. I want to cherish you every day of your life…as my wife. Will you marry me?"

His girlfriend squealed her answer, "Yes! You're my dream come true. Of course, I'll marry you!"

The rhyming proposal churned Holly's stomach. Spontaneous applause erupted from those standing nearby. The guy spun his gal around as she tossed her head up to the night sky, beaming with joy.

Holly forced a smile as she passed the happy couple. She would not let the familiar ache of being unattached overpower her growing appetite for dinner. Sometimes, being single made things easier, and sometimes, especially over the holidays, it stunk.

Holly pulled out her phone and whispered into it: "Reason #3: The Single Jingle."

"*Herzlich Willkommen bei uns. Kommen Sie rein.*" Ms. Claire Weber, decked in a floor-length black dress with an eyelet collar, greeted Holly as she entered the inn.

"*Danke schön*," Holly responded, thankful for Ms. Claire's welcoming countenance.

Prior to retirement, Ms. Claire had been the high school guidance counselor. When Holly's mom had been skeptical about

Holly pursuing art as a career, Ms. Claire had encouraged her to stay the course. Now Ms. Claire spent most evenings as head hostess at the inn, staying busy and in touch with the heartbeat of the community. Instead of advising students on class schedules and career paths, she advised restaurant patrons on where to head—booth or table—regarding their next culinary experience.

"Grabbing a bite before the main event?" Ms. Claire said.

"Yes, ma'am."

Elaine, dressed in her Colonial-style uniform with puffed sleeves and white pinafore apron, her crimpy curls tucked into a braid, hurried over to where Ms. Claire and Holly were conversing. "I've got to cash out two tables, and then I'm outta here."

"Sounds good, and so does the world-famous club sandwich," Holly used air quotes to emphasize her favorite item on the menu.

"You got that right." Elaine straightened her apron and pivoted toward the dining room.

"I'd be happy to place that order now to speed up your wait time." Ms. Claire positioned herself in front of the vintage cash register.

"*Vielen Dank.*" Holly curtsied as her stomach applauded with anticipation.

After Elaine's shift ended and they'd devoured the twin club sandwiches, Holly returned with her friend to Elaine's apartment so she could get ready for their night on the town.

"You sure you don't want to wear your stylish uniform for karaoke?" Holly twisted her mouth to the side, trying not to laugh.

"Yeah, right. This getup is no guy magnet, that's for sure."

Elaine turned on the TV before retrieving her out-on-the-town outfit from her closet—form-fitting black leggings and a square-neck, long-sleeved top. "I know it's still November, but whatcha think, green or red?"

"Hmm. Which one makes you feel more alive?"

"You're a weird one, Brigham. I'm alive either way."

"Green then. 'Cause the Grinch likes it."

"Naturally." Elaine pulled her sweater on and smoothed it out. "Hope the fellas don't think my heart is missing in this one."

"Not a chance. Your heart is bigger than Texas."

"I'm going to take that as a compliment."

"Good!"

Holly laughed easily around Elaine. There were no pretenses. No need to impress or flatter. Quirks and hang-ups weren't deal-breakers. Decades of friendship, even though there were fits and starts through middle school, provided solid ground beneath their feet.

Elaine got ready in the bathroom while Holly picked up a design magazine from the pallet coffee table.

The smell of jasmine filtered from the bathroom as Elaine spruced up.

"What is this?" Holly gestured to the show on TV.

"This is one of my new favorite Christmas movies."

"Oh, brother. The plots in those are so cookie cutter. I bet I can tell you what happens before it ends."

"Doubt it. This one has a big twist." Elaine spritzed herself with perfume.

"I'll bet. What's it called?"

"Pepper's Mint Twist."

"Come again?" Holly set down the magazine.

"Pepper's Mint Twist. The main girl, Pepper, is a broke college student studying law in order to defend small businesses against corporate takeovers. She cares for an elderly woman as a side job. Between studying and her job, Pepper barely has a social life. Surprisingly, when the elderly woman passes away, she leaves her fortune, a.k.a. her mint, to poor Pepper. But the twist is that in order for her to access the money, she has to date the woman's grandson for one month and give him a chance to win her heart. The grandson works for a big company that is trying to buy out a locally owned bakery. Needless to say, sparks fly in the form of heated arguments. But near the end of their required dating period, different sparks fly as Pepper and the guy lock lips under the mistletoe after finding a way to move forward together and save the bakery."

"Please tell me the bakery is not called Heart-Breakery?" Holly rolled her eyes.

"Um, no. But clever."

"And there aren't any homing pigeons in the movie, are there?" Maybe she should give up her art ambitions to write formulaic screenplays instead.

"What are you talkin' about?"

"Never mind."

"This one's different, I'm tellin' ya. You should give it a chance."

"Elaine, you are the Christmas Queen, aren't you? It's amazing we're friends after all these years. It's not my favorite, ya know?"

"I know."

Holly had been too much in her head for weeks. It was time to think about something other than her woes and wounds. It was time to cut loose and release her inner pop star downtown at Klingemann's Tavern. "How about karaoke?"

Elaine clicked off the movie, and they flung on their winter coats and headed down the stairs. No car keys needed since Elaine's apartment was only a few blocks from Klingemann's Tavern: home to German beer, a colorful array of locals mixed with a handful of tourists, and, most importantly, Friday night karaoke.

"Elaine, please reassure me that I'm not living out the lyrics to a country song." Holly's breath left white puffs in the air.

"Ha! You don't mean that one about the brown-eyed girl with big dreams who wanted to make it in the city but eventually realizes that all she's ever wanted is found in her hometown where she's famous in the eyes of the locals?"

"My worst fear is living a clichéd life that everyone can predict before I see it coming. Geez, is there really a song like that?"

"Sure is. It's called 'Hometown Famous,' and I just wrote it."

Holly punched Elaine's arm with her gloved hand.

"Ouch!"

They rounded the corner and took in the festive display. No matter how many times Holly walked these streets, the twinkling lights overhead stirred up a bit of childlike wonder within her. The picturesque scene begged to be entered into and enjoyed. You'd have to be Scrooge not to be moved by this idyllic town. Even though the holidays were a source of sadness for Holly, she was determined to put the ghosts of the past behind her—at least for tonight.

"Holly, my friend, tonight isn't about what was or what may be. It's about your right-now life. Look around. You've got a friend who is glad you're here, great music to boost your mood, and who knows, an eligible bachelor may have broken up with his girlfriend and is looking to meet a nice girl like you. Right now looks pretty good if you ask me."

"How do you do it, Elaine? You're so upbeat. You rock this single-jingle thing with your positive outlook. My jingle sounds more like a gong, dooming me to a life of loneliness. Alas, the disappointed artist who lives in her parents' basement and pines after what might have been."

"Good grief, Bestie. It's not that bad. Besides, you're living on the main floor of your parents' house, not the basement. And it's only temporary. You have a lot to offer. Snap out of it."

"I'm trying," Holly forced a semblance of her award-winning smile, pushing her apple cheeks up toward her ears, hoping to fool herself into a lighter mood.

"That's the spirit. Now, what are you waiting for?" Elaine returned a glove punch of her own before darting toward the castle-style doors. "Let's go."

Rousing music served as the soundtrack as bundled townies and tourists partook of the nightlife in Bavarian Falls.

Holly let go of her Eeyore-like mindset as she willingly followed Tigger into the tavern. She adjusted her posture, tossed her loose curls over her shoulders, and refocused her thoughts on the "pretty good" of her right-now life.

Klingemann's was hopping with local flavor. Elaine beelined toward an open high-top table. Holly joined her, ready to welcome the weekend by taking in the savory flavors, malted smell, and the crescendo of rich voices.

Holly scanned the growing crowd for hometown regulars, wondering what kind of friendly competition she'd be up against tonight. Midway through her scan, she spotted someone who stood taller than most.

"Frank?" she muttered.

Frank was surrounded by a co-ed group that seemed close to his age. Holly tried not to stare, but a magnetic force radiated from him, demanding her attention. It wasn't a chemical reaction but more like curious anticipation of what might happen next.

What happened next was that Frank, mid-laugh, turned his head and made eye contact before Holly could look away.

Her center of gravity a bit off-kilter, Holly steadied herself on Elaine's shoulder, diverting her gaze from Frank—trying to play it cool even though her sweater felt unbearably stuffy all of a sudden.

"You okay?" Elaine cocked her head toward Holly.

"Guy from work is here. Trying to avoid a run-in," she mouthed, attempting to channel untapped ventriloquist skills.

But was she trying to avoid Frank or avoid him noticing that she'd been watching him?

"I got your six," Elaine reassured her. "This is a place to escape work stressors, not face them."

Holly stole a glance in Mr. Magnetic's direction. He was still there but no longer looking her way. It appeared he was telling a compelling account to his captive audience. He was definitely cute in his own sort of way, but he was also younger than she was and lived in Bavarian Falls. He was everything she was trying to avoid—stuck in what her life had been a decade ago.

Holly shook off her conflicting feelings and pivoted her attention to her song selection for the evening.

"Oh look, there's Lena and Shayla." Elaine waved them over.

Holly tried to be open-minded about their party of two becoming a party of four. However, one of the plus-two headed their way was the size two, Miss Congeniality-sashed local who ran a successful nonprofit. Lena Albrecht, with her oval face and almond-shaped eyes, was one of the nicest human beings ever, which made it hard not to like her. But next to her, Holly felt like a flop.

"Hey, girls." Shayla bear-hugged Elaine and Holly.

"Happening place, per usual." Lena courteously side-hugged the others.

"Who's ready for a sing-off?" Elaine waggled her eyebrows, egging them on.

"Lena will have to pass tonight," Shayla said. "She's got a big date with you-know-who."

Lena blushed, smoothing her sleek, raven hair with her dainty palm.

Holly had no idea who you-know-who was. She and Lena hadn't exactly been hanging out much since Holly's walk of shame from failed city conquest to hometown seasonal employment. But Holly guessed he was probably tall, dark-haired, and practically perfect in every way.

"Spill it, girl. Are you Facebook official?"

"Oh, Elaine. The only time I'm on social media is for work. I don't put much of my personal life out there."

Thankfully, Lena did not own a bakery or a breakery. But she had founded Music Keys, a nonprofit that existed to help individuals with disabilities unlock their potential through music therapy, lessons, and performances.

"Hey, Lena, speaking of social media. Did you see that young man wow the judges on Hidden Talent with his soulful rendition of 'Music for Us All'?"

"Yes, I did. Wasn't it amazing? That's why we do what we do at Music Keys."

"It was incredible. We were a puddle of tears over at the inn when Ms. Claire showed it to us."

Shayla's eyes lit up, turning toward Lena. "Speaking of Ms. Claire—"

The exchange was interrupted by a screech of feedback from a mic.

All eyes turned toward the owner of Klingemann's, Klaus—rhymes with house.

"Sorry about that, folks. Just testing the system. About ready for your favorite pastime to get under way?"

"Woohoo!" Holly hollered. Her enthusiastic response

wasn't only because karaoke was about to start, but because it was bringing an end to Miss Congeniality's glowing success report.

"Gimme five minutes, and we'll be good to go." Klaus nodded.

"Let's get a few appetizers before the fun starts, shall we?" Shayla asked as her piano-playing fingers tapped the menu in a syncopated rhythm.

"Girl, I can't eat one more thing. Holly and I each had the club at the inn."

"I gotcha." Shayla winked. "That mouth-melting goodness will keep you full for a week."

"Remind me to tell you about the new initiative we're starting at the studio. It'd be great if you two would like to get involved," Lena called back as Shayla dragged her off to order their appetizers.

Stay down, Eeyore. Believe the best. Holly didn't need to look like Lena or to be like her. Lena was a beautiful, successful hometown girl, that was all. She was not the enemy. Holly was good enough, smart enough, and doggone it...

The conclusion of Holly's Stuart Smalley-ish pep talk was cut short by the main event.

"Who's first, ladies?" Klaus bellowed.

At the moment, Klaus was Santa incarnate, delivering cheer to Holly—wrapped in a mic chord.

"Hit me with your best shot, Mr. K.!" Elaine held her hand high.

"I've got next," Holly shouted.

"I'm after Holly." Shayla returned with a glass that sported a tiny umbrella.

"You fourth, Lena?" Elaine looked around for Shayla's companion. "Hey, where'd she go?"

"She went to fetch Mr. Dreamy. He texted while we were in

line. He thought they were meeting at the touristy bar. He hasn't lived here long. Rookie mistake." Shayla shrugged.

"Elaine, you're up." Klaus boomed.

"Ladies, watch out. I'm going to show y'all up."

The rest of the evening was filled with music, dancing, and fun.

Lena never resurfaced with her boyfriend, but Frank showed up and showed off with a charismatic version of ABBA's "Take a Chance on Me."

Holly's mom was a big *Mamma Mia* fan, so Holly was very familiar with the song. The crowd ate up Frank's antics and well-placed Elvis-like hip thrusts as he sang both the male and female vocals. He locked eyes with Holly several times during the song and smiled wide.

She reached for her beverage, trying to send the "I'm not as impressed as the rest of the crowd" message to him.

As the song ended, Frank shot a finger gun pose in Holly's direction with a wink.

Gulp.

Shayla whistled over the applauding crowd. "Way to go, Frank! That's what I'm talking about."

"That was impressive." Elaine turned to Holly. "Did he wink at us? What a character."

"Umm, yeah, something like that."

Holly wasn't sure what to make of Frank's playfulness, but karaoke at Klingemann's was exactly what the doctor had ordered. Although she wasn't sure what the next few months held, her right-now life, with a mic in hand, felt like a gift.

She unwrapped it with vigor, jingling her single with a smashing rendition of "Stronger" by Kelly Clarkson.

CHAPTER FOUR
Unmet Expectations

HOLLY HAD SPENT THE PAST DECADE of her life trying to get away from what had been, trying to start anew…yet there was a comforting familiarity to the hard-backed pew she occupied at the 9:30 am service at St. Schäfer's Lutheran Church. She had grown up in this congregation. Her physical growth was marked, year after year, by the distance between her dangling feet and the evergreen carpet until that gap eventually closed. But her spiritual growth continued long past the day her feet finally reached the floor.

The second Sunday of the month, St. Schäfer's hosted a German service at 11:00 am, which Holly attended on occasion. But today, she attended the traditional service with her parents. The hymns "Now Thank We All Our God" and "We Gather Together" aptly marked the coming Thanksgiving holiday. The pipe organ rang out with depth and vibrato as congregants sang the final line of the latter, "Thy name be ever praised! O Lord, make us free!"

Holly's silent prayer escaped to the rafters of the sanctuary. *Dear God: Help my dad experience freedom on this side of eternity.*

Her dad's job in the military had been to usher in freedom for others, yet through an unexpected turn of events, his freedom has been taken in many ways. That wasn't entirely true. Before his job involved preserving freedom, he transported military prisoners to Fort Leavenworth in Kansas—to remove freedom from those who had abused it.

Dad was eventually transferred from Leavenworth to work at the U.S. Army Department office located about half an hour from Bavarian Falls. So, they moved back to the Falls, since the commute wasn't long, and it was close to Mom's parents. It was a good thing, too. They'd needed her grandparents nearby when Dad was deployed as part of peace-keeping efforts overseas.

They had said a tearful good-bye to him shortly after Christmas. Holly had been freshly seven years old and Gabe ten. Dad hugged her so tight she could barely breathe. She couldn't stop the tears, but she bit her lip so she wouldn't demand he stay. Grandpa Dale and Grandma Bea looked on as the family of four clung to one another. Dad's wisdom thumped around in Holly's mind as her tears splattered onto his boots: "The place where you live is called courage."

Dad came home almost a year later, but he wasn't the same. During a routine supply transport, he'd suffered a brain aneurysm.

Holly once overheard her mom talking to Grandma Bea about the irony of Dad coming home wounded, not from combat, but from the time bomb that had been ticking inside his brain, unbeknownst to anyone until its explosion. Dad had been treated overseas until he was stable enough to return home on medical discharge. He was fortunate to have made it through. Holly's dad was still loving, determined, and strong, but his speech was slow, his memories disjointed at times, and his mobility limited—as evidenced by the cane he used to stabilize himself as he shuffled from his in-home hospital bed to the recliner. Sometimes, his anger flared at seemingly small things—a closed door, the television volume being too low or too high, his cane not being where he thought it was. Instead of laughing and talking with her dad like she used to, Holly often tiptoed around him, never knowing when he might explode.

Her untainted expectation as a young child, that her family

life would be relatively stable, was met with an uninvited, unexpected shattering. Like when Gabe accidentally knocked Grandma Bea's vintage snow globe off the buffet as he ran by. The keepsake splashed and splintered on the hardwood floor, pieces strewn about.

Since the year-end good-bye in 2000, Christmas marked the fault line between what life used to be like and what it was now after Dad's aneurysm. Her mom attended to Dad like Florence Nightingale, making him as comfortable as possible, carting him to doctor's appointments and physical therapy sessions. A woman of her word, she lived out the vows she had promised under a weeping willow in May of 1987. Mom tried to juggle her new responsibilities well, but Holly and Gabe had fumbled to find their footing in the aftermath of the aneurysm earthquake.

In many ways, the four-person Brigham brigade was disbanded in the wake of their new normal. Each member searched for true north in the foggy conditions, trying to prevent their battleship from sinking in the icy waters now that their captain was injured. Their anchor was compromised. Treading water was the only way forward. And Holly hated treading water.

Holly discreetly typed another strike against the holiday season into her phone: "Reason #4: Unmet Expectations."

Hollow footsteps on the church platform yanked Holly back to the present. "This morning's reading is from Philippians 4:6." Pastor Meyer opened his Bible and set it on the pulpit. "Please read along with me. 'Do not be anxious about anything, but in everything by prayer and supplication with thanksgiving let your requests be made known to God.'"

Nothing like having the pastor's morning selection point out your painful navel gazing.

Holly had a few words with God, trying to let her request be made known. In many ways, it had been easier to stay away from home. But she realized she needed the Big Guy's help to face what she'd rather avoid.

God? Hey there. It's me, Holly. I'm tired of feeling like I'm half here. I'm tired of living fragmented. It feels like a part of me is missing. I need a breakthrough. Will You help me out?

No answer floated down from the cathedral-style ceiling, but Holly felt a little better and a tad braver as she resolved not to let her sadness have the final say.

After the service, the Brighams made their way into the fellowship hall for coffee. Many of the eleven o'clock attendees were there as well, rubbing shoulders with the early risers before they entered the sanctuary.

Holly was thankful for the coffee and the chance to delay the uncomfortable Sunday meal that would likely ensue with her well-meaning but hovering mother and her disabled father. Holly couldn't wait until Gabe, his wife, Monica, and their sweet daughter, Claudia, arrived in a few weeks to celebrate Thanksgiving. Although she knew Gabe would tease her endlessly about anything and everything, she would appreciate the parental attention not being solely on her.

Her mom was engaged in conversation with the pastor's wife while dad sat nearby sipping his coffee. His longtime buddy, Walt, sat next to him shooting the breeze about the latest sporting event.

"Sorry to interrupt, but I'm going to go pull the car around to the side entrance for you," Holly announced.

Dad smiled at her and nodded.

"Can you let Chatty Cathy know?" She pointed at her mother, who, from the sound of it, was knee-deep in a debate about what shade of paint would best match the new carpet in the fellowship hall.

"Ya-yew got it. We'll be up soon...I—I think." Dad's eyes twinkled with a bit of mischief.

"Thanks, Dad." Holly headed toward the door that led to the parking lot.

"Oh, there you are, Holly." Ms. Claire called. She was dressed in a plum-paisley blouse and tan slacks—quite the change from her traditional hostess uniform at Edelweiss Inn.

"Here I am," Holly said.

"I want to introduce you to my nephew, Nik Beckenbauer. I'm trying to make the rounds during fellowship hour to connect him with the younger crowd, so he feels more at home here."

A dark-haired, steely-blue-eyed man put his arm around Ms. Claire, a genuine smile making its way from his mouth to his eyes.

Holly, taken aback by the attractiveness of said nephew, stretched out her hand, trying to appear calm, cool, and collected. "Hi there. *Willkommen.*"

Nik responded with a firm handshake. "Good morning, Holly. Nice to meet you."

The hot coffee cup in Holly's other hand misbehaved, splashing onto her Sunday best, Ms. Claire's tan slacks, and the carpet.

"Oh no! I'm so sorry, Ms. Claire," Holly gushed, aware she hadn't let go of Nik's hand through the spill.

"Let me help." Nik released Holly's hand to retrieve napkins from a nearby table.

"Are you okay?" Holly reached for Claire

"Oh yes, I'm fine. Nothing that a little laundry magic can't fix."

"I'm afraid I didn't make a good first impression." Holly lowered her gaze.

"More like a big splash." Ms. Claire chortled.

Her lighthearted response put Holly at ease.

Easy-on-the-eyes Nik returned with a handful of napkins.

He handed a stack of them to Holly and his aunt for their coffee-stained clothes as he attended to the floor.

"Let me do that. It was my fault," Holly insisted.

That felt like déjà vu. Didn't Frank say something similar to her when she tried to help him clean up his ornament spill? Almost like Groundhog's Day, except new guy and slightly different circumstances.

"I got this. It's no problem. Besides, I think my committed handshake played into this mess." Nik winked at Holly before returning his attention to the cleanup.

"Our hero," Claire clutched her purse "You know, he's such a help to me around the house, too. I keep trying to shoo him out, but he insists on completing my home repair list first."

Nik acted as if he didn't hear his aunt's accolades.

Holly definitely heard the praise Ms. Claire was showering upon him, elevating him to knight-like status. She also noticed that said knight, in the pale blue Oxford shirt, was stooping down to clean up the spill at her feet. If she only had a pair of glass slippers, the scene—minus the coffee stains on the new carpet—would have been the stuff of fairytales.

"Thank you again, I—"

"I don't understand why they put carpet in here in the first place." The pastor's wife rushed over to help Nik, Holly's mom following her.

"They thought long and hard about different flooring, but the noise decibel would have been much louder without carpet," Holly's mom said.

Holly wanted to fade into the outdated wallpaper in the fellowship hall as the pastor's wife and her mom's banter brought more attention to her ungraceful introduction.

While the women engaged in their lively debate, they didn't seem to notice first-time attender, Nik, who stood up with a handful of hazelnut-coffee-stained paper towels in his hand. Though Holly had recently met him, Nik's blend of steadiness and mystery, in addition to his good looks, drew her in like an Arthur Hughes painting. She couldn't look away.

Something about Nik made Holly feel as if she already knew him. She forced her dark eyelashes to blink in order to break up her stare, not in an effort to flirt. Well, maybe to flirt a little. It wasn't often that a man like this strode into town. Soon, he'd be swarmed by the single jingles spanning a wide range of ages, ringing out their plea, "Pick me! Pick me!"

Simmer down, Brigham. Blink, breathe. Act normal. Show some restraint...and dignity. She wasn't desperate. Besides, Bavarian Falls was not where she was going to stay. She was only passing through. She ordered her thoughts to move along before this newly relocated man displaced her vision board.

Holly touched her flushed neck. It likely matched the camouflaged pattern of the damp paper towels in Nik's hand.

The flooring debate continued with a lament from Pastor Meyer's wife. "There are ways to soundproof, you know. In fact, Donna Rasmussen was telling me they did something like that over at Blessed Epiphany. But I guess it's too late to change things now."

Ms. Claire, probably not wanting to be roped into the decorating committee's conversation, led Nik over to the trash cans. "Don't worry about it," she mouthed to Holly.

"Thank you." She mustered up the willpower to not stare at Nik's backside as he made his way to the other side of the fellowship hall. She was in church after all. And she was also a grown woman with healthy hormones. She peeked, once.

Mercy me. Just right.

Mom, seemingly oblivious to Holly's exchange with Nik, continued the spontaneous committee meeting near the damp carpet. "You're right. It's too late for a flooring change, but it's not too late to pick out the right color for these walls. Now, as I was saying, I prefer the Ethereal White over the Nebulous White."

Mom had a knack for stating her opinion as fact.

"The Ethereal has a bit more of a tan tint than gray. I see what you mean."

Mom beamed, anticipating victory. She'd never been a fan of gray.

A brief pause in the rapid-fire conversation made room for Holly to interject. "I'll go pull the car around."

"That is sweet of you. Are you okay? You usually linger at coffee hour."

"Ma-maybe she's ha-ha-hungry. I am!" Holly's dad exclaimed a little too loudly.

"I hear you, dear. Let's get you up and moving," Mom agreed before turning back to the pastor's wife. "Let's chat more this week so we can send the rest of the committee our paint color recommendation before Sunday."

"Sounds good. Chat soon."

"Now, Mr. Brigham, let's get you to your feet," Mom said, and Holly worked with her to assist him.

Midway through Dad's slow shuffle to the door, relying on his cane and his wife's arm to steady himself and with Holly leading the way, Nik rushed ahead of them to open the door.

"Thank you so much," Mom said.

"Always the gentleman." Lena joined him by the door, stating the obvious.

Lena knew Nik.

"Hi, Lena," Mom greeted. "How are you doing? I'm hearing great things about Music Keys. We're all so proud of you."

"Thank you, Mrs. Brigham. We're overwhelmed by the community's support. Oh, excuse my manners, have you met Nik?"

"Why, no. We haven't. Hi, Nik. Nice to meet you. I'm Anna Brigham and this is my husband, Carl."

Nik shook her hand. When he went to shake Dad's hand, he seemed unsure which hand to reach for—the one steadied by the cane or by Mom's arm. Instead, he patted Dad's arm like a teammate would do to another after a successful play but with more gentleness.

"Nice to meet you, Mr. and Mrs. Brigham."

"You too, Nik. Now, please, call us Anna and Carl."

"And this is our daughter, Hol—"

"Nice to meet you. Holly, was it?" Nik played along as if they hadn't yet met, offering a slightly less committed handshake than before. "Coffee?" he teased.

"Oh, no thank you. We're headed out," Mom intercepted.

"Nik is Claire Weber's nephew. He recently moved to town from out of state," Lena added.

"And Lena's boyfriend," Nik clarified, wrapping his arm around Lena's petite waist.

Glass slipper shattered before it was worn. How silly of Holly to assume he was an eligible bachelor. Mr. Blue Eyes was further proof that the holidays delivered unmet expectations on a hand-me-down platter.

Holly inadvertently wrapped her arm around her own side.

She was embarrassed by how quickly she had pounced on the possibility of Nik being a possible dating option after just meeting him. It wasn't usually her style. To make matters worse, Miss Perfect had one-upped her...again. Holly tried to shield her disappointment. She pulled her long bangs over her left eye, willing herself to teleport through the church walls, led by the Ghost of Christmas Present.

"That was fast," Mom observed, letting her thoughts spill out unfiltered.

"Oh, no! Wow, I see how you could think that. See, I don't usually do this sort of thing. But Nik and I connected long distance about six months ago. Then an unexpected turn of events allowed for him to move in with his aunt, so he relocated here, and...well, I'm not sad about it." Lena smiled as she looked up at Nik.

"That's great, Lena. Willkommen to Bavarian Falls, Nik. We're glad you're here. Now, I apologize, but we've got to scoot."

"I'm sorry I had to leave karaoke early," Lena tagged on before Holly walked through the arched doorway.

"That was my fault," Nik confessed. "I got mixed up and ended up at New Castle instead of Klingemann's."

"R-r-rookie move," Dad teased.

"Indeed, it was. Place was packed with out-of-towners, like me." Nik laughed.

"It doesn't sound like you're an out-of-towner anymore with Lena by your side," Mom observed. "Enjoy your Sunday."

"We will, thanks Mrs. Brig—"

"Anna. Please, call me Anna."

"Ah, heck, I left my phone at the t-t-table. Darn it! Walt was sh-show—"

"Oh dear," Mom stated, likely more of an apology about her husband's outburst than concern about his misplaced phone.

"I'll go get it while you make your way to the parking lot." Holly was thankful for a reason to exit the presence of the happy couple since teleporting wasn't a viable option.

"Thank you, sweetie. And nice to meet you, Nik."

Holly headed to retrieve her dad's phone and quickly located it under the table.

"I'm so glad I caught you before you left," Ms. Claire said.

"Oh, please let me know if you can't get that stain out. I'd be happy to replace your pants. Truly."

"I'm not worried about that at all, but I do want to fill you in about my nephew." She lowered her voice. "Since you've recently relocated here due to an unexpected turn of events, I thought you, more than anyone, would understand what Nik is feeling and could be trusted with this sensitive information about him."

For a split second, Holly's imagination ran wild in a swirl of assumptions. Had he received a difficult medical diagnosis? No, he looked too healthy and strong for that. Maybe he was a part of a witness protection program? No, that sounded incredibly far-fetched. Maybe he....

"He was recently released."

"Oh, that's too bad. Where was he?"

"He was in Leavenworth." Claire leaned forward, grabbing Holly's arm as if trying to steady herself.

Holly's eye widened, and her jaw dropped. "Whoa."

"I know it's shocking. Like I said, he doesn't want people to know. He's trying to start over with a clean slate. Pray for him as he starts over, please?"

"Uh, wow. I mean, yeah, Ms. Claire, I definitely will."

"Thank you, dear. I feel better knowing I've got a prayer partner to help share the load on this one. Nik is a great guy, and it's so upsetting that he got tangled up with the wrong sort of endeavor. I'm glad he's here now."

"Um, yeah, totally," Holly fumbled.

The wrong sort of endeavor? Being incarcerated in Leavenworth was not exactly the result of an endeavor, but a crime! Did Pastor Meyer know that a freshly released prisoner was freely roaming the church halls?

"Of course, he had other motivations for moving to Bavarian Falls besides li'l ole me living here." Ms. Claire clutched her purse.

Other motivations, indeed. Like robbing a bank perhaps? Or maybe something a little more discreet, like swindling money from unassuming folks at the assisted living facility? And why was Ms. Claire smiling? Nik seemed like a nice guy, and wow, those steely blues weren't hard to look at. But maybe that was how he got away with whatever it was that had landed him in Leavenworth—his good looks and firm handshake. She had sure dodged a bullet.

Holly made a mental note to require a background check on future suitors prior to a first date.

Flustered and more than a little bothered, Holly politely excused herself and darted to the parking lot.

Once she was buckled up, her mom dove right in. "Claire's nephew was quite the gentleman."

"You mean the criminal?" Holly's voice escalated. The words accidentally escaped before she could contain them. How was she going to dismiss her outburst and keep the secret she'd been entrusted with under lock and key if she had already disclosed it?

Her mother pulled down the car visor and slid open the mirror so she could converse with Holly without turning around,

"Holly! What are you talking about?"

"Not sure why I said that. Must be the hunger talking. I'm starved. You too, Dad?"

"Y-y-y-es." He answered from the passenger's seat.

"The Chicken Kiev should be ready in the crock pot when we get home. But back to Nik, surely you aren't accusing him of wrongdoing without any evidence?"

"Maybe it was that murder mystery podcast Gabe shared with me. I shouldn't listen to that stuff before bed, it revs up my imagination." Holly was fairly certain her fast talking and back-pedaling were unconvincing to her mother. She who was one of those moms with eyes in the back of her head. If mothers like her were allowed to be Catholic priests, there would be a whole lot more confessing going on.

Silence. Measured silence from the driver's seat.

Holly repositioned herself, determined not to snitch under the interrogation that was about to ensue.

"Carl, dear, remind me to call Claire later and see if her nephew might be willing to help us winterize the house."

There it was. The poke, the prod, the counterattack, the "I'm on to you and about to expose the holes in your testimony in three seconds flat" approach. Maybe a prosecuting attorney would better suit her mother, instead of a priest?

"I'm not sure that's a good idea, Mom."

"Why do you say that?" Holly's mother locked eyes with her daughter in the rearview mirror.

Rookie mistake. Never make eye contact with your interrogator. This wasn't Holly's first rodeo, so why didn't she look away? She felt herself weaken under her mother's questioning.

Holly tried to discreetly shrink down in her seat. It did not go unnoticed.

"It's settled then. If there's no good reason we shouldn't hire Nik to help us, then I'll call Claire after lunch."

"Lunch." Holly's dad smacked the dashboard as if to get the vehicle moving from its parked position.

"Maybe I should run back into church and see if I can catch her now?"

"She's probably occupied, Mom. Let's just head home."

"I'm happy to, once you level with me."

If Holly and her dad wanted to enjoy her mom's delicious Chicken Kiev anytime soon, Holly knew she'd have to abandon her weak arguments and deflections.

"Okay, okay, but, promise me you won't tell any of the other busybodies."

"Holly, watch your mouth."

"Mother, please!"

"How about you speak a little kinder about my friends?"

From the backseat, Holly volleyed her response. "Fine. Listen, keep this between you and Dad, but Ms. Claire told me that Nik was recently released from prison."

"That can't be right. Nik was a delight." Holly's mom repositioned a stray hair the visor mirror had revealed.

"That's probably his tactic, Mom. Charm his way into the hearts of unassuming hometown residents, and *bam*! Your TV is missing…or your life savings."

"Now, Holly."

"He was in Leavenworth."

Her dad's eyes flickered when she mentioned the familiar place where he used to transport military prisoners.

"His build and manners should have tipped me off that he was military. But prison? Carl, what do you think he did to land himself in Leavenworth?"

"Could b-be a na-na-number of things. Are you sure, Holly-ee?"

"Have you known Ms. Claire to be a liar?" Holly challenged.

"Heavens, no," Mom said.

"Let's get out of here, shall we? I'm starved. And I'd rather not wait around to see the con again." Through the car window, Holly scanned the church parking.

"Does Lena know?" her mom pressed.

"I can't imagine she does. I mean, why would she willingly date a criminal? Unless she's in on it with him. But that can't be right. Lena's squeaky clean."

"Wouldn't Claire warn her, though?" Mom demanded.

"I'd think so. Although, when Lena puts her mind to something, there's no stopping her."

CHAPTER FIVE
Ribbon Curling Standards

BESIDES THE STRANGE ENCOUNTER WITH THE criminal at church, the rest of the weekend proved uneventful. The bank wasn't open on Sunday, so no robbery to report—yet.

On Monday morning, Holly was back at Christmas Wonderland, red apron, nametag, and messy bun in place.

"Hello, Sunshine. Ready to roll?" Andy greeted Holly with his signature snicker before presenting her with an ooey, gooey cinnamon roll from Neumann's own Stocking Stuffers' Eatery.

"Ha! Nice Dad-joke. I see what you did there—roll and roll."

"You got me."

"How was your weekend?" Holly asked.

"It was fantastic. I had Oliver this weekend. River isn't frozen yet, so we couldn't ice fish. But we took a road trip to the city to watch the Snow Birds play. My ex-wife's boyfriend, Bill, offered us the hockey tickets last minute because he couldn't go. Normally, I wouldn't give him the pleasure of one-upping me, but they were Bird's tickets."

"Lucky. Don't blame you a bit. Did Oliver love it?"

"You know it. He talked nonstop and convinced me to spend an arm and a leg for one of those souvenir cups. I swore him to secrecy so he wouldn't tell his mom it'd been filled with enough soda to fill the Danfield River twice over."

"What a special memory."

"It was memorable, all right. We had to stop about fifteen times on the way home for him to use the bathroom after all that liquid sugar."

"I'll bet!"

"You know the crazy thing? Oliver tried to convince me to let him pee in the souvenir cup instead of stopping to use the bathroom. He said that Bill told him that when he was growing up, his mom would let him pee in an empty juice container that she kept in the car so she didn't have to stop so much."

"That's disgusting."

"Right! Wouldn't want to confuse the pee jar for lemonade."

"Gross." Holly shuddered.

The jingle jangle of Betty Jo's Christmas socks filled the room before she magically appeared in front of the ornament customization station.

"How are my favorite Station 8 employees?" she sang.

"Thirsty," Holly said.

Andy tried to restrain his laughter.

"Well, you know you can get a complimentary beverage at Stocking Stuffers. The hot cocoa is divine."

"Thanks. I'll keep that in mind. But right now, I need to get to these orders, or I'll never finish on time."

"You're doing great work, Holly Noel. Mrs. Rasmussen made a point of telling me that on Friday—and compliments don't usually free fall from her lips." Betty-Jo perched her fists on her wide hips. "Now, Andy, will you show Holly how to curl the ribbons to our standards today, please?"

"You got it, ma'am."

And with that, the jingles headed off to another section.

"There are ribbon standards?" Holly turned toward Andy.

"But of course. Don't worry. You'll get the hang of it."

"Reason #5: Ribbon Curling Standards."

"What was that?" asked Andy.

"Oh nothing, I'm just counting the reasons why I'm not a

fan of Christmas."

"Hey, watch it. You don't want the boss man or Betty Jo overhearing that. It's pretty much blasphemy around here not to adore Christmas."

"Naturally."

"Now, let's get your ribbon curling tutorial underway."

Holly swallowed, trying not to let Andy see her shaking fingers.

Truth be told, this wasn't her first ribbon tutorial. Her inaugural lesson had taken place right after her Norman Rockwell childhood was overshadowed by a Pablo Picasso abstract.

Dad had been transported home a few days after Thanksgiving in 2001. After his arrival, Grandpa Dale had taken Gabe bowling, and Grandma Bea had picked up Holly for early holiday shopping. They wanted to keep their grandchildren busy while their daughter tended to their brain-injured son-in-law. They did their best to be strong for the Brigham children, although Grandma Bea kept wiping her eyes when she thought Holly wasn't looking.

She helped Holly pick out a holiday coffee mug for mom, the latest Hootie & the Blowfish album for Gabe, and a large-print Tom Clancy novel for dad. Afterwards, they went back home to Grandma's house to wrap the presents.

All the shiny paper and Christmas decorations would normally put Holly in the holiday mood. But the lump in her throat and ache in her tummy made her feel as though she'd swallowed the holly instead of placing the prickly leaves on the mantel. She was glad her dad was home but sad about the circumstances that had brought him back. Her mother told her that something bad happened to his brain, and he was trying to get better. Daddy looked the same except for the wormlike scar on his head. But he didn't act the same. He seemed far away. Holly hoped he'd be all better by Christmas and that he'd like the book she was wrapping.

Once upon a time, Grandma Bea had worked at a fancy department store, so she took great care in showing Holly how to carefully wrap each package. The apple didn't fall too far from the tree between Holly's grandma and Holly's mom as there was a right way to wrap packages. Holly thought it was silly to spend so much time measuring and fussing over the wrapping paper when the gifts would be opened so quickly. Except for Dad's present. Maybe she should put his in a bag instead, in case he had trouble managing the tape and wrapping paper.

"Here's how you make the curliest ribbons on this side of the Mississippi. Watch carefully." Grandma Bea worked her magic. Long pieces of shiny, crimson ribbon became a perfectly formed nest of festive curls. "Please hand me that strip of tape, dear, so we can secure it in place."

Holly had done her best to make sure the tape did not stick to itself.

After Grandma Bea's impressive demonstration, it had been Holly's turn.

"Be careful. I don't want you to cut yourself with the scissors."

Holly crinkled her nose and tightened her bottom lip as she concentrated on the task. She tried to emulate Grandma's technique with the ribbon, but Holly's best attempt resulted in uneven curls.

"This looks terrible." Holly hurled the ribbons in the direction of the wicker wastebasket.

"Don't give up. Keep trying, and before you know it, you'll be making ribbons so curly that even Shirley Temple will be jealous."

Holly didn't only want to give up the ribbon curling. She wanted to give up her present reality with a disabled dad and preoccupied mom. She wanted to return to family laughter around the dinner table and watching the Lions play football on Thanksgiving Day. This year, instead of watching the game, Grandpa Dale had taken Gabe and Holly to the community Thanksgiving meal hosted in St. Schäfer's fellowship hall while Grandma Bea and her mom readied the Brigham home for Dad's arrival.

The previous day, a hospital bed had been delivered to 725 Kühn's Way. Since her dad was experiencing headaches and compromised mobility, the hospital bed would allow him to sleep in a slightly elevated position and would make it easier for him to get out of bed.

Instead of slaving in the kitchen over turkey and dressing or joining the community church dinner, Holly's mom and grandma rearranged the home so there would be a clear path for her dad to walk.

The meal at St. Schäfer's was designed to serve anyone who didn't have family nearby. Grandpa Dale had plenty of friends to talk with, but Gabe and Holly stuck out among the tables filled with seasoned attendees. The aroma of sage and thyme wafted through the air, but it hadn't sat well with Holly's upset stomach. She picked at her food. After two refills of bright red fruit punch, Gabe ripped tiny parts from his Styrofoam cup until there was nothing left but a pile of broken pieces.

"You gonna eat that?" Andy interrupted Holly's flashback as he pointed to the untouched cinnamon roll.

"Definitely. I'll eat while you teach?" Holly bargained.

Andy flashed a mischievous smile. "Confession time." He looked around to make sure Betty Jo hadn't returned unexpectedly. "I'm terrible at the ribbon thing. So, I convinced Teresa over at Station 3 to do them for me."

"You're awful! Poor Teresa." Holly closed her eyes as she bit into the tantalizing treat.

"Hey, don't feel too bad for her. We arranged a trade. Teresa curls my ribbons, and I warm up her car about ten minutes before she leaves work. That way she doesn't have to get into a cold vehicle."

Holly's eyes flew open as she swallowed quickly. "What century are we living in? The dark ages? Where men can't curl ribbons and women are too fragile for winter?"

"Hey, watch it. For starters, I tried to curl the ribbons to standard, but my sausage thumbs don't allow for it. And before you jump to conclusions, you should probably know that Teresa struggles with rheumatoid arthritis, and the cold aggravates her symptoms."

"Insert foot. Although not until I finish this pastry. But seriously, I feel terrible. I had no idea." Holly wiped her sticky fingers on a Neumann's branded napkin.

"I know."

"Isn't Teresa around your age?"

"Yes, early forties. Only a few years younger than me," he explained.

"Does the ribbon curling trigger her arthritis too?" Holly lowered her voice and tilted her head.

"She assured me it didn't."

"You're in luck. My Grandma Bea was a ribbon-curling professional, so I think I can manage. I'll go double check my work with Teresa, though, to be sure."

"Hey, I'll come with you," Andy offered a little too eagerly.

"Oh, I see what's going on here."

"What do you mean, Holly girl?"

"You know, Andy, I'm only ten years younger than you. That hardly makes me a girl."

"Holly lady doesn't have the same ring as Holly girl, now, does it?"

"Oh, brother."

"Shall we?"

"As fun as it would be to have a field trip to Teresa's station, one of us has to stay here in case customers arrive, right?"

Andy tried to camouflage his disappointment—unsuccessfully.

"How about this? I'll send you over with the curled ribbon, and you can have your lady friend check my work. If it's not up to par, you can negotiate another deal with her. Maybe a dinner date this weekend?" Holly teased.

"I don't know about that, but I'll take one for the team and go solo to the field trip."

"Very generous of you." Holly laughed.

After serving several customers and no sight of Andy returning, Holly retrieved her clipboard with the day's custom orders.

"I'm back!"

Holly spun around, startled by Mrs. Rasmussen.

"Hello. How can I help you today?"

"I'm actually here for the big reveal of the latest installments to the Christmas village. But I wanted to swing by to show you a picture of my darlings. You worked so hard on their ornaments, I wanted you to see how adorable they are."

Mrs. Rasmussen unlocked her smart phone to retrieve the picture of her darlings. Holly fully expected to see Hildebrandt, Bo-Bo the Third, Elora, and Huffy-Jack decked out in their Sunday best, the boys in bow ties and the girls in smocked dresses. Instead, she saw a picture of four fancy dogs decked in Christmas hats, posed in front of a massive white-brick fireplace with monogrammed silk stockings hanging from the mantel behind them.

"Excuse me, Mrs. Rasmussen, but where are your grandchildren?"

"My grandchildren? Wait, do you know something I don't?" The color drained from her very tanned face.

"I don't think so. Is this the wrong picture?"

"Nope. These *are* my little darlings. My doggies. I can't wait to give them the ornaments you made them."

Speech eluded Holly.

"I have to keep an eye on Huffy-Jack. He tried to eat last year's ornament. It was probably my fault because I picked out dog bone ornaments."

"Hi, Mrs. Rasmussen. Whatcha got there?" Andy returned.

"I'm showing Holly a picture of my darlings."

"How is Hilde doing? Man, she's a pretty breed. Think you'll enter her into the show this year?"

"I might. It depends on whether she can keep the weight on. I've been hand feeding her to make sure she gets it all down."

Holly still had no words to offer and no bone to throw the eccentric dentist's wife.

Andy didn't miss a beat. "I'm sure she'll be good as new in no time."

"Thank you."

"Are you headed over to the big reveal of the new Christmas village pieces?"

"Indeed. I'm going to go chat with Betty Jo first, and then I'll head over. Ba-bye."

"Bye," Holly managed. As soon as Mrs. Rasmussen was out of earshot, Holly leaned closer to Andy. "Her little darlings are dogs?" she whispered in amazement.

"You didn't know?" Andy chuckled.

"How would I know? Who gets hand-painted glass ornaments for their pets?"

"Mrs. R., of course."

"But of course."

Andy greeted a customer while Holly returned to her checklist. About five minutes into her setup, she was interrupted. It was going to be a long day.

"How is my favorite Station 8 employee?" Frank asked. He stood before Holly with a goofy grin, holding a box stamped *Fragile*.

"Hi, Frank."

"These are for you and Andy. Don't worry, no leg lamp inside this 'fra-gee-lay' box."

Holly resisted an eye roll at his reference to the movie *A Christmas Story*. "What a relief."

"But it does contain new, customizable ornaments. Can I put them on the shelf for you?"

"That'd be great. Thanks."

"Oh, the pleasure is all mine." He waggled his eyebrows and leaned across her worktable.

Uh-oh. Warning, warning.

Holly blushed, trying to avoid contact with overeager Frank. He shelved the ornaments in the prep room before returning to Holly's counter.

"I hear there's a great new band coming into town this weekend."

"Oh yeah? Hadn't heard." Holly tried her best to keep her tone steady and casual.

"I realize you don't know me from Adam, but um, what do ya say about checking it out with me?"

Holly had never been good at masking her emotions, and Frank's inquiry induced feelings of watercolors trying to mix with oil-based paint. The thought of dating a hometown boy went against her plans to get out of Dodge after the holidays. But Frank made her laugh, and if anyone could use a few laughs, it was Holly.

"Huh, well, gosh…" She struggled to offer a burnished response.

"Oh, sorry, do you already have plans?"

"Not exactly, it's just that…"

"Stupid me, you probably have a boyfriend, don't you?" Frank slapped his forehead with his palm.

"No—definitely not." Holly scrambled for a response that might put space between them. "But um, my friend Elaine and I usually hang on the weekends." It was technically true and would buy her time to figure out how she felt about Frank and boyfriend in the same sentence.

"Oh cool. Elaine Lewis who was with you at karaoke, right? She can totally come with us."

What did he mean by come with? As in a third wheel or just as friends?

"Hey, how do you know her last name?"

"This *is* the town where almost everyone knows your name. Elaine and I played on the same team a handful of times during pick-up basketball at the community center."

"She never mentioned that."

Elaine and Holly were going to dish about this later, so Elaine could tell her what to do.

"Why don't you ask her? It'd be fun. Maybe Andy wants to come too?"

Now Holly was entirely confused. Did Frank want to go on

a date or invite the entire store to the concert?

"Oh hey, Frank. How are you, man?" Andy extended a bro-handshake to Mr. Magnetic.

"Doing good. I'll be even better if you join Holly, her friend, and me for the concert downtown on Saturday."

"I wish I could, but I'm already booked."

"Too bad for you. My grandad can get us front row seats."

"Oh man, maybe next time. Keep me posted."

"Will do."

Frank swung his attention back to Holly. "How 'bout I pick you and Elaine up at seven on Saturday? I need your address."

"You know, Frank. I don't…"

"Holly, you should go," Andy prodded.

Holly paused for a beat to collect her thoughts as she did before attempting her first stroke on a canvas. She didn't want to lead Frank on, but maybe he was looking for friends to hang out with. As Frank and Andy waited for her response, she felt like a piece of plastic fruit on display, ready to be sketched by curious onlookers.

Make a decision already. It's not a marriage proposal, it's a casual outing with a coworker. Stop overthinking it.

"Look, I'm sorry. I shouldn't have been so direct. I thought you'd enjoy some weekend fun in the 'ole town. And who better to take you than Frank from the Falls?" He offered his wide smile that was equal parts silly and endearing.

"I'd need to check with Elaine."

"Of course. Swing by my office on Wednesday to let me know what you decide. Really, no pressure, but think about it."

"Will do," Holly said.

And with that Frank exited, this time without a crash or jingle.

Holly turned to confront her coworker. "Thanks for nothing. I thought you had my back."

"Frank's a great guy."

"Wait—office? Frank has an office?"

"You don't know, do you?" A cheeky grin covered Andy's face.

"Spill it!"

"I'll give you three guesses."

"Oh, come on. We've got work to do. I don't have time for games."

"It'll be fun. Promise."

"All right. Let's see… Frank is an oversized elf from the North Pole who's here to reconnect with his biological father."

"Seriously. His name is Frank, not Buddy the Elf."

"There's not a sequel yet?" Holly joked, referring to one of the only Christmas movies she didn't mind.

"You have two guesses left."

"Hey, not fair," she protested.

"You snooze you lose, princess."

"Let's see. Frank is a local college student who is interning for the head honcho, but his secret plan is to take over this holiday empire."

"Nope. But you're getting warmer."

"Oh, I've got it! Frank is actually the boss, and he's gone undercover to make sure we're all doing our jobs. Hey, maybe he'll agree to be an investor in my collective art space if I tell him about it at the concert."

"I can assure you he's not the boss."

"Shoot."

"But he is the boss's grandson. And he may run the family

business one day. For now, he's in charge of purchasing. Tomorrow, the moon."

"You're kidding me. Frank is a Neumann?"

"Nope, he's a Walker. His mom was a Neumann before she married Drew Walker."

"The meteorologist?"

"Yup. The Weather with Walker on Channel 5."

Miss Congeniality walked by. Holly ducked, but too late. Lena turned and saw her.

"We'll have to continue this small-town gossip later." Holly tried her lackluster ventriloquist skills again in case Lena overheard.

"Oh hi, Holly."

"Hi, Lena."

Holly tried to play it cool and not let on that she knew Lena was dating an ex-felon. But didn't Lena know? How could she not?

Holly worked to recover. "Can I help you?"

"No, thanks." Lena held up a Neumann's bag. "I have a meeting upstairs in a few minutes, but I was looking around since I'm early."

Holly didn't press about the meeting.

"Hey, since karaoke didn't pan out, we'll have to try a night out another time. It'd be good for Nik to get his mind off his previous residence. He relocated recently from out of state." Lena looked around before adding, "It wasn't an ideal situation."

She could say that again. Being locked up for a crime was not at all ideal.

"Yeah, well, keep me posted on your plans," Holly managed, attempting to keep things as normal as possible.

"Our plans?" Lena raised her manicured brows.

"About a night out?"

"Oh yes, that." Lena straightened her blazer. "I've been quite busy lately…"

Holly glanced down at the order sheet on her clipboard as if it were a script that would cue her next line.

"Oh! I know." Lena snapped her fingers. "There is something you could help me with. Maybe you could volunteer with this new program we're doing at work. I think you'll like it. It'd be easier to show you than tell you about it. Why don't you stop by this week after work around six, and you can see it in action?"

"Yeah, maybe."

"Great! Hey, before I go, would you mind wrapping this for me?"

Lena opened her bag and laid a singing angel ornament and a receipt to prove her purchase on the counter. "It's for Chase. You'll get to meet him when you stop by Music Keys. And can you put those perfectly curled ribbons on top?"

Reason #5.

CHAPTER SIX
Risky Gift-Giving

THUMP, THUMP, THU-THUMP THUMP.

Holly knocked on Elaine's apartment door. "I come bearing gifts."

"Of the caffeinated variety?"

"Naturally." Holly offered the cardboard cup holder to her friend with two peppermint-striped cups nestled in it.

"Come on in. It was crazy town tonight at the inn. The closer the holidays get—"

"The more tips you get." Holly said.

Elaine set the cupholder on the island. "True story. And I am thankful. But we were almost at capacity already; imagine what it'll be like after Thanksgiving."

"Crazier town." Holly sat down on the bar stool, leaving her coat on. "I can't stay long. My mom needs me to grab my dad's prescription at the pharmacy before they close. But I wanted to run something by you."

Elaine leaned on the island, sipping her beverage. "Lay it on me."

Holly told her about Frank's concert invitation, inserting numerous reservations from her time spent overthinking it.

"I think it'd be fun," Elaine said.

"You sure?"

"Oh, come on. Frank's quirky cool. His three-point shot isn't too shabby, either. And we'd be stupid to pass up front row seats."

"You're right. And it's not like I'm agreeing to a lifelong commitment to a hometown boy who'd keep me stuck here. It's a date, that's all. And you'll be there, too. What else would I do anyway, stare at my bedroom ceiling and listen to depressing songs while feeling sorry for myself?"

"You know I'm in your corner, girl, but you seriously need to snap out of this. You're not a failure. Repeat after me: A failed project does not make me a failure."

"Why is that so hard to believe?" Holly cupped her beverage in her hands.

"Listen, I know it stinks that the creative space thing in Chicago didn't work out. But you can't let one dead end hold you back. Let's call it a detour instead. One that led you back here where you get to hang with fun people like me *and* Frank, sing your heart out at weekend karaoke, and custom paint ornaments for purebred pets."

Holly laughed out loud and then imitated Hildebrandt's cocky pose in the picture that Mrs. R. had shown her. The laughter lowered Holly's guard. "All right, I'll tell Frank that we're in for the concert."

"You don't have to twist my arm. It's a date."

Midway through Holly's workday on Wednesday, Andy leaned against the counter. "I'm treating you to lunch at Stocking Stuffers. Bratwursts are in your near future—unless you're vegetarian?"

"Nope, not anymore. I was for a few years in college, but that had more to do with the questionable meat they served," Holly explained.

"Then brats it is!"

"It's nice of you to offer lunch, but if we take a break at the same time, who's going to keep our station running?" Holly gestured to the line-up of ornaments awaiting her flourishing.

"Never fear, Holly dear. I worked it out with Betty Jo. She's sending someone over."

A few minutes later, Leslie from customer service arrived to take over while Andy and Holly went to lunch.

They walked over to Stocking Stuffers near Station 11, which was crowded with customers. Holly managed to snag a table while Andy ordered.

He eventually returned, precariously juggling four plates of food.

"That hungry, huh?"

"Yes, but I'm trying to slim down a bit. This is actually for the other two who will be joining us. Did I forget to mention that?" Andy set the steaming entrees on the table, one at each spot.

"Hulllooo!" Betty Jo jingled her way over to their table. "Ooh, doesn't that look good?" She wiggled into the chair next to Andy, making herself quite comfortable.

Holly tilted her head at Andy as if to ask why he had invited the jovial store manager to join them during their break.

Andy diverted his attention. "I'm so glad you could come."

"It's not often other employees invite me to lunch. You both are so kind." She beamed.

"Sorry I'm late." Frank slid into the seat next to Holly, nearly stepping on her foot.

Holly tried to take Frank more seriously now that she knew he was upper management, but his boy-next-store vibe mixed with his inability to gracefully maneuver his lanky frame made it challenging.

As they ate, they made small talk about weather and work.

"Ladies and gentleman, truth be told, I invited you to lunch to ask for advice." Andy interrupted the conversation.

"Ooh, I'm all ears," Betty Jo said.

Frank rubbed his palms together, fidgeting beside her. Holly tuned out the hubbub around her to give Andy her full attention.

"I'm trying to make a decision, and I think womanly input will help. And Frank, I think your spirit of adventure will come into play."

"Bring on the fun. That's my motto." Frank rested his arm on the back of Holly's chair.

She pretended not to notice, but she was most certainly aware.

"Is this about someone who needs her cold car warmed?" Holly surveyed Andy's body language for clues to confirm her hunch.

"Kind of yes and kind of no. I don't know. Maybe this isn't a good idea."

"Oh, do tell," Betty Jo said.

Andy stroked his lumberjack beard, as if deep in thought.

"Okay, well, when Tammy and I split, my whole world split in two. It was hard to imagine life beyond what we'd built. Oliver was only four at the time. It was so unfair to him. I even suggested that Tammy and I take turns staying at the house, so Oliver didn't have to be the one to shuffle between us. Since we had uprooted his stability, I thought we should be the ones to inconvenience ourselves for him, not the other way around."

"That sounds quite sensible," Betty Jo said.

"Fast forward three years, and here we are. I think Bill is about to propose to Tammy. I've been living in an apartment since the divorce, but Tammy asked me if I wanted to move back into the house or sell it after she moves out."

"What do you think you'll do?" Betty Jo drenched her brat

in stone ground mustard before taking a bite.

"Here's where it gets weird. I have this strong sense that I'm..." Andy looked around as though checking to see if anyone was listening in.

Betty Jo's eyes were as big as Shopkin dolls.

Holly tapped her foot under the table in anticipation.

Frank scooted closer to Holly, his extended forearm grazing her back.

"...that I'm supposed to give the house to someone." Andy delivered the outlandish news so quickly that Holly wondered if she'd heard him correctly.

"Rad, man!" Frank nearly clocked Holly in the head as he offered Andy a fist bump from across the table.

Holly ducked.

"You okay?" Frank patted her head.

"I'm fine," Holly assured him.

"I concur," Frank muttered with a nod at Holly before turning his attention back to the conversation at hand.

Subtlety was not his strong suit.

"Oh my goodness, Andy. This sounds like a scene from *Miracle on 34th Street*. The black and white version, not the latest one. The original is so much better, in my opinion."

Leave it to Betty Jo to add her two cents about a Christmas classic when a whole lot more than pocket change was on the table—that, and the mostly devoured bratwursts.

"Say that again?" Holly pushed her plate to the center of the table.

"The black and white version is far superior..."

"Not that. I want to hear what *he* said again." Holly's eyes were fixed on Andy who was adjusting and readjusting the collar of his plaid flannel shirt.

"I know it sounds crazy, but I feel like I'm supposed to give the house away. And I want to know what you all think about that. Not that I need your permission or anything, but I mean, I've, um, never done anything like this before and, to be honest, I don't want to come across as a lunatic to the person I think I'm supposed to give the house to."

"Oh my stars and bars, you already have someone picked out for the house? Oh, do tell! I won't tell a soul." Betty Jo leaned over her plate, reaching for a napkin. Holly was afraid her "girls" might land in the ketchup of her half-eaten brat. "To the grave."

Holly held in a burst of laughter. Work was never dull, that was for sure.

"Spill it!" Holly egged, a little too loudly, as evidenced by concerned customers who looked her way. She waved them off and quickly turned her attention back to a slightly squirming Andy. He was typically easygoing, but this give-the-house-away epiphany and subsequent confession seemed to have him out of sorts.

"Let's see. It's someone who could really use the house. But I don't want her to get the wrong idea."

"A her, huh?" Holly's eyes danced. "I knew it."

"Smooth, man. Totally smooth," Frank said.

"Ooh la la, what a Romeo! Usually guys ask a girl for her digits, but not you, no siree, Bob. You, Andy Schroeder, give a girl the farm—I mean, your house. Technically the house that you and your ex-wife used to live in. But I digress. Whew! What I'm trying to say is, it's a grand gesture of love that's sure to make the lucky girl swoon." Betty Jo fanned her face with her hand.

Good grief.

"Oh no, I was afraid of this. All due respect, Ms. W., but this is not a grand gesture of love. Well, I guess it kind of is, because it was the Big Man's idea for me to help this person out. But I definitely don't want to scare her off or give her the wrong idea. This kind of gift-giving is risky business. There's no tellin' how it will be received or if I—I mean *it*—will be rejected."

Holly noticed his slip-up. While she wasn't familiar with the ache of divorce, she was no stranger to risky gift-giving and the rejection that can accompany it.

All those years ago, when Holly's dad opened the Tom Clancy book she had picked out for him, he labored to retrieve it from the gift bag and dropped it.

Her mother picked it up and set it on the tray next to her husband. "Oh, Carl, look, your favorite author. That was sweet of you, Holly."

"If he can still read," Gabe muttered.

"Gabriel, enough!" Mom had scolded, obviously weary from the cutting words Gabe had started to render since Dad's return home.

Young Holly hadn't considered that. She knew her dad had frequent headaches, but had he lost his ability to read too? Her eyes glassed with tears as she hugged her knees.

What a dumb gift I picked.

"You with us, brown eyes?" Frank nudged Holly.

"Yeah, of course. Hang on a sec."

She bossed the painful memory into a corner of her mind, but not before adding to the list on her phone: "Reason #6: Risky Gift-giving."

"What'll y'all think? Am I crazy to go through with this thing?" Andy grabbed his cup and crunched the last bit of ice in it.

"I think it's amazing!" Betty Jo clapped her punctuation.

Holly admired Andy's willingness to follow through on this

wild idea, yet—partly because of her past hurts and partly because she knew some of his—she felt protective of her new friend.

"Do it, man. It's so smooth," Frank urged.

"Almost tempts me to like Christmas again," Holly muttered.

"Oh, Holly, this is no time for jokes. This is serious business. Not liking Christmas? That's not funny at all," Betty Jo scolded.

Andy and Holly exchanged a knowing smile.

Frank leaned closer to Holly. "Not liking Christmas, huh? I'm pretending I didn't pick up on that. Not sure I can take out a girl who has an aversion to Christmas." He shook his head. "No matter how fantastic she is."

Holly raised her eyebrows to Frank as if to challenge the validity of his claim.

"Good thing I'm not that shallow. My invite still stands." The tips of his fingers grazed her back before returning to his plate to reach for the last few fries.

"Does it now?"

"Besides, now my mission is clear—to make you fall in love…with the best holiday ever."

"Good luck."

The store clock chimed, signaling twelve-thirty.

"Gotta run, man. But I say go for it. Who wouldn't want a free house? Let me know if you need help pulling off the big surprise," Frank offered. As he rose to leave, he gave a casual salute. "I've got my eye on you, Holly Noel."

She was pretty sure the color of her face looked more festive than desired as a result of Frank's obvious flirting. Thankfully, he left Stocking Stuffers before reading the conflicted expression that had to show on her face—one part apprehensive, another part amused.

"Oh dear. I'm afraid I have to go soon. A manager can't munch for long. Duty calls! But I'm all ears if you're going to tell us who she is."

"Yes, do tell," Holly said.

"I will, if you promise to keep it a secret." Andy brushed a stray crumb out of his beard.

"Like I said…to the grave."

"Pinky promise." Holly locked her pinky fingers together as proof.

"It's—"

Only in "a mile of Christmas joy for every girl and boy" would a trio of employees be interrupted at the pinnacle of a fascinating conversation by the announcement over the loudspeaker: "Attention employees. Code Rudolph. Code Rudolph."

"Promise me we'll finish this later?" Holly jumped up and pushed her chair under the table.

"Deal," Andy said as he rushed off.

Code Rudolph did not mean there'd been a red-nosed reindeer sighting or a bloody nose incident. It meant that a small army of red-aproned employees were needed to search for a missing child in the mile-long Christmas store.

"I've gotta skedaddle." Betty Jo sprung to her feet, nearly causing a spill.

Holly steadied the wobbling cups.

As a member of the Code Rudolph team, Andy had already pulled up the store's emergency system on his phone to gather the details:
- Ten-year-old male
- Blond hair
- Hazel eyes

- Down syndrome
- Last spotted near the lighted houses display at Station 6
- Part of North Star Elementary School field trip

"It's Chase." Wide-eyed, Andy mouthed to Holly, "A boy from Oliver's school." And with that, he darted out of sight.

As Holly cleared the table, she shot up a prayer for lost Chase to be found. She decided to take the last few minutes of her lunch break to get fresh air before relieving Leslie, that way she could help search without getting in the way of the trained recovery team.

She grabbed her down coat and gloves before heading outside. Warmth and cold collided as she left the store and stepped onto the sidewalk surrounding the Christmas mecca. As she walked past the life-sized Nativity figures, she tried to sort through her swirling thoughts.

Was she still feeling brave enough to say yes to Frank's concert invitation? Or should she back out? Did he like her, or was he simply having fun?

Who was Andy going to give the house to? She had a hunch, although she could be wrong. But was it a good idea?

Who was Chase? Where had he gone? And why did his name sound familiar?

Movement near the Nativity caught her eye. A boy knelt in front of a ceramic rendition of Baby Jesus, his head bowed and hands outstretched.

Holly drew near.

"Chase? Is your name Chase?"

The blond-haired worshipper looked up but kept his hands straight out. Without coat or hat, he was shivering in his position of adoration. His ungloved, stubby fingers held a Charlie Brown tree ornament. An apparent offering to the newborn King.

"Hey, buddy. Wow, that's a really neat thing you're doing. But we need to get you inside. People are worried about you."

Chase looked back at Jesus and then at Holly. His lip quivered. She wasn't sure if it was from the cold or because he didn't want to leave his post or both.

"My name is Holly. Let me help you get inside where it's warm."

Chase set the tree ornament on top of Jesus' swaddling clothes and double-tapped it for good measure.

The risky gift-giving of both the child and Christ about did Holly in. The two of them stood with open hands, readily offering, even if others chose to reject the gift.

Holly offered a gloved hand to steady Chase as he slowly rose from his kneeling position.

"Th-th-th-thank ya-yew." Chase's lips protruded as he formed the words.

"My pleasure, young man."

Chase took another look at Baby Jesus as if to make sure his humble offering remained in place. Then he linked arms with her, and they made their way to the west entrance of the store.

Before they reached the double doors, Nik rushed toward them.

"Oh, thank goodness. There you are, Chase." He let out a sigh of relief into the crisp air. "Holly?"

"Hi, Nik."

"What are you doing here?" they asked simultaneously. Nik's inquiry sounded more curious while Holly's was a little accusatory. She adjusted her tone slightly in an effort to ward off any suspicion that she knew about his shady past.

"I work here," Holly pulled her glove on tighter. "I was on a quick break when I found Chase."

"I'm serving as a chaperone for the school field trip," Nik said. "I was supposed to be keeping an extra close eye on this guy, but another student tripped, and I got tied up helping her, and then Chase was gone."

An ex-con working with children? Surely, he had to fill out a background check first?

"S-s-sorry," Chase stammered, looking down at his Velcro sneakers.

Nik bent down, sliding an arm around Chase's shoulder. "Listen, buddy. You're okay. We were worried, but I'm so glad Miss Holly found you. Please don't go disappearing on me again. All right?"

"J-j-jee. Jesus."

"What's that, Chase?" Nik asked.

"I found him by Baby Jesus. I think he was trying to gift him with a 'borrowed' ornament from the store," Holly explained, gesturing with air quotes.

Nik's concern faded into amusement. "Oh, I see, buddy. That was really special. Next time, let me know, and I'll come with you, okay?"

Chase nodded.

"It's cold out here. Let's get you inside." Nik rested a hand on Chase's back as Holly reached for one of Chase's hands, trying to keep him warm.

Holly's nurturing instinct kicked in as she gently pulled Chase closer to her than Nik, trying to widen the distance between this precious boy and his chaperone with questionable character. Once inside, they escorted Chase to the information station, where the attendant's tense expression melted into relief at the sight of them.

"Attention Neumann's employees, Rudolph has landed. I repeat, Rudolph has landed."

Chase looked up to the rafters as if he anticipated a reindeer sighting.

The red-aproned brigade was called off since Chase had been safely returned to his teacher and classmates, Holly went back to her post.

After a debriefing with the Code Rudolph team, Andy joined Holly at their station.

"Well done, Holly girl. Maybe you should join the safety team."

"I don't know about that, but I'm relieved Chase was found. I have no idea how long he would have stayed out there."

"What made you look near the Nativity?"

"Nothing in particular. I was trying to burn off calories from that delicious lunch—when I spotted him. He was so sincere, kneeling beside Baby Jesus."

"Reminds me of one of the songs Oliver's class is practicing for his school Christmas concert."

With a slight country twang, Andy sang the last verse:
What can I give Him,
Poor as I am?
If I were a shepherd,
I would bring a lamb;
If I were a Wise Man,
I would do my part;
Yet what I can I give Him;
Give my heart.

"'In the Bleak Midwinter'! My Grandma Bea loved that song. Gabe and I sang it each year, while she played the piano."

"Maybe Chase's version went something like this: Yet what I can I give ceramic Jesus, give Him a stolen Charlie Brown tree ornament."

"Way to ruin the moment."

"Consider it my specialty."

"Hey, that reminds me…who's the lucky lady?"

"Whatever do you mean?"

"You're not going to tell me?"

"Tell you what?"

The rest of the work day continued like clockwork. Andy acted as if he had never disclosed anything about his grandiose house plans at lunch, so Holly decided to try—or pry—again tomorrow.

She turned her attention to the steady stream of custom orders. After avoiding an important matter all day, time was running out. If only she could decide what to do about the concert, say yes to Frank or no? One minute she felt good about it. What was the big deal? She didn't have to decide if she wanted to spend the rest of her life with him. But on the other hand, what were Frank's intentions? Was he trying to be nice, or was there more there? Was he secretly plotting to gift her a house…or his heart?

Reel it in, girl. One baby step at a time. Stop overanalyzing it.

Holly's feelings ping-ponged inside as she tried to maintain a steady hand while painting ornaments.

A few minutes before five, Holly headed upstairs to the Neumann's family offices. Hoping no one would notice her, Holly kept her head down while she located Frank's office. As she lifted her hand to knock, the door opened simultaneously. She fell into Frank's chest.

"Well, well, hello there, Holly Noel. Fancy running into you here."

His long arms were semi-wrapped around her like a lopsided Bavarian pretzel.

Oh dear! This was not the nonchalant vibe she was going for.

"I'm sorry. I was, uh…"

Holly managed to untangle herself from Frank. She took a step back and brushed her hands on her black pants to avoid further inadvertent bodily contact. No doubt her flushed face was its own sort of Code Rudolph.

"Oh no, I'm sorry. I should look before I leap."

Holly tucked a rogue curl behind her ear before announcing with auctioneer-like speed, "Hey, Frank, you've got two yeses for the concert. Elaine and I will be there. Okay, thanks."

"Why, that's fantastic! You sure know how to make someone's day."

"Gotta go." She turned, trying to collect her pride off the floor. Putting herself out there was risky business.

"All-righty. I'll see you there."

"Sounds good," she added without turning around.

And with that, Holly hurried down the stairs with a spring in her step—in the opposite direction of Frank.

Thump, thump, thu-thump thump went her heart. 'Was that due to her taking the stairs so quickly or because the boss's grandson was proving to be more endearing than annoying?

CHAPTER SEVEN
Fainting Spells

Holly opened the door to Music Keys and ushered Elaine in before her. In true Lena form, the interior of the building was tastefully decorated in calming hues of cream and tan. Pops of emerald were present in a few statement pieces. The focal point of the reception area were large bronze notes that spelled out "Music Keys" mounted on classical sheet music. Lena never did anything halfway—except when it came to her most recent selection of a boyfriend.

Had Lena been so consumed by her work at Music Keys that she'd gotten sloppy in her choice of companion? That seemed unlikely.

Deceptively handsome Nik was plunked down on a stool in the reception area. He was probably crafting a master plan to line his pockets with the grant money Lena had been awarded—swindling innocent children like Professor Hill in *The Music Man*.

"Earth to Holly. You with me?" Elaine waved her hands a few inches from Holly, trying to get her attention.

"Uh, yeah, sorry."

Elaine followed Holly's gaze to Nik.

"He's taken," she whispered, much to Holly's shock and disgust.

"I know. I also think this town's about to be taken—" Holly stopped herself mid-sentence, realizing she had almost broken her promise to Nik's Aunt Claire.

"What are you talking about?"

Busted.

"Never mind. Forget what I said," Holly backpedaled.

Regal Lena entered the room. Nik rose to greet her.

Per usual, she looked as polished as a porcelain doll—her posture, the glow of her skin. A coordinating pencil skirt and blazer complemented her silky jade blouse. Lena's raven hair was parted down the middle and pulled back in a tidy bun at the nape of her neck. Dainty pearl earrings served as the crowning finish.

Holly usually felt pretty comfortable in her own skin. But in the presence of people like Lena, she reverted back to the thirteen-year-old version of herself, at least on the inside—feeling frumpy, clothed in an oversized sweater of insecurity. Her signature messy bun didn't feel so fun and attractive at the moment. She—and it—felt a little too messy.

"I'm glad you're here. I can't wait to show you around," Lena announced.

Elaine was two and O when it came to getting her way. First, she had convinced Holly to branch out and say yes to Frank's concert invitation. And now she had swayed her to stop by Music Keys to hear about Lena's new initiative. Both of those yeses went against Holly's better judgment, but the alternative was less than appealing—home alone, minus the threat of burglars and Kevin McCallister's arsenal of booby traps.

A few measures of Puccini's "O Mio Babbino Caro" rang in the air. Lena reached for her phone and answered the call. Deep in conversation, she exited the entryway.

After a few moments, Nik announced, "Ladies, looks like I'll be your tour guide."

Or prison guard.

Nik led Holly and Elaine past the reception area and down a short hallway. The emerald accent pieces matched Holly's envy as she was confronted by Lena's success on display throughout the tour. She tried to wrangle her wayward thoughts by turning the channel to a lively pep talk that went something like this...

Don't let Lena intimidate you. Her success doesn't mean you're doomed for failure. Things come more easily for her. Don't let her accomplishments trip you up. Lena isn't flawless. Whether she realizes it or not, she's fallen in love with a convict. Hopefully, Nik won't get her locked up, too. Hmm, I wonder if they have female prisoners in Leavenworth? She definitely won't be able to wear her coordinating power suit there. Unless it's orange.

"You look a million miles away." Nik's observation halted Holly's internal dialogue.

"More like eight hundred miles away," she muttered under her breath.

Holly had Googled it, discovering that it was exactly seven hundred and ninety-two miles from Bavarian Falls to the U.S. Penitentiary in Leavenworth, Kansas.

She smirked at her inside joke.

Nik looked confused.

"What's with you today?" Elaine asked.

"Must be the brats talking or the adrenaline wearing off from the Code Rudolph."

Nik smiled. "You really saved the day, Holly. How can I repay you?"

Oh, now you want to give me money? Are you a bank robber or Robin Hood?

"Code Rudolph, huh? Do tell," Elaine pressed.

Holly recounted the story of lost Chase being found kneeling beside Baby Jesus.

"Truly, you were an answer to prayer." Nik patted Holly's

shoulder in admiration.

She resisted the urge to recoil and brush off the convict's compliment.

"Well done, you," Elaine added.

"I was trying to clear my head during my break, and there was Chase, shivering in the cold."

"Did you say Chase?" Lena rounded the corner.

"Yeah."

"I'm assuming we're talking about the same one. The ten-year-old with blond hair and the voice of an angel?" Lena raised her arm gracefully to the heavens, err, ceiling.

"I can vouch for the first two descriptors, but he didn't break out in song during our interaction," Holly said.

Lena linked her arm through Nik's. "Let's show them, shall we?"

"We shall. Right this way."

Nik held open the door to the newly refurbished studio. Lena entered first. She slowly spun around, gesturing to the various features of the soundproof space. On the wall hung a professional photograph of a motley crew gathered around a microphone, grinning from ear to ear.

"This is where the magic happens," Nik snapped his fingers.

Lena went on to explain that Music Keys had been the recipient of a large grant, enabling them to record a Christmas album with their attendees. The grant covered the cost of the equipment needed for the studio, hiring a sound engineer to produce the album, and the funding for the mastering, distributing, and marketing of the project. The sales from the album would be used to provide scholarships to cover voice and music lessons for participants with special needs throughout the year.

"It's a win-win." Lena beamed.

"The best part is how stoked the kids are to be a part of a professional recording. They think they're rock stars," Nik ran his hand along the framed picture like a proud parent. "The other day, little Julie asked me if I'd be her bodyguard when the paparazzi come to town. I told her that her wheelchair is so fast, she'll probably get away from them pretty easily."

Lena pointed to one of the young people in the portrait who towered over the rest. "You should hear Tony's rendition of 'What Child is This?' Cue the waterworks." She plugged a mic chord into a monitor. "He's on the spectrum. Pretty much nonverbal except when he sings. It's amazing. Music has unlocked so much for him."

"I see what you did there." Elaine smiled back at Tony's likeness. "Music Keys…unlocked his potential."

"Exactly. Here's where you two come in, I hope. One of the grant's requirements is for veterans to benefit from the project. I've been wracking my brain trying to come up with a creative way to include some of Bavarian Falls' military personnel. I know both of you have family members who served. I could use your help incorporating this important element."

Black and white war-torn scenes projected in Holly's mind. At the mention of military personnel, the flashbacks strobed through conversational fragments from her childhood:

"There's been an accident, Holly." Her mom's voice wavered as she pulled young Holly in close. Her whole frame shook. "Your dad is alive, thank God, but he's not the same. I'm so sorry, sweet girl." She rocked her daughter back and forth like a metronome.

"I want Dad back!" Gabe erupted a few weeks later. "Why can't things be like they used to be?" Glass exploded as Gabe flung a basketball through the living room window. Holly looked up from her coloring book in stunned silence.

Next, the voice of the counselor assigned to her and Gabe hung in the air. "How do you really feel, right now?" Holly blinked, keeping up her guard. She was afraid she'd break like the living room glass and Daddy's brain if she answered honestly.

And then, the most painful soundbites of all: "Daddy, are you awake? It's time for Saturday Workshop. Can we listen to our favorite song? Can we…Daddy, why are you still in bed?" Holly had bounded into her parents' bedroom, holding hope that their favorite pastime could continue.

"Hol-Holly, stop it! I-I-I can't. Go play with Gabe. My ha-ha-head hurts. Be quiet!" Dad yelled.

Holly couldn't remember an instance of her daddy losing his temper prior to the aneurysm. But his verbal explosion that morning rattled her, as did his subsequent, sporadic outbursts throughout her childhood.

"But, Daddy—"

"Quiet! Can't you s-s-see I'm not the same?" he moaned.

At that moment she had felt as if an arrow had ripped through her chest, exposing her harsh, altered reality. The gaping hole became a dull ache over time, but the conclusion was the same—something was missing that once belonged to her, and she didn't know how to get it back or if it was even possible.

Silence hung thick between father and daughter for a few uncomfortable moments.

Holly wanted to crawl into her own skin, like a cocoon, never becoming a butterfly. Maybe a moth though, so she didn't have to stay in the dark forever. But if she were a moth, people might shoo her away or even squash her with a paper towel…or their foot.

Her dad closed his eyes and laboriously rolled away from her. Holly backed out of the room slowly so she didn't further disturb him.

Holly never did play with Gabe that day. Instead, she ran to her room, closed the door, and ripped up a damp painting. The one she had made for Dad of a caterpillar on a leaf.

As the replay of heartache reached a crescendo, the studio walls seemed to be closing in on Holly. Lena's voice became muffled and distant. Holly's ears rang, and she felt hot from the inside out as the room started to go dark. Like a tree that had been hit by the final blow of a lumberjack's ax, she started to go down.

Timber.

Two strong arms grabbed her.

"Holly!" Elaine called out.

Fifteen minutes and a glass of carrot juice later, Holly was feeling quite a bit better. Chalking it up to low blood sugar, she assured her companions she was fine. Holly didn't tell them that Lena had unintentionally triggered the grief, that unwelcome house guest that barged in often and knocked her off balance.

It was as if Holly's body remembered what her mind was trying to ignore. The holidays were coming, and with them a wave of loss that hadn't dulled as much as she'd expected. Her dad wasn't who he used to be, yet even after all these years, she wanted to rewrite the story—to rewind to B.C. Not Bible times, although that might not be half bad, but Before the Christmas when Dad left and didn't return the same. Before the Crisis that rocked her childhood. Instead, Holly was forced to live in A.D.— the Aftermath of Dad's aneurysm.

Holly thought she'd been doing okay, but her near fall seemed to connect the dots between her brain's avoidance techniques and her body's muscle memory of the pain. Fascinating, how the days on a calendar could alert grief in the soul, long past tally marks and vigil keeping.

After catching her fall, Nik had walked her to the pleather couch in the studio so she could regroup from a sitting position.

"Are you sure you're okay?" Lena asked for the third time.

Elaine sat beside Holly, rubbing her back in a gesture of comfort and understanding.

Holly was not a wimp. She hated how her episode might've given her present company a different idea. Although her head was still foggy, Holly made a mental note to add "fainting spells" as another reason she was not a fan of the season—not that she was planning on making fainting a holiday tradition or anything, but one couldn't be too careful.

"Would you look at the time? I've got to get going. My mom is expecting me to swing by Greta's Grocery before I head home and get the items on the list she sent me."

Nic shook his head. "I'm not sure you're in any condition to drive."

"Oh, I'm fine. Really. I'm feeling much better after sitting here for a while and drinking this juice. Thanks for that, Lena."

"Nik is right. Why doesn't he drive you home? I'll go grab the items from the store and meet you back at your house."

Holly had hoped Elaine would come to the rescue, but she was no help.

"I wish I could take you, but I picked up a shift at the inn tonight, and I'm going to be late if I don't leave now. I'm sorry. I'll text you after work to see how you're doing. Take it easy, okay?" Elaine hugged Holly and then grabbed her coat, heading for the door.

Elaine stopped at the door. "Thanks so much for thinking of us, Lena. I'm sure once Holly is feeling better, she and I can come up with a plan to help with the grant."

Holly was usually in perfect sync with her friend, but Elaine was now O and two. First of all, she was leaving Holly with Miss

Congeniality and The Jailbird—although, to be fair, Elaine only knew about Lena's claim to fame, not Nik's. And secondly, she had volunteered them to help with the veteran component of the grant. How was Holly's heart supposed to heal when she was thrown headlong into dealing with her source of hurt?

"Wonderful. It's settled then. I knew you two were right for the job." Lena clapped her hands daintily, about as uncomposed as she allowed herself to be. "Now, Holly, where's your mom's list?"

"Hang on, it's on my voicemail," Holly groaned.

"She doesn't text?"

"I'm working on it."

Holly sat in the passenger seat of her car as Nik pulled the vehicle into the driveway of her brick home on Kühn's Way.

Great, now the criminal knows exactly where I live. Maybe I should text Lena to see if she'll pick up glue, feathers, and a blow torch, so I'll be prepared for a home invasion.

The ride had been pretty uneventful, much to Holly's relief. The weirdest thing that happened was that a Harry Connick, Jr. song came on, and both she and Nik admitted he was one of their favorites.

Was he a favorite before Nik's incarceration or had Harry come and done a concert in the slammer? The latter seemed less likely.

Holly shifted in her seat looking in her chauffeur's general direction but avoiding eye contact. "It was nice of you to drive me home. And thanks again for catching my fall."

"Any time. Well, I guess I should ask first—does the fainting thing happen often? You know, so I'm armed and ready with my guns."

It took Holly a few beats to realize that Nik was referring to his muscles, not actual firearms.

"No, I'm not prone to it. Haven't done that in years. Like I said, I probably needed a pick-me-up."

"If you say so. Sure there wasn't more to it?"

Holly wasn't ready to admit the other reason to herself, much less to Nik.

"Lena should be here soon. I'll walk you in."

"That's not necessary."

"Selfish motives. I don't want to stand out here in the cold or sit creepily in your car until Lena gets here."

"Oh yes, of course. I mean, come on in. I think you met my parents at church? They'll be surprised I brought you home—err, I mean that you came home with me. I mean..."

Nik laughed. "You better stop while you're behind."

Holly's cheeks flushed for the third time that day—first in front of Frank and then when she fainted at Music Keys and now while standing in her driveway with a guy whom she knew very little about yet enough to not let her guard down. It didn't help that he was good-looking.

Where did that come from? Holly lassoed that stray thought to the ground and tried to stay focused…just not on his eyes, guns, or charming nature.

"Think fast," Nik announced right before throwing Holly's car keys in her direction.

Plunk.

Apparently, Holly hadn't thought fast enough. And Lena wasn't returning fast enough.

Holly picked up her keys and bolted toward the front door. Feeling childish and unsteady, she was determined not to let it show.

"I'm home!" she called out too cheerily as she entered her childhood home and current residence.

"Oh hi, honey. How was the tour? Thanks again for grabbing the groceries. I really—"

Spotting Nik, Mom stopped talking.

"Hi, there, Mrs. Brig—I mean, Anna. Lovely to see you again."

Oy vey. They're on a first name basis? This is the weirdest—and longest—day ever.

"Welcome to our home. What brings you here?" Mom kept her voice light, but her eyes searched Holly's for answers as she rose from the table and moved to the sink.

"Well, ma'am, Elaine and Holly were at Music Keys, and Lena was recruiting them to help, when..."

Holly could see where this was going, and she definitely didn't want her mom to know about her incident.

"Nik rode with me because I wasn't feeling well, and Lena should be here any minute with your groceries. I wonder what in the world is taking her so long."

"Technically I drove, but..."

"Alone with my daughter?" Mom blurted, much to Holly's horror.

Mom seemed to realize she had nearly blown it by admitting her awareness of Nik's incarceration. Thankfully, she gracefully deflected by doing what moms do best.

"Snacks, anyone? I made chocolate chip cookies, and if Carl didn't get into it yet, there should be vanilla ice cream to serve with them."

"Sounds great, thanks." Nik agreed a little too enthusiastically while Holly resisted the urge to make a swift exit. At least he didn't seem to have picked up on her mom's slip-up. That or he was as thankful for the culinary diversion as Holly and her mom were.

After the cookies, bowls, spoons, and mostly full ice cream

container were retrieved, Mom left Nik and Holly sitting around the Amish-built kitchen table while she checked on her dad in the den.

"We're livin' the dream," Nik said mid-bite.

"I don't know about that."

"Seriously, this is such a welcoming community. I tried finding this kind of camaraderie in Leavenworth, but unfortunately my time there was cut short."

Holly almost choked on her mom's famously soft chocolate chip cookies, dumbfounded that Nik would freely admit to being locked in the slammer. And why did it sound as though he regretted his early release? Wasn't it a good thing to not have more time there? It wasn't exactly the place you'd go to look for a new bestie.

Ding dong.

Lena finally arrived in all her goodness with the bag of groceries from Greta's. The only thing missing was her wand and bubble encasement as she floated in like Glenda the good witch from Oz.

"Let me help you," Nik offered, rising from his seat.

"Thanks. But I'm more than capable of carrying a few groceries," Lena scolded as sweetly as honey. She carefully set the bag on the counter. "Sorry it took me so long. No less than three people stopped me to talk about all that's happening with Music Keys."

"That's my girl. The hometown hero, unlocking kids' potential one music note at a time."

"You sound like an infomercial." Lena scooted the grocery bag further from the counter's edge.

"Hey, that's a good idea." Nik patted the open seat next to him at the kitchen table, inviting Lena to come sit down.

"It's already on my to-do list." Lena walked over and stood

behind the chair.

"The one with 101 items on it?" Nik teased.

Lena's serious expression melted into her awarded-winning smile—the one that, along with her nightingale voice, had won her several beauty pageants.

Mom returned to the kitchen with Holly's precious dad in tow. His anger had mostly subsided over the years as his brain made healing strides, but the gaping hole between what had been and what was still ached.

"Lena, thanks so much for doing the grocery run. Is there anything you can't do?"

Holly willed her eyes to not roll back in her head as her mother gushed praise. Holly's annoyance and insecurities were magnified under the lens of the two high-achieving women, cut from similar, color-coordinating cloth. She brushed stray cookie crumbs off her sweater.

"Actually, she's lousy at bowling," Nik offered. Lackluster bowling skills were hardly kryptonite, but they were a start.

"Hey now." Lena protested, still standing.

"I, on the other hand, am basically a pro. I took a bowling class in college for one of my electives," her boyfriend boasted.

"Impressive," Holly's dad said.

"Mr. Brigham, we meet again." Nik rose to extend his hand to Holly's flannel-pajamaed father. "I don't know how you keep your figure with your wife's famous cookies around the house. They're delicious."

Dad patted Mom's arm.

"Can I help you put away the groceries?" Lena asked.

"I'm feeling better now. I've got it," Holly intercepted, not letting on that her head still throbbed a little.

"Glad to hear it. We need to get going, but let's touch base soon about your creative ideas for the grant requirement."

Her mother paused in the act of tugging a carton of milk out of the bag. "Ooh, do tell."

"Later, Mom, okay?"

"Oh, all right. Please, take a few cookies for the road."

Nik obliged.

Lena politely declined.

Within minutes, the unlikely couple had left the house.

"Well, that was delightful," Holly's mom commented as the door closed.

"Mom. Have you forgotten Nik's history? Don't let him fool you. Aren't you concerned that he knows where we—and your famous dessert—live? He's bound to come back, either to steal Dad's flat screen or a few dozen cookies."

"Now, now, ladies. Nik seems ha-harmless."

"And not too hard on the eyes, either."

"Mom!"

"Oh dear, did I say that out loud?"

"Now, Anna, I th-think…you and I need to find some…pr-pre-season mistletoe," Dad coaxed.

"Don't worry, dear. He doesn't hold a candle to you."

With that, Holly's parents retired for the evening.

Holly grabbed her AirPods and listened to Harry Connick, Jr. while she put the groceries away. She wasn't sure how to process the strange evening. But she was sure of one thing: she was determined to say no to Lena's invitation. She didn't want to risk another painful walk down memory lane—or fainting spell around Nik—again.

CHAPTER EIGHT
Big Crowds

ON FRIDAY THE 13TH, HOLLY FEARED the concert might make the day live up to its name. Still, the hours at work dragged on.

"Ready for your hot date?" Andy nudged Holly, almost causing her to mess up the ornament she was working on.

"Hey. This is serious business—the ornament, not the date—although I don't know if I'd call it a date exactly. Some friends and I going to a concert, that's all. Besides it's cold outside, not hot—thank you very much. Don't you have a deer to hunt?"

"Soon…very soon. I'll be back on Tuesday with a photo of a trophy buck to prove it. Never fear, they'll send someone over to fill my place while I'm gone."

When Holly lived in Chicago, November 15 was an ordinary sort of day. But in Bavarian Falls, opening day of rifle season was pretty much an official holiday.

Holly was relieved she wouldn't be winging it on her own while Andy was occupying his hunting blind. With Thanksgiving approaching, the die-hards were already Christmas shopping. Ornament customization orders were stacking up faster than you could say "Christmas ornaments" in German—although that wasn't saying much, since *weihnachtsschmuck* didn't exactly roll off the tongue.

As an artist, Holly had adopted her high school art teacher's philosophy that "art takes time." But the in-store "Countdown to Christmas" clock wouldn't allow for that. There was no time for art to take in this case, as impatient shoppers flocked to Station 8.

There were the typical requests that came in:

- Personalize a child's name on the Baby's First Christmas ornament.
- Paint the wedding date on the Mr. and Mrs. wedding bell ornament.
- Write a teacher's name in calligraphy on the chalkboard ornament.
- Add grandchildren's names to the back of snowman collectibles.

Only yesterday, Andy had received an order to add a couple's first names to the We Still Do ornament for their tenth anniversary. Picking up on Andy's subtle sadness, Holly offered to take that one for him. Andy and Tammy hadn't made it to their tenth, and the customization request seemed to prick her co-worker—even though he clearly tried to appear nonchalant about it.

As Friday the 13th continued to unfold, the custom ornament requests went from slightly weird to full-blown mind-boggling.

There were the more unusual requests, like:

- The non-traditionally spelled names: Jennyffer, Justeen, Caspurr, and Tommee, to name a few—all humans, not pets.
- The senator's wife who wanted to add her kids' names—Kennedy, Carter, Wilson, and Rosie (after Roosevelt, apparently)—to a donkey ornament.

Would Clinton or Obama be next?

And then there were the ones she really didn't want to ask about, such as the request to add *will you pluck my chicken?* on the farmer ornament.

While the demands on her time were a bit stressful, Holly was usually fascinated to learn a little about the customers through her interactions with them and their requests for customization.

There were many requests to add Mrs. Jackson to teacher ornaments. Holly safely concluded she was a favorite among the local students. One customer came in and bought fourteen figurines for her daughter and son-in-law's slew of children. Holly marveled at how each of the children came to the family—a blend of international adoptions, biological children, and several sibling sets adopted through the foster-care system.

All the talk of children reminded Holly that she wasn't exactly a spring chicken anymore. She tried to mute her biological clock that tick-tocked louder than her singleness could shush.

It helped that she had a date tonight. Frank struck her as the kind of guy who would want a baker's dozen when it came to offspring. Not that she was imagining their future or anything. Besides, she couldn't picture herself driving around in a fifteen-passenger van, although she did love children.

As her shift neared its end, an attractive middle-aged couple approached the counter. They held up a glass ornament—a stocking with gifts pouring out the top. There were ten spaces on the stocking, ready to be customized with tiny letters by an artist's steady hand. The couple was visiting from Tennessee, and within a few minutes, they hit it off with Holly.

They confided in her, recounting their newlywed life as Broadway stars and their transformation from fame to faith. They had left their success in New York to lead a quieter life and start a family. In the wake of heartache and health issues, they were unable to fill their home with the children they longed for. Miraculously, they conceived one child. A daughter. They raised her to develop her innate talents and work hard without compromising her integrity. Now she was a successful musical artist with her name in lights at concert venues all over the country. But, more importantly, she and her husband had been blessed with five children of their own.

The couple beamed with pride as they pulled up a picture of their adorable grandkids.

"We once thought our names would be on marquees and that we'd have a minivan full of our own children. But we have no greater joy than to see our only child shining brightly in a dark world, filling the world with wholesome music and filling our hearts—and vehicle—with grandchildren. It wasn't the story we would have written, but in many ways, it's better."

Holly was stirred by the sincerity and transparency of this couple. It was clear they had faced disappointments, yet it was evident how grateful they were to be a part of a bigger and grander plan.

"When we saw this ornament, we knew it was the one. Look! It has exactly ten slots to be filled with names—for my daughter, her husband, their houseful of kids, and for us, too."

"And what would you like on the last line?"

The husband chimed in, "That one's for Rocky. Our dog."

Holly laughed easily. "No problem. Dogs are my specialty."

"Do you know how long it'll take? I know this probably isn't typical, but we really need it before the weekend is over. We're only in town through late tomorrow."

Holly glanced at her ever-growing stack of orders. The current wait time was two weeks out.

"For you guys? It'll be ready tomorrow morning by nine. I'll leave it up at the customer service desk with Leslie. Don't let on that you ordered it today, or my manager will give me the naughty elf slip," Holly joked.

"Thank you so much. We really appreciate it. I know it might seem silly, but it's pretty special to have an ornament like this, serving as a tangible reminder of God's faithfulness and how He brings good out of difficulties."

"It's my pleasure, truly. Thanks for coming in today."

And with that, Holly's mind was changed. Maybe she could make something helpful and useful out of her dad's difficulties. Maybe she would look beyond her past and herself and invest her time in others for the greater good.

She'd call Lena tomorrow.

Holly had convinced Frank to meet her and Elaine downtown near the life-sized Glockenspiel Clock instead of picking her up at home. It was bad enough that Nik knew where she lived. She didn't want to add to the list of ineligible suitors showing up unannounced at her front door or inviting themselves in for dessert. Well, at least she was trying to convince herself that Frank was an ineligible suitor. She rehearsed her list again. *He's younger, he's committed to Bavarian Falls long-term because of his job and family, he's funny, he's amusing, he's...*

Wait—this was supposed to be a list of the reasons why this shouldn't go anywhere. Oh dear, Holly needed to get out more.

Bavarian Falls felt like Christmas all year long—even in mid-July, minus the snow. However, as the end-of-the-year holidays drew near, an electrical current radiated from the Christmas enthusiasts who crowded the streets and filled local businesses. The intensity permeated the air. There was no avoiding what was coming.

Holly didn't even attempt to park at Edelweiss Inn because it was the night of the big concert. Instead, she opted for public parking near the visitor's center and then walked the few blocks to the inn to meet up with Elaine.

"Sorry, I know I'm cutting it close," Holly apologized.

"Almost thought you backed out."

"Nope—had a rush order I needed to finish before my shift was over."

"You're here now and this is going to be fun," Elaine reassured her.

"I think you're right. Thanks for giving up karaoke for this."

"Don't get used to it," Elaine joked. "I doubt Klingemann's will be hopping tonight, anyway. It's not every day that an artist of this caliber comes to town."

A rush of people swept past the friends.

"Let's hurry. It's almost six."

Elaine and Holly crossed Main Street to the iconic landmark, the Glockenspiel Clock located near the Engel Haus Restaurant. The monumental clock was housed in a bell tower. Several times a day, wooden figurines emerged on a moving stage, portraying the story of the Pied Piper of Hamelin. Gabe used to make fun of Holly for being afraid of the trail of ceramic rats that were a part of the Pied Piper depiction. Holly still wasn't a fan of the life-size rodents, but thankfully, they no longer haunted her dreams.

Rats aside, the wonder of the clock delivered joy to the year-round crowds, young and old alike. The illuminated clock face brought locals and tourists together in close proximity, as they indulged in a Bavarian-style slice of history. Even Christmas-averse-Holly appreciated the Glockenspiel's cheerful carillon bells and Westminster chimes that echoed throughout town. The German and American hymns it played were part of the soundtrack of her childhood.

The intricate time-keeping hands clicked into place on top of the gold-covered numerals of six and twelve. This shift in time initiated the music proceeded by the presentation of the tragic tale.

"Never gets old, does it?" Frank sneaked up on Holly and Elaine while their attention was fixed upward.

"Ahh!" Holly startled.

"What, the rats or my sneak attack?" Frank grinned.

His timing was the worst. Or impeccable, depending how you looked at it.

"Both?" Holly shrugged.

"We've got about an hour until we need to be at the concert. VIP tickets have their advantages. We can bypass the line. So, my question is: carriage ride or dessert?"

"Dessert," Holly and Elaine blurted out.

"Jinx!" Frank yelled.

It wasn't that Holly was opposed to the carriage ride itself. But it sounded romantic, like something you'd do with a boyfriend, not the boy next door. Or, in this case, the boss's grandson.

"It's really nice of you to treat us to a night on the town," Holly said.

"My pleasure."

What was this? Chick-fil-A? Or a fun-loving guy trying to leverage his social life?

"You sure no carriage ride?"

Apparently, Frank had booked both a carriage ride and a table at the Engel Haus restaurant ahead of time so they'd have no waiting with whatever option they selected. He was either over-eager or thoughtful. Over Black Forest torte, he admitted he clocked about sixty hours a week during the holiday season, so perhaps it was a good excuse for him to take a break.

"Doesn't the store only close a few weeks a year?" Elaine asked. "When do you get a break?"

"When Great Grandpa was alive, he instituted a mandatory

family break so we could all have time off together. He trained other staff to fill in during that two-week period. After his business took off, he acquired land. He eventually built a place big enough to house all of us."

"Please tell me it's in Florida, where you can thaw out and chill at the beach," Elaine said.

"Do you know my family? We're basically the official Christmas ambassadors." Frank leaned back in his chair.

"Not a beach house?" Holly deduced.

"No, a massive chalet in—wait for it…North Pole, Alaska."

"Stop it!" Elaine waved her hands.

"Not joking. Population 2113, or 2147-ish when the Neumann entourage arrives every June." Frank alerted the server that he was ready for the bill.

Wow. Vacationing with extended family every year at the same place? Sounded equal parts sentimentally sweet and slightly suffocating. And definitely far removed from her vacation experiences.

Besides the Mackinac Island trip and a few other day trips to nearby cities, Holly's family had stayed close to home because of her dad's health complications. When Holly was thirteen, Grandpa Dale and Grandma Bea surprised Holly with an adventure trip to Chicago where she experienced a new art museum each day. Holly had felt as if she had been transported to another country. Her senses had been wide awake, painting with a broad stroke of diverse colors while a cacophony of different languages swirled overhead and the El rattled as it approached its next stop.

Holly's soul had been stirred as she took in the varying styles, textures, and feelings of each museum exhibit. Pursuing art as a career went to the forefront of Holly's mind, as did a resolution to not stay in Bavarian Falls after high school. She had seen a glimpse of what was out there beyond the borders of her hometown, and she couldn't wait to leave her mark—preferably on the bottom right corner of a canvas hung in The Art Institute of Chicago. She adored the opportunities the city afforded. Her only complaint was the large crowds—pushing past her on the subway, bumping into her on the sidewalk, and encroaching on her contemplations in front of the art exhibits. It was ironic that, although her hometown was small, it was usually flooded with tourists, especially the night of a concert.

After more small talk and the last bites of Black Forest torte, the trio exited the restaurant and drove five miles out of town, in bumper-to-bumper traffic, to the packed concert venue. Before they arrived, Holly added Reason #8 to her growing list of holiday hate: Big Crowds.

Frank pulled up to the entrance and instructed Holly and Elaine to give their names at the window to pick up their tickets. He'd meet up with them at their seats after he found a parking space.

"I'm surprised he doesn't have VIP parking with his family connections," Holly said.

"Looks like he's a VIP in your book," Elaine teased.

"Can't a guy and girl be friends without everyone assuming there's more?" Holly stuck her hands in her coat pocket as they walked briskly to the entrance.

Elaine raised her hands in surrender.

"Can you imagine vacationing with your immediate and extended family for two weeks straight in Bavarian Falls' sister city?"

"Is that true?"

"The sister city thing? I don't think so. But it might as well be. On the drive over, I did a little investigating of North Pole,

Alaska. You should see the Santa house there." Holly opened the heavy door to the venue.

"Sorry about teasing you. I think Frank's a nice guy looking for friends outside of work." Elaine rubbed her hands together.

"But I'm from inside his workplace."

"That's true, but—"

"Hey there, ladies. We meet again."

Holly pulled her prickly shell up like a turtleneck in the presence of the guy who had once been guarded himself—literally.

"Oh hi, Nik."

Everywhere Holly went, Nik showed up. Was he following her? Maybe she was being paranoid. It was a small town, after all—must be a coincidence that they kept running into each other.

"Lena's meeting me here after her video call with a nonprofit out of Atlanta."

Of course. He was here for Lena. *Get out of your head, girl.*

"She's definitely committed," Elaine nodded.

Nik crossed his arms and rocked back on his heels and then forward again.

After a few uncomfortable moments, Holly said, "I hope you enjoy the show."

She led Elaine over to the ticket window. An elderly man with an official-looking name badge that read *Barry* handed them their tickets along with swag bags filled with merchandise from the headliner and her opening act.

Once they were settled in their front row seats, Elaine laughed.

"What's so funny?"

"It's really too bad that Barry was too old for you."

"The ticket guy? I think he was in his seventies. What are you talking about?"

"Holly and Barry sound like a match made in heaven. Get it? A holly berry?"

"Oh boy."

Speaking of "oh boy," a few minutes later, Frank and his lanky legs arrived and sat next to Holly.

He leaned over the arm rest. "Ready for this?"

His peppermint-y breath lingered, and Holly fought the urge to back away. He wouldn't try to kiss her here, would he?

"Um…for the concert?" Holly blurted. "Yeah, it's a good change of scenery. Thanks for inviting me."

"No problem-o. I'm glad you said yes, by the way. You kept me guessing." He turned his head toward Holly.

"I like to keep things a bit mysterious."

"It's no mystery that you're beautiful. You know that, right?"

"Thanks, Frank." She patted his arm, acknowledging his compliment yet trying to put the brakes on the freight train of thought barreling down on her.

Frank received a text message and responded, his thumbs typing rapidly.

She turned her attention to the stage, taking in the elegant beauty of the set design. Her appreciation for the various stage elements was soon interrupted by what was becoming a familiar voice.

"You sure it's okay, man?" Nik directed his question toward Frank.

"Totally. I'm sorry that your girlfriend had to bail." Frank stood up to give Nik his seat while he moved to the empty seat on the other side of Holly.

Mayday, mayday! What is happening?

"Nik and I ran into each other in the lobby." Frank leaned

close again to explain the situation to Holly. "Lena canceled on him, so he was going to leave, but I insisted he come sit with us and not miss out."

"Where did you get the extra front row ticket?" Holly kept her voice low.

"I've got connections." Frank tilted his head slightly, pointing at Holly while clicking his tongue on the inside of his cheek and adding a wink for emphasis.

Elaine initiated small talk with Nik, probably to distract him from Lena not showing.

Thankfully, the show was about to start. Holly wondered if Frank would try to hold her hand in the dimmed venue. Her palms beaded with sweat at the thought of it.

Sandwiched between a boisterous Frank and a stood-up Nik wasn't ideal. Still, Elaine had it worse—although she didn't know it. At least Holly was also sitting next to a guy who hadn't broken the law...not that she knew of, anyway.

Soon after the concert began, the less-than-ideal seating arrangement was forgotten.

The five-piece band started playing, unleashing joy into the atmosphere that reverberated off the walls and bounced back to the crowd. Holly realized that, since returning home, she had allowed a gray cloud to loom overhead, tempering lightheartedness. It was as if she was stuck on a back road and needed a push out of the ditch. The wailing trumpet served as that shove as Holly willingly let her guard down, drinking in the wonder of the concert. She laughed freely as the crowd rose to their feet. She clapped to the beat and danced as if no one was watching.

A few times during the show, Holly looked over at Elaine, who appeared to be having a grand time. Holly couldn't help but notice that Nik seemed to be enjoying the experience too, as evidenced by his bright eyes and steady smile. She couldn't imagine what he might have done to land in jail, but she could definitely see why Lena was attracted to him. And there was no doubt Frank was having the time of his life with his flailing dance moves and loud, slightly off-key singing. He nearly gave Holly a black eye during one zealous spin. He profusely apologized with a quick peck on her temple that left her paralyzed.

He'd basically claimed her as his without asking how she felt about it.

Holly glanced over to see if Elaine had witnessed Frank's unusual concoction of clumsy mixed with spontaneous affection. Elaine's attention was elsewhere, but Nik raised an eyebrow at her and shook his head a bit. Holly flushed and shrugged, turning her attention back to the stage.

If the lead singer, Jana Bonparente, hadn't been so talented or authentic, Holly might have mulled over the moment for the rest of the night. Instead, Holly was mesmerized. In a culture of celebrities compromising their morals and toppling under the weight of fame, there was something different about Jana. It radiated from within.

As the concert neared its conclusion, the band members faded into the background, except for the musician at the grand piano. Jana's heels clicked on the stage as she walked over to a stool positioned under a flood of sapphire lights. The audience seemed captivated by Jana's crystal voice as she performed a ballad that built and swelled as it unfolded.

The key to peace is turning to face that which holds you down.

The way to freedom is not out of reach.
Turn the knob, let yourself be found.

There's an echo of hope that you have forgotten
As you've lost your way in the crowd.
But don't give up, I've come for you.
I'm your Everything...even in this.
I never leave. I never change.
I see you.
Even when life causes you pain.
I'll be with you.
The key to peace is turning to face the One who loves you best.
The way to freedom is not out of reach.
Take a seat, let your soul find rest.
There's a pattern of purpose you've overlooked
As you've made your way back home.
But don't miss out on what's to come.
I'm your Everything...even in this.
I never leave. I never change.
I see you.
Even when life is not like you planned
I'm here with you.
I'm your everything.
And that's everything.
Ooo...everything.

The hush of the crowd replaced applause. Sacred silence was their amen. Nik on her left, Frank on her right, and thousands at her back, but Holly felt like the only one in the room for a moment. It was as if the song had been written for her, for this moment. A gift from above, carried on sound waves and tucked inside her heart for safekeeping.

The way to freedom is not out of reach. Turn the knob, let yourself be found.

CHAPTER NINE
Frank Conversations

As Holly set up her station Monday morning, she wondered who had been assigned to fill in for Andy. Whoever it was, she hoped they'd be able to keep up.

Was it Teresa? No.

Was it Leslie? No.

Was it Betty Jo, accompanied by her jingling feet and bubbling enthusiasm? No!

It was…Frank! He who had sent one hundred texts in three hours after the concert Frank.

"I'm all yours," he announced as he approached Holly's workstation. He had exchanged his crimson vest for an apron that matched hers, minus the "Holly Noel" nametag.

Holly spent forty minutes trying to teach Frank how to paint customized ornaments, but there are things that can't be taught; they're innate. Not that Frank wasn't trying hard enough. In fact, he was trying too hard. The apprentice stopped his sensei frequently, making sure his brushstrokes were up to standard.

"Thanks again for the concert. Jana was amazing."

"You're welcome. I liked the first band better 'cuz I could jump around like a fool to their sick beats."

Touché.

"How about that carriage ride sometime?" he asked.

Gulp.

She willed Andy to fill his hunting tags early, come show off his prize deer, and relieve Frank of his duties.

"Uh…I'd need to check with Elaine first. Her work schedule's pretty crazy at the inn right now."

"Elaine is nice and all, but I was meaning you and me. Like a date."

Double gulp.

"Oh no. I have to check with Leslie about something. You're doing great on that order, by the way. Keep it up. Be right back."

Holly tried to keep her stride to a swift walk instead of a full-on sprint, as she bolted over to customer service. She needed to buy time to process what had happened and to figure out what to do next.

"Hi, Les. I wonder if you can help me?"

"Sure can."

"Did a middle-aged couple stop in on Saturday morning?"

"Let's see. There were about two hundred middle-aged couples here from all over the country and the world. You're going to have to specify."

"They were picking up a custom ornament. The stocking one, with presents in it. They were from Nashville and as kind as they could be."

"Yes! They were here. Why didn't you ask if Jana Bonparente's parents stopped by instead of being elusive?"

"Are you kidding me?"

"Come on. Surely you knew who they were?"

"No way! I had no idea."

"Look them up. You'll see. There's a great photo that pops up online of them with their grandkids. Looks like the sweetest bunch."

Holly replayed her conversation with Jana's parents, making sure she hadn't said anything stupid.

"By the way, your secret is safe with me."

"What do you mean?"

"You obviously rushed their order and gave it priority over others to get it done."

"Guilty as charged."

"My lips are sealed."

"I owe you."

"Oh, don't worry about that. The shock on your face was worth the price of admission."

Holly walked slowly back to her station, shaking her head along the way. Who knew? Apparently, everyone in the store but her.

She'd left Frank hanging long enough. It was time to respond to his direct request for a solo carriage ride.

"What was that all about?" he asked.

"Looks like you're really getting into your work." Holly pointed to the stray paint mark that had wound up on his temple.

She grabbed a cloth from the drawer and offered it to him, trying to avoid his probable request that she wipe it off for him…or return a temple kiss of her own.

"Did I get it all?"

"Almost. One more spot, right there," she directed.

"Back to my question. How about you, me, and a horse and carriage?"

So much for Elaine's idea that Frank was looking for friends to hang with outside of work. He was trying to work it in his own sort of way. Holly didn't want to be mean, but she also wanted to be clear. She decided to rely on a bit of humor to lighten the blow.

"Let me be frank…"

"Wait a minute. I'm not sure I like the sound of that. In my estimation, it could mean one of three things, one, let me be Frank, meaning you're going to shoot straight and give me your answer, either declaring your affection or aversion to me or telling me you can't go on a carriage ride because of a horse allergy. Two, let me be Frank, meaning you think I'm so cool you actually want to be me. Three, let me be, Frank, meaning you want me to leave you alone, forever. *Auf Wiedersehen*."

Holly laughed. "I see what you mean. So many options. Let's see. I'll take what's behind Door #1. I'm going to be frank…"

Frank gave her a quizzical expression.

"Whoops…I see how that's still confusing. What I mean is, let me be direct. There, is that a better word choice?"

He nodded.

"Thanks for asking, but I'm not interested."

"Not interested in the carriage ride or me?"

"That sounds a little harsh when you put it that way. I'd like us to be friends, Frank."

"Famous last words."

"I'm sorry."

Frank held up his hand like a patrol guard stopping traffic for young children to pass. "You don't owe me an explanation. I'll speculate the reason. One, you think I'm too young for you. Two, it's a conflict of interest to date the boss's grandson. Three, I'm out of your league, and you'd feel insecure around me. Four, the thought of a honeymoon in the North Pole is not your cup of tea—I mean cocoa."

"Uh, whiplash! We went from zero to sixty there. First a carriage ride, now we're getting married?"

Ingrid Meyer, the pastor's wife, was shopping within earshot when Holly delivered her last line. Which made Holly's timing impeccable—or the worst, depending on how you look at it.

"Holly? And Frank! How are you, darling? I still can't get over how tall you are. It seems like yesterday when you were in Sunday school, keeping things lively and terrorizing poor Mrs. Schulz."

"My claim to fame!" Frank boasted.

"I didn't know you two were an item. I can't believe your mom didn't tell me," Ingrid said to Holly.

"Nope, we're partners today," Holly assured her.

"Oh dear, young people are so progressive these days."

Holly, horrified by her own word choice, added an important clarifier. "We're *work* partners today—not a couple, we're checking offline items for these one-of-a-kind ornaments. That's all."

"Is that a fact?" She looked for confirmation from Frank.

"It's a fact that Betty Jo is, as we speak, adding the newest additions to the clergy ornaments at Station 10. You won't want to miss snagging up the latest and greatest for Pastor M.," Frank said.

"Thank you. I'll head over there right now. And don't worry, you two. Mum's the word." She mimed locking her mouth with a key and tossing it away.

Holly's stomach tangled like a string of unruly Christmas lights. It wouldn't be long before Ingrid told Holly's mom what she'd overheard—and had clearly misunderstood.

"We're working side by side, but Mrs. Meyer acted like we were hand in hand." Frank checked off a finished order on the clipboard.

"You think?" Holly said a little more sarcastically than intended.

"Come on. It was sort of funny, right? Who else could we convince that we're an item?"

Oh dear. Here goes Round 2.

"Let me be Frank…"

"I hear ya loud and clear. Friends, it is. I hope?"

"Sure thing. But can you lay off the antics a bit?" Holly picked up the delicate ornament in front of her.

"Your wish is my command. Wait. Let me try again. How about, as you wish? Nope—romantic movie line, too much. How about this—final answer—you've got a friend in me?"

Holly hoped the eye roll, coupled with a smile, communicated her feelings precisely. Frank was both annoying and slightly amusing. Time would tell if he remained hung up on Holly. Their kind-of date at the concert had been fun, but Frank's overzealous text barrage induced the sort of claustrophobic reaction that Holly experienced on elevators and under the watchful eyes of Bavarian Fall's busybodies.

While sometimes necessary, candid conversations—whether at work, on a date, or over a meal—were no picnic, especially when they were partially overheard and entirely misunderstood. So, they earned their spot on Holly's holiday hangups' list. Reason #9: Frank conversations—not the person, but the type of convo. And her addition to the list did not merely refer to direct dialogue with a prospective boyfriend, but boundary-setting with adults who had forgotten Holly was grown up, even if her present circumstances fed into a "failure to fully launch" narrative. Besides, it was only temporary. With a little more time and effort, she hoped to be far from here. But not as far as North Pole, Alaska.

The rest of the morning went off without a hitch and without any more talk of them getting hitched. On her lunch break, Holly decided it was time to act on the important decision she had made after her encounter with Jana Bonparente's parents.

I'll bet they were at the concert! It would have been fun to see them there. Heck, they were probably in the front row, too.

Holly pulled out the Music Keys business card that Nik had given her on the tour last week. Like Lena herself, the business card exuded professionalism and poise. It was baffling how Lena could walk hand in hand with the likes of Nik. Although, had Holly not known about Nik's dark side, she would've been easily won over herself.

Holly decided to exercise her adulthood and call instead of text after asking herself, what would Lena do?

After several rings, it went to voicemail. "You're reached Music Keys, a five-o-one-c-three committed to unlocking children's potential through the universal language of music. Please leave a message, and we'll get back to you as soon as we're able...Beep."

At the sound of the tone, Holly told Lena that she could count on her to come up with a creative solution for including veterans in the grant-funded project.

She sighed as she hung up. It wouldn't be easy to face what had held her back—and had literally knocked her down—the last time she was at Music Keys. But she was committed.

Andy arrived back to work on Tuesday without bragging rights of a trophy buck but satisfied with a good-sized doe, which meant meat in the freezer. He relayed to Holly how Oliver had helped him process the deer in their garage.

"You're a straight up pioneer."

"You know it. Hey, how'd it go while I was gone?"

"It was entertaining, all right." Holly shared the bullet points, including the inordinate number of texts she'd received from Frank. How anyone could type that fast on a phone was beyond her.

Andy's raspy laugh swelled when Holly got to the part about the pastor's wife misinterpreting her and Frank's relationship status.

"You're going to start a town scandal, Holly-girl."

"That's the last thing I need."

"Frank's a great guy, though. I hope you let him down easy."

"I tried, truly. He seemed like a pretty good sport about it. I might have considered another date with him after our concert experience, but it's all a little—or a lot—too much. Besides, Frank belongs in Bavarian Falls, and…I'm only passing through, ya know?"

"That's what you keep saying. We'll see."

"Not you, too."

"Just kidding, Holly. We'll be lining up to pay admission to view your art exhibit one day."

"At this rate, my art might only make it onto local Christmas trees."

"Speaking of, let's tackle these orders so we don't get backed up."

After they worked in silence for a while, Holly broached the subject of Andy's house. "Since I shared with you, are you finally going to let me know more about the mystery woman?"

Andy explained how he did his best thinking in the woods. With looming oaks and squirrels as witnesses, he was able to slow down long enough to gain perspective and clarity.

"It's Teresa," he blurted out.

"I knew it!"

"But please don't say anything to anyone about it."

"Do you like her? Is that what this is about?"

"See, that's what I'm afraid of."

"Liking her?"

"No, that she'll think I do if I offer her the house. This is more about being true to the prompting I had. I know this house would be an answer to her prayers for her and her kids. She has confided in me about her difficult financial situation—mainly due to all her unexpected medical bills because of her arthritis."

"Oh, Andy. This is big. How are you going to present it? With a mile of ribbon wrapped around the house?"

"I'm not sure. I'm still thinking that through. Any suggestions?"

"Maybe dinner at Edelweiss Inn and a letter from Santa that lays out the details? That way you'd simply be the messenger."

"I think you've been getting ideas from Betty Jo and that movie she likes. Hopefully, Teresa won't shoot the messenger." Andy chuckled.

"Obviously you've still got hunting on the brain."

"Always."

"When do you think you'll ask her?"

"Before the end of the month. Oh, did I tell you that Bill proposed to Tammy this weekend?"

"You thought that was coming, right? How are you feeling about it?" Holly asked.

"I can't change the past. But this arrangement has been our reality for a while now, so I'm making the most of it. Trying not to live with regret."

"How's Oliver doing?"

"Ebbs and flows. Bill bought a new puppy, so he enjoys chasing the dog around. He'll be with me for Turkey Day, and we're going to go hunting, just us. That'll be fun."

"Gabe, his wife, and my niece will be home for Thanksgiving. It'll be nice to be together again under one roof." As soon as the words were out of Holly's mouth, she regretted what she'd said. Andy would give anything to have his family under one roof. She put her head down and tried to erase the unintentional hurt she might have caused.

"I think that's great, really. When you don't have something you once did, you appreciate the small things even more."

"How profound, Mr. Pioneer. Or should I call you Mr. Frost?"

"Why, because I'm ice cold?"

"No, because you're a poet, and you don't even know it."

"Far from it."

The next few weeks were packed with thousands of customers and what felt like thousands of ornament projects. There was little room for friendly banter between Holly and Andy, as their attention was needed elsewhere.

Andy mentioned that he was formulating a plan for telling Teresa about the house, based on Holly's suggestions. He'd let her know if he needed further assistance.

Holly was counting down the days until Thanksgiving, a much-anticipated day off for all Neumann's employees. She was also looking forward to her brother's arrival and, to be frank, she was more than ready to let Gabe and his family gobble up Mom's attention for a while.

CHAPTER TEN
Crossing Boundaries

ON HER DAY OFF, HOLLY PLANNED on sleeping in—but her mom had other plans, starting with an early intrusion into Holly's bedroom. Her conspicuous objective? To locate the fancy Thanksgiving placemats housed in a plastic storage container under Holly's bed. The retrieval process was more like a search and rescue mission than a covert operation.

"Mommm, seriously. It feels like I'm on a waterbed."

"Oh, don't mind me. I'm only sneaking in to grab decorations."

There was a lot of tugging and pulling and not much sneaking. With one last tidal wave of exertion, the stowed container was finally freed.

"You'll be up soon, right? So much to do, so little time!"

"Twenty more minutes. Is that too much to ask? And could you please knock next time?"

The door closed, most of the way.

Holly's disturbed slumber and her mom's oblivion to—or disregard for—her personal space, was motivation to add Reason #10 to her list: Crossing boundaries.

To be fair, Holly's parents weren't charging her rent or anything. It was their house, but they had given her access to this space, for now. And her bedroom door had been closed.

Still groggy, she opened one eye to scan her list. "10 Things I Hate About Christmas" had a nice ring to it. Although, if for some reason Holly's list was turned into a screen play, it probably wouldn't make it on the holiday movie channel with a title like that. Plus, with December right around the corner, Holly had a feeling her list was not yet complete.

"Auntie Holly! Are you up?" the exuberant voice of her six-year-old niece, Claudia, called out not more than five minutes later.

"Give me a minute, sweetie."

"Nana told me to come wake you up."

Holly coached herself...happy thoughts. Think happy thoughts. You can do it. You can make it through today without a meltdown. You're a grown woman. You can cooperate without being controlled. Deep breaths.

"It's gobbly bird pick-up time!" Claudia added.

Holly's mom, in her high-achieving, gold-hearted fashion, coordinated a collection of thirty cooked turkeys for the local shelter on Thanksgiving Day. Her friends and neighbors dropped off the "gobbly birds," as Claudia called them, that they'd cooked the day before. It was a sight to see, as giant coolers lined the front yard, proof of the early morning turkey drop-off. A truck from the shelter was due to pick them up mid-morning, which was why Claudia was anticipating and urging her auntie to get up.

Holly finally rose to the occasion. Her hair nest and dragon breath were proof of her disgruntled awakening. She left the nest but opted to brush her teeth in hopes it would freshen her mood.

She emerged in tapered gray sweats and a monochromatic orange crewneck, ready for comfort food and a day at home. The televised parade was going strong in the Brighams' household, as was the savory aroma of turkey and stuffing.

"Hey, little sis. About time you joined us." Gabe bear-hugged her and added a few noogies for good measure.

His wife of eight years, Monica, greeted Holly with a normal hug void of noogies, thankfully. Her ginger beach waves reached her mid-back and had long been a source of covetousness for Holly.

"Auntie!" was the only warning Holly received from her freckle-faced, pigtailed niece who sneaked up from behind, squeezing her around the waist.

"Claudi-boo. It's so good to see you!"

"Not Claudi-boo. But Claudia. Or Claudia Ann."

"Hey now, don't be rude to your auntie," Monica instructed.

"Claudia or Claudia Ann, please." And with that she curtsied and ran to the bay window to look for the truck.

"Kids these days," Gabe added. "Speaking of, when are you springin' this place and moving out of your old room?"

Monica elbowed him.

"Nice, Gabe. Way to make me feel awesome within the first few minutes of our reunion. That hurt."

"So did my wife's side jab."

Holly pursed her lips and flared her nostrils. How dare Gabe waltz in here with his precious family and rub it in Holly's face that she was such a loser because she'd moved back home for a hot minute? Never mind the fact that she tried her best to avoid a scenario like this.

Holly's stare down and her concerted effort to bite her tongue instead of lash out like usual seemed to help Gabe realize his teasing had crossed a line.

"Look, sis. I'm sorry. I'm sure this isn't your end goal."

"You think?"

Old habits died hard.

"You were so insistent that you'd never live here again, and now..."

Holly stood, armed crossed, trying to hold her ground. But she couldn't hold the tears back anymore. They fell freely, locked up for too long.

"Hey, Hol—look, I'm sorry, truly. Can we have a redo?"

Silence.

The altercation between them was Monica's cue to attend to her daughter. She shot Gabe a look as she left.

"I know it's like our 756th redo, but what do ya say?"

Holly swiped at her tears, trying to brush away the vulnerability.

"It's me. Your big bro who acts like a jerk every now and then but cares about you, more than you know."

"That was really low." Holly rubbed the toe of her sock into the carpet.

"Hey, maybe Dad still has that triple XL shirt they used to make us wear when we fought."

"Oh man, that was the worst!" Gabe whistled.

"Right? What was it called again?"

"The Get Along Shirt—oh, the memories." Holly scanned the framed pictures on the mantel, a timeline of her and Gabe's childhood, but, alas, no photo had been taken to commemorate the unpleasant experience of said shirt.

"For sure. We have a long history, you and me. Let's not give up now."

"No more snide remarks about my living arrangements?"

"Deal." His hand shot out to take Holly's.

She couldn't help smiling when he nearly shook her arm out of the socket. "I've been looking forward to you being here so Mom can micromanage somebody else for a change."

"She means well, Sis."

"I know, but my tolerance has gone down with age. I'm a

grown woman now...even though my current circumstances don't exactly scream *adult*. But I'm saving up and trying to make the most of my short stint here."

"Does that mean you're dating again?"

"Gabe!"

Her brother held his hands up in surrender as Holly reached for the decorative *give thanks* pillow from the couch. Gabe, anticipating her next move, counter-attacked with the *count your blessings* pillow from the recliner.

"Kids! Knock it off. Come on. The truck is due any minute. I need help loading the birds," Mom hollered from the kitchen with a mix of amusement and irritation.

Mom's partially empty nest was now full again—temporarily—and both her smile and instinctual bossiness signaled that she felt quite at home with the arrangement.

Dad wasn't saying much, per usual, but his pleasant expression indicated that he was enjoying the holiday hubbub.

Holly stood beside her niece, looking outside. Claudia's round face was pressed up to the cold glass of the bay window as she tried to get as close as she could to the outdoors without actually being there. Her mom had vetoed her plea to wait in the yard for the shelter's truck. Surprisingly, Claudia was more dedicated to the truck's arrival in the driveway than she was to witnessing a life-size dog balloon float down Fifth Avenue in the televised Thanksgiving Day Parade.

Finally, the big moment arrived, and Claudia squealed with delight, "It's turkey time, everybody!"

Holly reached the mass of warm clothing first, and in a scurry and flurry, Mom, Holly, and Gabe and his family threw on their coats, mittens, hats, and boots, and tumbled out the front door to greet the truck's driver, Stan.

Gabe was the first to reach him. "Stan the Man, good to see you again."

The passenger door opened as Stan's helper got out.

"My sidekick is going to help us load up. Everyone, this is Nik Beckenbauer."

And there he was again. Did he help everyone in this town? First his aunt, and then Chase, and then Lena at Music Keys, and then he'd driven Holly home, and now he was volunteering at the shelter? Was Nik casing this town, or had he turned over a new leaf and was now trying to make up for lost time?

"Oh, we know Nik," Mom cooed.

"Sure do. Already been a recipient of the Brighams' wonderful hospitality and Anna's famous chocolate chip cookies," Nik affirmed.

"Great to meet you," Gabe said as he shook Nik's hand. "A friend of mom's cookies is a friend of mine. This is my wife, Monica, and my sweet and spicy daughter, Claudia."

"Claudia Ann...please."

Nik bent down to her level. "It's certainly nice to meet you, Miss Claudia Ann."

She giggled before running over to grab Holly's hand.

"When I insisted Stan let me tag along, I had no idea where we were headed. But when we turned on Kühn's Way, I remembered this is the street where you live." Nik spoke directly to Holly.

Monica's turn of the head and raised eyebrow were not subtle.

Holly couldn't help but notice Nik's nod to the Harry Connick, Jr. song, "On the Street Where You Live"—or was it a coincidence?

"I assume you're also a friend of my single sister?"

And there it was, Gabe's knack for throwing her under the bus…or, in this case, the shelter's truck.

"Yes, you could say that. We're getting to know each other through my girlfriend's nonprofit."

Nik seemed to emphasize *girlfriend* a little more than necessary, probably trying to set the record straight that he and Holly were just friends.

Famous last words. Where did that come from? Probably a little word association from her interaction with Frank. Nik had a girlfriend. And even if he didn't, Holly was not interested in dating an ex-con.

Get it together, girl. Sheesh!

Holly's face felt as crimson as the pick-up truck in her driveway. She tried to act unfazed by her brother's teasing and her own stream of consciousness.

Stan picked up one of the turkeys. "Hey, folks, it's cold out here. Let's get these birds en route."

Stan to the rescue.

The crew set their mittened hands to the good work so the needy in Bavarian Falls would not go without for Thanksgiving.

Halfway through the loading process, Nik almost dropped one of the turkeys that Claudia insisted on handing to him. Holly rushed in to intercept the near spill at the same time that Nik was adjusting his grip. Their hands collided, Nik's insulated gloves covering Holly's as they both held on to the foiled pan. Time seemed to stand still for a moment.

Holly's mind raced. *Pull away! Don't cross that boundary. Resist his captivating eyes. Back away from the turkey pan.*

"Why are you staring at each other?" Claudia asked, cocking her head.

Holly and Nik shifted their eyes.

"I've got it," Nik assured Holly as he repositioned his hands.

Holly nodded and turned back toward the waiting turkeys.

After Stan and Nik drove away, the Brigham women gathered in the kitchen to finish their own meal prep.

Holly had long been annoyed that the men got to sprawl out on the couch, half-watching the dog show, while the women cooked. She knew it wasn't like this in every household. Remembering her resolution to not revert back to a tween or toddler, she bit her tongue for the second time and chose to look at the bright side, like the protagonist from the movie *Pollyanna*.

In Holly's childhood, applying Pollyanna's Glad Game used to include things like:
- I'm glad we went out for ice cream today.
- I'm glad that Mom let me stop taking clarinet lessons.
- I'm glad that Gabe stood up to Penelope Jorgerson for me on the playground.
- I'm glad Daddy didn't die from his aneurysm.

Today, it included things like:
- I'm glad my brother married someone so nice.
- I'm glad my parents have stuck it out for all these years.
- I'm glad I have a sibling even when he drives me crazy.
- I'm glad Dad didn't die from his aneurysm, even though things aren't the same.

"Do you think you guys will ever move back to the area? Bavarian Falls is such a wonderful town to grow up in. Claudia would fit in well at the elementary school," Mom primed Monica.

"Mom, can't we enjoy the time we have right now?" Holly interceded.

Monica mouthed a quick and silent, "Thank you."

"Oh, I am! Isn't it wonderful to be together? Sure wish Grandpa and Grandma were still here."

"Me too. But aren't we glad that Grandma Bea's corn casserole recipe lives on?"

"Yes and amen," Monica said.

"It makes me miss her, but it also feels like—in a small way—she's still with us." Mom sniffled.

"Remember when I turned ten and she decided I was old enough to learn the secret recipe? It was a rite of passage of sorts."

"A very messy one, I might add." Mom laughed.

Holly retrieved Grandma Bea's handwritten corn casserole recipe from her mom's recipe box. Her flawless cursive and the buttery-smudged fingerprints comforted Holly as she gathered the necessary ingredients.

Not long after the casserole went into the oven, Mom assigned the women other tasks—Monica peeling potatoes and Holly making the apple pie. As Holly cut butter into the flour for the pie crust and rolled it out, her mom recounted the success Gabe had achieved in basketball, baseball, and as a leader on the award-winning debate team. She mentioned that Holly had been selected as a seventh grader along with a few upperclassmen to design and paint a mural of Bavarian Falls at the community center for the Bavarian Festival. She reminisced about holiday traditions like visiting Santa at Neumann's and getting their annual family picture taken by the covered bridge. The long monologue was most likely to fill Monica in on stories she hadn't heard yet.

But what her mom didn't include was how long it took Dad to get into position for the family picture, or Gabe's near expulsion after Dad's incident, or how much pressure her mom had put on Holly about her contribution to the mural. Holly remembered many sleepless nights due to her mom's insistence to always put her best foot forward. The pressure had nearly imploded Holly on more than one occasion. Now, her mother's sidelong glances at her back-at-home daughter and her hints on slicing the apples thinner didn't help matters.

"I'm glad all your memories are rosy—or that you've managed to view them through rose-colored glasses. But mine aren't like that. Some of them still sting," Holly admitted, slamming the cupboard door.

Her mom's slanted recollection had pricked holes into Holly's outer shell. It was inevitable that the steam was about to escape as the conversation heated up.

"What do you mean?"

"I know you were doing your best, Mom. But I didn't feel like I could compete with Dad's disability. It felt like it was all about him. And no matter what I did or didn't do, it didn't hold up when compared to this big thing that none of us asked for or expected but that we all had to deal with. I know no one asked for this, and we were all trying to find our way through. But it hurt. And I feel guilty for even saying any of this. But I can't keep it in anymore."

Holly sat down at the table, crumpling a tea towel she had been using to clean up her mess.

"Oh, honey."

"And while I'm laying it all on the table, I might as well say that I felt like you were too busy for me. I don't want to say that because it will make you feel bad. But if I don't admit it, I'll grow more resentful."

Holly gripped the towel as if trying to draw strength from it.

"Can't you put yourself in my shoes for a moment?" Her mom threw her own towel on the counter.

"My feet are two sizes bigger than yours!" Holly stood up, her chair wobbling from the force, and walked over to the sink.

Her mother sank onto the seat across from the one Holly had vacated. "Dad needed me, you and Gabe needed me, and our dwindling bank account needed me to work once we had respite care for Dad. I never wanted either of you to feel like you were on the back burner. It was so..." Mom gasped, taking in deep breaths, her lips beginning to quiver, her eyes filling with tears. "So...so hard. I was trying to be enough for everyone, but there wasn't enough of me to go around."

"I feel like a jerk." Holly walked slowly back to her chair.

"You're not, Hol. It was hard on everyone. And as much as it hurts to hear, I'm glad you're letting it out. I mean, I think we've all tried to hold it together, but eventually the hurt has to escape our hearts so it doesn't break us in half."

"Did you hear that in counseling?" Holly sat down.

"That obvious, huh?"

They both smiled, easing the thick-as-flannel tension in the room.

"Honey, I love you so much. I'm so proud of you. And I am truly sorry for the hurt."

"I guess I never really thought about it from your perspective. I was young, and it was like I got stuck there. Cycling 'round and 'round, rehearsing the pain, and then feeling bad about how I felt. I wanted Dad back...and you back. And our life back before all of this."

"I know. My coping mechanism was to muscle forward, to do the next thing so I wouldn't have to face the pain. Because if I did—if I like, really did—I was afraid it would overtake me and paralyze me." Mom returned to her bowl, forcefully stirring the batter.

"I was oblivious to all that, Mom. How lonely that must have been for you."

Tears fell in the place of words. Strong and put-together Anna Brigham letting her guard down. The crack in Mom's armor was showing, and it wasn't a flaw. It was light.

Holly had put her mom on a pedestal, even when she was annoyed with her. The pedestal had a light shining up on it, like an art piece in a museum display. But until now, Holly couldn't recall ever noticing light radiating from it.

There in the weakness, in the humanness, in the break, a ray shone through. The drone of the dog show could be heard from the den. In the kitchen, a few wall-demolishing swings at the past liberated Holly, and she joined her mother near the corn casserole batter.

This breakthrough wouldn't fix everything, but it was a start. A pivot away from resentment and a lunge toward honesty and health.

Monica cleared her throat, gently reminding the mother and daughter that she had served as witness to the emotionally charged exchange. Though usually soft spoken, she sounded as though she was gearing up to speak, and both Holly and her mother looked over at her. "I wanted to let you both know something. Please hear me out. This isn't easy, but I think it's important to consider how all this has affected Gabe. He was ten when it happened, and he had to grow up overnight. He said Grandpa Dale and Grandma Bea helped a lot. But at the end of the day, he strapped on a layer of responsibility that he tried to mask with his jokes and charisma. In the quiet moments—before bed, on a walk, on long car rides—it's there. The face like flint. The tense jaw. The distant eyes. The *am I doing this right?* The *do I have what it takes?* The second guessing." Monica's blotchy face and shaking voice indicated that this admission was uncomfortable, but it was necessary.

In part, Gabe had fooled them. There was more to the story than his apparent steadiness and frequent punchlines. He was hurting in his own way. Of course, he was.

How had Holly been so blind and oblivious to the pain of her family members?

"It's been a long time since it happened, yet it's fresh in many ways." Monica paused, as if calculating her words. "This is good, though, getting it out in the open so we can get stronger and softer, too. Gosh, this is hard for me."

"For all of us," Mom added.

"Mom, you always seem to have it together." Holly scooped the batter from the mixing bowl into the baking dish.

"Ha! If only you knew the persistent, inner critic and its exhaustive commentary about my missteps."

"I don't get it." Monica peered into the den where the other half of the family was watching TV.

"What's that, dear? About my strong inner critic that tries to improve everyone and everything—mostly myself?" Mom used a spatula to swipe the remains of the batter Holly had left behind. She tapped the remnants into the baking dish before placing the beloved corn casserole into the oven.

"No, not that. I was talking about the dog show. I don't get all the hype."

Holly blinked a moment, processing what her sister-in-law had said. Then a giggle escaped. Leave it to Monica to break the ice and melt the room with her warmth and a well-placed conversational reset. It wasn't that she was trying to avoid the tough stuff altogether, but headway had been made. The rest of their time together didn't need to be dominated by discord.

Mom laughed too. "I'm grateful for you girls. I know this situation isn't easy, but it's ours, and God will help us at every turn. Now, I think this calls for hot cider and a slice of butter almond *stollen*."

"Let's not let the couch potatoes know we're slicing into dessert," Holly stood and walked over to the silverware drawer to retrieve a butter knife. Monica grabbed three mugs out of the cupboard and brought them back to the table.

Some boundaries were meant to be crossed, at least when it came to clearing up long-held, wrongful assumptions and enjoying dessert before dinner.

Over their indulgence, Mom stirred the pot. "It's really too bad about Nik. He seems like a great guy."

"You mean, too bad he has a girlfriend, right?" Monica cupped her steaming mug of cider while looking up at Holly.

Holly made eye contact with her mom, telepathically trying to decide whether they should share the inside scoop.

"It's a little more than that," Mom said.

"Mommy! Mommy! Look!" Claudia rushed into the kitchen, tugging on her mom's hand to come see. "The golden doodle is going to win. That's the one I picked."

"In a minute, sweetie."

"Please, Mommy. Come on. You're going to miss it!"

Holly had expected Gabe to be the center of attention, but it was his daughter who gobbled it up—and that was fine with her.

CHAPTER ELEVEN
Frenzied and Fanatic Shoppers

THE DAY AFTER THANKSGIVING WAS ALWAYS the busiest of the year for the mile-long Christmas store. Thousands of customers descended upon Neumann's to tackle their holiday shopping lists.

Hundreds of employees were aproned and ready to make spirits bright and exude the love of Christmas, melting grinchy hearts with hospitable smiles and helping hands.

"Oliver is coming to the store to see Santa," Andy announced.

"Today?" Holly asked.

"Yup. Tammy insisted, even after I told her the line for Santa will feel like it's a mile long today."

"No fear of missing out for him."

"Or her. Listen, I'm all for Claus spreading holiday cheer and my son getting a keepsake photo with him, but of all days, Black Friday is not the day I would choose for him to do so."

"Agreed."

Andy manned the counter, taking orders and answering questions so Holly was free to execute the custom orders. Holly tucked a stray hair behind her ear as she leaned over an ornament shaped like a fir tree and plotted how to fit Merry Christmas in German—*Frohe Weihnachten!*—on a Tannenbaum ornament.

Holly wished she could put in AirPods to tune out the peppy sleigh ride music and the peppering of questions Andy received while she tried to work:

"Can you change the date on my ornament from last year to this year so I can re-gift it?"

"Can you personalize this ornament with Baby Girl

VanHusen for a gender reveal party? They're going to pull this out of a stocking and be tickled pink. Her family has all boys in it. Bring on the tutus and crowns, right? And the Legos and trucks for good measure, of course. We have to prepare her to be an engineer and a ballerina."

"*S'il vous plaît ajouter Voulez-vous m'épouser? À cet ornement?*" A phone translator helped Andy understand that this request was to add *will you marry me?* in French to the customer's ornament of choice.

The questions got weirder as the day went on.

"How long will it take to personalize twenty black ornaments with Doug Doug the Tattoo Thug for my work party?"

"Sir, can you fit her full name on the ornament? It's a bit above the letter count, but my goddaughter doesn't have anything with the whole thing on it, so it'd be really special. It's Matilda Jenaye Gertrude Perry-Harrison."

Amid the flurry, Reason #11 was clear for Holly's case against Christmas: Frenzied and Fanatical Shoppers.

For once, she was thankful for the larger-than-life showroom. Its high ceilings helped curb claustrophobia as the waves of shoppers kept surging.

During one such tidal wave, Andy's ex-wife, Tammy, fought her way through the crowd with Oliver hanging onto her faux leather purse. A man Holly assumed was Bill stood a few yards away, unusually preoccupied with the stocking display.

"Psst. Psst." Tammy motioned to Andy.

Andy tried to politely excuse himself for a moment from the godmother of Matilda Jenaye Gertrude Perry-Harrison.

"What is it, Tam? I've gotta get back to work."

"I know you're maxed out right now, but you'll never believe what your son asked Santa for."

"A Red Ryder carbine-action 200-shot range model BB air rifle with a compass in the stock?"

"Come on. I'm serious."

"So am I."

"Your son asked St. Nick for a six-pack."

Oliver shook his head. "No, I didn't ask Nik the Elf, I asked Santa Claus."

"Nik the Elf?!" Holly interrupted the conversation between Andy and his ex-wife.

Warning bells went off in Holly's mind: Nik was in the store interacting with all those kids?

"St. Nick and Santa Claus are basically the same thing, buddy," Andy calmly explained to his son.

But definitely different from Nik the felon.

"Andy! Back to the six-pack." Tammy stomped her foot.

"What?"

"I was mortified by his request. We were standing in line by Pastor Meyer, his wife, and their grandkids."

A sheepish Oliver peered out from behind his mom.

"And get this," Tammy said. "When Santa asked him to explain further, Ollie said, 'My dad has some of those, so I want 'em, too.'" Her voice escalated with each syllable.

Holly set down her brush and squared her shoulders, preparing to step in to defend her friend from the woman who had broken his heart.

"Listen, Tammy. I told you before, I have a few cold ones on the weekends. That's it. Maybe he saw them in the garage fridge."

"It was humiliating."

Oliver tugged on his mom's arm. "*Mom*...Mom!"

"Wait a sec, bud."

"I've gotta go, Tam. Can we talk about this later?"

"Mom!"

"What, son?" Tammy snapped.

"Why am I in trouble? I just wanted some of these, like Bill." He looked to the man still perusing the stocking display. And I think Nik the Elf has some, too." Oliver lifted up his shirt and pointed to his abs. "A six-pack of abs. I've been trying to do sit-ups, but they aren't doing much. I thought Santa could help."

Tammy's cheeks pinked. But Andy, who had every right to be angry at his ex-wife's accusations, burst into a merry laugh that could've rivaled the big sleigh driver himself. Tammy tittered and glanced at Bill, who joined in. Holly released a snort and bent over her work.

Oliver looked confused.

"Oh, buddy, you'll get there," Andy assured his son. "But maybe not this year."

Eyes lowered, Tammy collected Oliver. "I'm sorry I jumped to conclusions."

"It's okay. I'm used to it."

"Andy, don't start."

"Gotta get back. Come here, little man."

Oliver ran over to do his part in their father-son secret handshake.

"I love you the way you are…two-pack and all."

"Thanks, Daddy. Love you."

And with that, Oliver left with his mom and his soon-to-be-stepdad, Bill with the six-pack abs.

Andy watched them disappear into the massive crowd of shoppers.

"You okay?" Holly mumbled.

The line of people at their station were growing more impatient by the minute.

"Later," Andy replied, turning his attention to the godmother whose stern expression resembled Marlon Brando in *The Godfather*.

Station 8 was so riddled with traffic that later ended up being a few hours. When Andy and Holly finally had a chance to recount the six-pack mix-up, they had another good laugh. Then Andy got quiet, his shoulders slumped.

"What's wrong?" Holly placed a comforting hand on his shoulder.

Andy muttered, "Oliver called him *dad*."

"Who, Santa?"

"No, Bill. Oliver said he wanted a six-pack like his dad. Tammy thought that meant me. But Oliver meant Bill."

Words escaped Holly at her co-worker's realization. He lifted his hand to hers and gave her a double-pat.

"Excuse me, sir." The female Brando lookalike was back.

Holly hadn't forgotten how Andy had saved her hide when Mrs. Rasmussen needed help, so she stepped up and took one for the team. "I'd be happy to help you, ma'am."

"We're getting ready to load the tour bus, but I came back to make sure he spelled Matilda's first middle name right. It's J-E-N-A-Y-E. People mess it up often. But she was named after my second cousin once removed, and it's important to me that it's spelled correctly."

"Attention shoppers. Last call for all riders on Bus #1228 headed to Oak Haven for the North Pole Express tour. Doors to the bus will be closing soon. Please finalize your purchases at checkout #4."

"Oh Mylanta, that's me."

"Andy is one of the best there is, ma'am. I'm sure he wrote

it down correctly when you spelled it out."

"If you're sure…"

"I'll double check myself if that will make you feel better," Holly assured her.

"Oh, it would. Thank you."

And with that, the godmother left the station.

During a brief parting of the seas, Mrs. Rasmussen sauntered up to the counter decked out in a red-and-green business suit, a Christmas hat, and elfin heels. She'd make Betty Jo herself look as though she didn't have enough holiday spirit.

"I'm back!"

"Yes, you are," Andy replied. "Anything I can help you with?"

"Honestly, I'm taking a stroll around the store to give Doc breathing room. He said I was driving him crazy. And he wasn't meaning it in the usual way. He shooed me away from Santa's line. Apparently, I was trying to squash the vision of sugar plums dancing in little heads with my timer and whistle."

"A timer and whistle?" Holly asked.

"I thought these tools from my former profession would help keep things running smoothly so the little darlings wouldn't dillydally in line, but I guess not."

"Your dogs are here?"

"No, of course not—they'd destroy the place. I was referring to all the kids in line waiting for Santa."

"Mrs. R. used to be a gym teacher at North Star Elementary," Andy turned over the sheet on his clipboard.

"Wow! I never would have guessed that." Holly hid a smile and avoided a chuckle.

"I know. It feels like another life. I'm glad to have exchanged my windbreaker getup for fancy clothes, but I do miss wearing tennies on my dogs—my feet, not my pets," she clarified.

"Heels have taken their toll on these Cinderellas." She lifted one foot, twisting her four-inch heel back and forth as proof.

Holly was trying hard to keep her face neutral, but Mrs. Rasmussen's vernacular wasn't making it easy.

"Still, I wouldn't trade this life for anything, even when Henry drives me nuts. He's good to me. I simply wish he would've let me go to that special school, so I'd be more prepared for my role today."

"I guess I'm a little lost. What is it that Dr. R. is doing at the store?"

"You don't know? I guess you're a little old for it, but I thought everyone knew. He's on his fifth year, after all."

"He's wearing the beard and velvety suit," Andy explained.

"That's right, Santa Claus has the best-looking teeth in the store. Gosh, he looks good in red." Mrs. R. sighed.

"He's a patient man, that's for sure," Andy observed. "I mean, because he's coming in contact with so many kids and all."

"Yes, he is. I practically forced him to take his Vitamin C, D, garlic capsules, and kale smoothie this morning to ward off any potential germs from snotty hands and close talkers."

"He's definitely a trooper."

"By the way, did you hear what Oliver asked for?"

Andy's jaw clenched. "About that, I'm really sorry."

"Sorry for what? I didn't catch the second thing he said, which seemed to cause quite a stir with Tammy. But the first thing he asked for was a BB gun. I was a little shocked myself, but when Santa asked him why, he explained how he loved spending time in the woods with his dad, looking for deer. You should have seen the adoration on his face. He sure loves you."

Andy straightened. "That means a lot. Thanks for telling me."

"Of course. Now, I think I've stayed away long enough. It's

time for the chief elf to take her place back at Santa's side—minus the timer and whistle." Mrs. Rasmussen tucked the timer into her suit pocket. "Nice talking to you two. Let me know if you want to pop a few Vitamin C tablets for good measure—I'm amply supplied."

"Thanks, but we're good." Andy offered a thumbs up.

"I'm off. Ta-ta!"

Mrs. R. returned to her post next to Santa. Andy's burden was eased, and Holly had quirky material for a Bavarian Falls tell-all book one day—if, that is, she decided to give up art and take up her other childhood dream of writing a novel like Jo March and Anne Shirley did in two of her favorite books. Books Grandma Bea used to read aloud to her. It was the books' covers that ultimately drew Holly to pursue art. She was awed by the way they encapsulated a slice of the story, serving as gatekeeper between imagination and reality.

Not long after Mrs. Rasmussen left, a masculine elf ran up to Station 8.

Nik the Elf was decked out in a red belted top with striped sleeves and evergreen shorts, complete with candy cane leggings and belled felt shoes.

Sheesh! He even looked good in that ridiculous outfit.

"Hey, guys. Santa got called in for emergency dental surgery, and Mrs. R. sent me to find a fill-in for a few hours until Doc can get back," Nik explained. Turning to Andy, he asked, "Can you do it?"

"I've never suited up at work."

"Listen, you'll do great. I offered to fill in myself, but Mrs. R. insisted my lack of beard and the fact that the kids will recognize the elf is now Santa could cause issues. So, she sent me to retrieve you."

"I could do it, but I don't want to leave Holly hanging here."

"I can step in for you. Holly can show me the ropes. There's another elf named Teresa over there who can hold down the fort while I stay here. Can you let her know I've been detained?"

Andy's conflicted expression morphed into confident determination. "Absolutely. I'll go get changed."

"Thanks, man. There's about to be a mutiny over there."

Here they were again. Holly going about her business and then bam! Nik appeared out of thin air, now in a different role, yet once again offering his time to help others.

This small town kept getting smaller.

"Sorry you lost your partner in crime," Nik joked.

"How many hours do you volunteer a week?" Holly drilled, suddenly realizing that his helpful spirit might cloak the fact that he was actually fulfilling required community service hours. She discreetly tried to spot a tether hidden near his ankles, where his elf leggings met his felt boots. Nothing appeared out of the ordinary—except that she was working side by side with Lena's elf boyfriend.

"Honestly, I've lost count. I don't mean that in a prideful way. But with this relocation, I'm committed to figuring out what went wrong in Leavenworth."

"By volunteering at as many places as possible?"

"When you put it that way, I now realize I've filled my schedule with so much volunteering and a few side jobs like this gig," Nik gestured to his elf getup, "that I haven't had much time to sit and figure out what I really want."

"Speaking of not having time to figure things out, I don't suppose you're a student of Bob Ross?" Holly picked up her paintbrush.

"The happy little tree painter? Um, nope. Is there another way I can help?"

"Sure. You take down orders, and I'll paint happy little

names and phrases on these ornaments. Ask the questions on this form and record the customers' answers on the spreadsheet. Make sense?"

"You got it, boss. I'll do my very best."

After a few more instructions, Nik quickly caught on. Holly attended to her pile of mounting orders. They managed sporadic conversation as they worked. Nik proved more than competent as he systematically took orders and engaged in small talk with customers.

"What's Lena up to today?" Holly forced herself to think about her friend—his girlfriend.

Nik smiled. "Oh, you know…changing the world one song at a time. I'm headed over to Music Keys after this, but Lena had meetings scheduled all morning, so I told Frank I could help out here today. You and Frank are a thing, right?"

Nik had most likely observed Frank's kiss on her temple at the Jana Bonparente concert and made the probable conclusion that they were an item.

"Stranger things have happened," Holly replied.

Why did she say that? Maybe it was a protective response from years of being single? But why would she say that to Nik? It wasn't as if he was someone she needed to impress or a well-meaning yet meddling friend of her mom.

Thankfully, no more strange encounters happened. In some ways, the rest of the day flew by. In other ways, it dragged on as customer after customer oohed and awed and hemmed and hawed. Andy returned shortly after lunch to swap places with Nik and reported that no punches had been thrown or hair pulled even in the endless line of antsy kids waiting for Santa. Maybe because Mrs. Rasmussen's whistle still hung around her neck, ready to intercept shenanigans with a shrill warning.

Mid-afternoon, the familiar face of Ms. Claire Weber surfaced from amid the flurry of shoppers.

"Holly, I'm glad you're here. I have a special order, and it needs a real artist's touch. No offense, Andy."

"None taken, ma'am. We all know Holly's skills are authenticated with an art degree and all."

"It appears that my nephew is in it for keeps with Miss Lena Albrecht, so I wanted to do something special for them."

From behind her back, Ms. Claire produced a circular emerald ornament and a bronze key charm.

"I'd like you to affix this key with a ribbon to the top of the ornament and also hand letter 'Nik & Lena' on the front in gold foil."

"That'll be beautiful," Holly admitted. Should she stop there or continue verbalizing her thoughts? She realized she cared too much about Claire and tolerated Lena enough to not speak up.

"Pardon me, Ms. Claire. But aren't you a little concerned about this?"

"Don't worry about a thing. I've been saving up for it. I know it's a bit extravagant, but I think it will mean a lot to them."

"I wasn't talking about the price." Out of the corner of her eye, Holly made sure Andy was still occupied with other customers, "I meant Nik's history…with Leavenworth."

"Ah yes, I see what you mean. It definitely was upsetting, but I think he's recovered from that quite nicely, don't you?"

"I don't know all the details of his release, nor is it my business really, but Lena is okay with it?"

"I'm sure they've talked about it and worked through it. Even though Lena is successful now, she started Music Keys from the ground up. She had to move out of the nonprofit's original building before moving into its current location. It was a huge setback. I think she, like you, knows what it's like to be forced to relocate and start over when things falls apart."

Holly couldn't believe a smart woman like Ms. Claire would minimize time behind bars as a *relocation* and a crime as *things falling apart*. Wait a minute—maybe Nik had been accused of something he didn't do? Based on Holly's interactions with him, he was either a professional deceiver or he was actually the considerate and kindhearted guy he appeared to be.

This new possibility gave Holly courage to ask, "Was it his fault?"

"It's hard to tell. Maybe partially, maybe not. These sorts of things can be unclear."

Again, Holly was taken aback by the nonchalant way Ms. Claire conversed about this serious matter.

"You don't think he'll return?"

"I don't think so, dear. At least not now. I think it would take a lot for him to go back. It's hard to face that which has hurt you most, isn't it?" Ms. Claire's compassionate inflection signaled that she knew her last sentence hit close to home.

Holly was temporarily distracted by the lump in her throat. The lyrics to Jana's song, "Everything," swirled in her mind.

The key to peace is turning to face that which holds you down.

"That's it. That's the key I've been missing."

"What, this one?" Ms. Claire still clutched the bronze key.

"Not exactly." A rebel tear escaped down Holly's cheek.

"Are you okay?"

"Yes, ma'am." Holly collected herself as best she could. "This is going to be the loveliest ornament."

Upon Ms. Claire's exit, and with throngs of Black Friday shoppers as oblivious witnesses, Holly decided she was going to face what had been holding her back. Come Monday, she would schedule a counseling appointment after a dozen-year hiatus.

CHAPTER TWELVE
Heart-Breakery

HOLLY AND ANDY WERE STILL STANDING after the shop 'til you drop mayhem. They wiped down their counter and boxed up finished ornaments. "My friends Elaine and Shayla have convinced me to join them for a Christmas movie marathon tomorrow," Holly scrubbed a stubborn paint stain. "I tried to tell them my eyes were already strained from painting a gazillion ornaments, but they insisted."

"Don't shoot your eye out!" Andy warned.

"Probably the best line from *A Christmas Story*. Please tell me you're going to watch that one."

"It's a rom-com marathon, so I doubt it will make the cut."

"What did you say?"

"Rom com—you know, romantic comedies?" Holly clarified.

"Like Christmas chick flicks? Why didn't you say so? Yeah, I don't care for those. It never turns out like that in real life."

"I couldn't agree more." Holly returned the spray bottle and roll of paper towels to their cupboard, under the counter.

"Want to know my weekend plans?" Andy untied his apron.

"Of course. Gotta be better than mine."

"I'm going to offer the house to Teresa. Like you suggested—a meal at Edelweiss Inn, note from Santa, the whole nine yards."

Holly punched Andy's arm playfully. "This is huge! Wow, let me know how it goes. You could even dress up like Santa again."

"I think my Santa days are over. That was intense. You can pray I don't need to overdose on antacid to get through it."

"You'll do fine. But maybe avoid the grilled onions on your bratwurst…for more than one reason."

"Duly noted."

"Are you going to the work party tomorrow night?" Holly grabbed her car keys from their shared drawer.

"Absolutely, I am. Mr. Neumann does it up right. You don't want to miss it."

"I don't mean to sound ungrateful, but I was kind of surprised to hear that the party is going to be here. I mean, it's already decorated, so that makes sense. But we spend a lot of time in this place, especially this month."

"I hear ya. But where else can you house hundreds of employees at this time of year?"

"Good point."

"It's lot of fun. You'll see." Andy waved as he left their station.

Soon after, Holly clocked out and hurried to her car. Once inside it, she made a phone call. She kept a promise to herself and scheduled an appointment with a counselor—one she'd seen advertised on the church bulletin board. Thankfully, the counseling office was about forty minutes away. The miles were a welcome buffer between that which she was trying to distance herself from and that which she was attempting to face.

Holly had been to counseling briefly as a child and then again after she graduated from high school, but now she was more determined to face the fog.

The counseling office was especially busy during the holidays, but miraculously they'd had a cancelation, and Holly was scheduled for next week.

She reached for her seatbelt and buckled up.

Relief and anxiety duked it out as she typed the appointment into her calendar app. Before she closed down her phone, she spotted an invite reminder for the work Christmas party. She moved her response from "Interested" to "Going."

Droves of employees arrived for the big event. The arena-like showroom felt even more festive than usual. Through the sound system, a synthesized orchestra amplified songs from *The Nutcracker*. Servers in tuxedos walked around with silver trays filled with mouth-watering appetizers. Bacon-wrapped water chestnuts, figs stuffed with goat cheese, and crispy flatbread crackers laden with pesto were headliners in the aromatic food prelude. A bird's eye view would've captured a real-life Whoville minus the sky-high hairdos of the Whos—unless of course, you took Betty Jo's bouffant into consideration.

Holly entered the party with the ambition to blend in. Thankfully, the absence of a guy on her arm would not be noticed in a crowd this size. After hors d'oeuvres, plated with a side of mingling, Frank's grandfather—the son of Neumann Sr., the store's founder and North Pole vacation acquirer—stepped up to the mic.

"Good evening, everyone. What a great turnout. We know this is a busy time of year, especially as a Neumann's employee. We host this annual party to express our deepest appreciation for each of you. We wouldn't be successful as a company without your commitment to making spirits bright for all those who visit our store. Folks, you're in for a real treat this evening. Over the years, I've rubbed shoulders with many well-known people all over the globe, from actors to business owners, from political figures to musical artists. But it especially blesses my heart to discover talent right here in the Falls. I've invited a special guest to grace us with holiday music. Ladies and gentleman, our local angel, Miss Lena Albrecht."

In walked Lena with the posture of a ballerina. Apparently, she had listened to her mother's advice about standing up straight as a child. That, or she'd taken a lot of dance classes growing up. Probably both. Her sleek French twist, white cashmere sweater, black leggings, and high boots exuded elegance.

The room erupted with applause.

"Thank you for that warm Neumann's welcome. What an honor to sing for you this evening. Shayla Johnson is going to accompany me on the piano."

Shayla, Lena's karaoke comrade and pianist at Music Keys, gave a full-faced smile to the crowd as she took her place at the grand piano.

Lena gracefully removed the mic from its stand. Her polished voice was amplified throughout the massive room. "The first song I'm going to sing is a familiar one to many, but you may not know the history behind it. 'I'll Be Home for Christmas' was recorded in 1943 by Bing Crosby. It was written from the point of view of a World War II soldier who wouldn't be able to celebrate Christmas with his family because he was serving overseas. The holidays looked different than he would have liked. His heart was home, but his feet were a world away from those he loved. Millions of people visit Bavarian Falls every year, and as you know, most of them come to Neumann's. You play an important role in helping them get a taste—or rather, a feast—of Christmas. The tourists are kind of like that soldier, wanting to remember the childlike wonder of the season, even if they are far from home. Even when life hasn't turned out as they planned, it's here that they can reconnect with that which grounds us all, the love of God and the hospitable hearts of people. Thank you, Mr. Neumann, for overseeing a place that welcomes the world and offers them the uncomplicated message of the true meaning of Christmas: good news of great joy, for all people."

The sea of employees cheered.

It was evident that Lena had participated in many beauty pageants. Her wording, inflection, and gestures worked in unison. It was also clear this wasn't an act. Lena's sincerity and admiration for Bavarian Falls was genuine.

"For this first song, one of my friends at Music Keys is going to accompany me on the cello. Come on up, George."

George, head down, arms at his sides, marched to the front and took a seat near Lena. A man, most likely his dad, carried his cello and bow and placed them in front of him. Once he was situated, George placed his left hand on the neck of the cello and lifted the bow with his right. He waited for his instructor's cue.

With an assuring nod from Lena, George began the first few measures of "I'll Be Home for Christmas." The rich tones of the cello served as a current of lament, carrying along Shayla's floating arpeggios and Lena's lilting soprano voice. Holly broke her gaze from the stage to glance at the audience. The rest of the party attendees seemed entranced. She spotted Andy across the room and waved to him, but he appeared to be deep in thought.

Holly looked around for another familiar face. Leslie was by the punch bowl, laughing with another employee. Teresa was nowhere to be found. And she wasn't sure she wanted to hang out with Frank all night. Although he had honored her just-friends request, she couldn't be one-hundred percent sure that he wouldn't try to lead her over to the mistletoe, which she had spotted hanging from the rafters, a little too close to the food table.

Continuing to survey the showroom, Holly spotted Ms. Jingle Jangle herself sniffling over her eggnog, in a corner of the store.

"Everything all right?" Holly approached her.

"I'm sorry for this less-than-cheery display," Betty Jo replied. "But that song gets me every time."

"It was lovely, wasn't it?"

"Yes, it was. Lena's voice is a gift straight from heaven. But it also made me sad, reminding me of a dream that never came to fruition."

You and me both, Betty Jo.

At Betty Jo's admission, Holly's unfulfilled ambitions surfaced. She kept the attention on her boss, intentionally avoiding the spotlight that could expose her own disappointments.

"Did you want to be a singer?" Holly asked.

"Not really, but my choir teacher did say I could break glass with my overactive vibrato."

"Did you want to start a nonprofit, like Lena has?"

Like I wanted to.

"That's a nice idea, but no, not that either."

"Then what made you sad?"

Betty Jo crumpled the festive napkin in her hand. "Well, dear. I'm going to blurt it out. I was almost engaged once. But it didn't end happily." Her voice cracked as she seemed to will her vulnerability to behave.

"I'm so sorry. What happened?"

"Oh, you don't want to hear about it. You should go be with your friends, not stuck here listening to the store manager's sob story."

"I'm not going anywhere. And besides, this sounds a lot like one of the storylines from *Anne of Green Gables*, so I'm here for it."

The truth was, not only was Holly interested in hearing what Betty Jo was about to reveal, she couldn't shake the feeling that there might be a key dangling in this conversation that she was meant to find.

"If you're referring to Marilla and Mr. Blythe's courtship not working out, then you have an inkling of what happened."

"Oh, no."

"I met Clark Köhler when we were both working at Rudolph's Reindeer Farm. I was in charge of the holiday tours, and he was training to be a large animal veterinarian—like that charming Dutch doc on TV.

"We hit it off and started dating in the off-season. A family emergency called him back to Milwaukee. Once things settled down, he invited me to come visit him in Wisconsin. It sounds silly now, but the city intimidated me. I'm a simple lady who is comfortable in the country. Navigating that way of life was easy for him, but it was out of my comfort zone. I was scared to commit, not knowing if we had enough in common for the long haul. I waffled. I was preoccupied with losing what I had always known, not willing to leave the safety of home to make a new one. He ended up not finishing vet school and our phone calls became fewer and further between. And with no way forward, because neither of us would budge, the relationship disintegrated."

Betty Jo's distraught expression was enough to make Holly sob herself. Her boss's heartbreaking story of missed love, all because she couldn't picture herself flourishing elsewhere, was a tragedy. It also provided fodder for the next line item on Holly's list. Reason #12: Heart-Breakery—possible bakery name for a cheesy rom-com and the current theme of conversation at the company Christmas party.

Holly wrapped an arm around Betty Jo. "I'm so sorry."

They stood side by side for a few moments.

"I can't change what happened, and I try not to let it get the better of me," Betty Jo added. "But when I hear that song, it reminds me that my home could have been elsewhere. Yes, it would have been different, but it might have been even better. Love takes guts, doesn't it?"

"You've got that right, especially when there's no guarantee it will end up like you envision." Holly shifted her weight. She felt compassion toward her manager, as well as a newly discovered kinship.

Passion for art and a hunger for adventure had driven Holly to put herself out there and relocate to Chicago even though there were enormous obstacles in the way. Securing competitive grants, navigating the bustle of city life, and cutting through the red tape of bureaucracy was no picnic. Month after month, Holly persevered, determined to find a way to make her dream a reality. But eventually, the little grant money she was able to secure ran out, the doors closed shortly after they opened, and her vibrant imagination had to face reality. Reflecting on the unsuccessful launch of her community art space in Chicago was a prime example of things not ending up the way she'd envisioned.

Betty Jo turned to face Holly. "Over time, I was able to take the love I had for Clark and use it to help others. It brings me such joy to see each face, young, old, and in between, different nationalities and languages all coming together here, under the banner of Christmas and what it means."

"You know what I realized?"

"What's that, dear?"

"Even though you were afraid to go out into the world for love, you have been strategically entrusted with a position where the world comes to you. You impact people from all over with your kindness and care. The circumstances are not like you thought they'd be, but the impact reaches far beyond these walls."

Betty Jo's jovial demeanor returned to its rightful place.

Holly longed for that same kind of impact...one that reached beyond herself and the walls she felt barred behind.

"I think you're right. All this time I felt like I missed the boat, but actually, trains, cars, planes, chartered buses, minivans, and maybe, somehow, a few boats have made their way here. The void caused by my parting from Clark hasn't necessarily gone away altogether, but all is not lost. Repurposed, not wasted. Maybe I haven't missed my one chance. I've been given thousands of opportunities to love."

Holly sighed. "That's the most beautiful thing I've heard in a long time."

"Well, now—Lena's voice, that was incredible," Betty Jo said.

"I prefer your epiphany."

"Thanks, dearie. Now, you better run along. Go hang out with people your age. Frank and Nik spent quite a bit of time hanging that mistletoe over there."

Oh boy.

Holly avoided any mistletoe mishaps by heading to the Christmas tree display during Lena's next two songs. Never had she imagined she'd have a heart-to-heart with her manager during the party or that their conversation would teach her so much—not only about Betty Jo, but about herself.

Holly couldn't help but notice the contrasts between her history and Betty Jo's. While Holly's manager had never wanted to leave Bavarian Falls, Holly had never wanted to stay. But here she was, in the place from which she had tried to distance herself.

Lena's rendition of "I'll Be Home for Christmas" had touched something deep in Holly's heart, too. No longer hearing the song as a verdict on her detour back home, she heard an invitation to come home to who she once was—not an exact replica, but one that was repurposed, as Betty Jo had said. What would it be like to allow herself to uncover joy in her present circumstances, even if the circumstances felt lopsided and unfinished? Even when they weren't wrapped up with three pieces of tape and a symmetrical bow?

"Deep in thought?"

"Andy, you scared me!"

One look at her coworker and she knew something was wrong.

"You okay? Did Lena's song do a number on you, too?"

"Kind of. But probably not in the way you're thinking. While she was singing about not being home for Christmas, I got the impulsive idea to speed up my weekend plans. I didn't want Teresa to have to wait any longer, wondering how she was going to make it. And I didn't want to delay the inevitable. So, I found her across the crowded room—"

"South Pacific?"

"Huh?"

"Never mind…keep going."

"I was already feeling nervous, and the change of plans made me more so, but I didn't want the moment to pass. It felt right, ya know?"

"What'd she say?"

"I tried small talk, but it fell flat. And since Teresa's pretty shy, she wasn't providing much feedback. So, I kind of went for it. I said, 'Look, I know this sounds weird, but I feel like I'm supposed to offer you my house to live in.'"

"And what did she say? You're killin' me, Smalls." Holly elbowed Andy.

"Sandlot?"

"Ding ding."

"She didn't punch me, but what she said next pretty much did."

"Oh no, why?"

"At first she thought I was asking her to move in with me. But once I assured her I wasn't, she thought my offer was too much, assuming—as I feared—that I was declaring my affection. Then, because I was flustered, I started mumbling stuff about the inn and dinner and a note from Santa. And I think I lost her."

His jaw clenched as he paused, obviously affected by Teresa's negative reaction. "It was awful. Reminded me of when Tammy and I were trying to work through things, but it was like we were speaking different languages. I was trying to follow this crazy prompting and help a friend out, but it backfired."

Holly couldn't help but notice the juxtaposition between the celebratory work party in the background and the gravity of the current conversation.

"I don't know what to say. I mean, I'm so sorry about the misunderstanding. Do you think she'll come around?'

"Doubt it. She seemed pretty overwhelmed. And that's what broke my heart. I was trying to ease her mind and her load, but I guess I messed it all up and made things worse."

It pained Holly to see her friend this way.

"Do you want a house?" Andy's shoulders slumped forward.

"What?"

"Thought I'd see if I had better luck with someone else. But I know deep down it's for Teresa. I can't force her to receive the gift, though. That's up to her."

"I hope she comes around. Maybe give her a little time?"

"I'm certainly not planning on putting myself out there any time soon." Andy shoved his hands in his pockets.

"This work party is breaking my heart," Holly admitted.

"Don't say that. It's one of the highlights of the year. Just wait. I'll be fine, promise. And if Teresa doesn't change her mind, well, I'll put the house on the market and see what happens. I don't like playing the fool, though, especially when I had noble intentions."

"You're a good guy, my friend."

"I don't know about that, but I try. Hey, since I won't be using the Edelweiss Inn dinner reservation this weekend, why don't you and your gal pals take a break from the movie marathon and eat up. My treat."

"See what I mean? That's so nice. Here's the thing, though—and I don't mean to sound ungrateful—but I think we're going to pass. Elaine works at the inn, and I'm pretty sure it's the last place she'll want to hang out on her day off, especially since it's December."

"Makes sense. Don't blame her."

"Thank you, though. That was really thoughtful." Holly leaned against the wall, surveying the crowd. Minus present company, everyone seemed to be having a holly jolly good time.

"Maybe I'll see if Nik wants to use it for a date with Lena. I hear she's been putting in a lot of time after hours with the album coming up. They could probably use a night out together."

"Probably."

"Hey, this is your first work party. You should go have fun and not worry about me. I'm fine, really. Pride's hurt. I'll bounce back."

"You sure?"

"Positive. You won't want to miss out on the Bavarian feast and the after-dinner entertainment."

"You're not sticking around?"

"I think I'm going to call it a night."

As Andy turned to leave, Holly stood in place, contemplating how the night had unfolded. Bittersweet conversations had induced so many feelings—she felt inside out.

"Hey, Holly. Have you seen Frank?" Nik caught her off guard. He'd exchanged his elfin garb for handsome party digs. "We've got drooping mistletoe, and I'm looking for the ladder before it drowns in the punchbowl."

"Nik to the rescue again, eh?"

Nik rubbed the back of his neck as if trying to divert Holly's observation.

"I actually haven't seen him, which may be hard to believe, but I've been detained with…" her voice trailed off with a sniff as she processed the weight of Betty Jo's and Andy's disappointments that mirrored her own.

"You okay?"

"You must think I'm a piece of work, huh? First nearly fainting, now a mess of emotions at the Christmas party. I'm usually a lot more fun than this, but coming home has magnified what's missing and it aches, ya know?"

Why was she telling him this? He was the last person she should feel safe to talk to—he was dangerous, right? Or maybe all that was behind him now?

"I do."

"You do?"

"Yeah, I get what you're saying. Of course, I don't know exactly what you're feeling, but I've been through some hard stuff, too."

Holly had to keep from letting on that she knew what that hard stuff might be. "You have?"

"My old job nearly killed me. I put it all on the line, but it wasn't enough. I tried doing the right thing and then it all went south. Nothing like I pictured, you know?" Nik rubbed his neck again and looked back toward the party, clearly conflicted.

"I do."

"You do?"

"This is definitely not how I pictured my life turning out. Since I was thirteen, I dreamed of my big move from small town to big city. I wanted to use my art skills for the greater good and inspire others to exercise their creativity, too. But when my execution of a collective art space in Chicago fell through and the money ran out, I was forced to come back home to regroup. Which was not part of the plan." Holly crossed her arms and pulled them in close, trying to feel less vulnerable.

"I think it takes courage to regroup. And hey, you're still using your talents for the good of others. I heard that you're the best custom painter on staff. And think of how many homes your ornament art will be displayed in this season."

"Huh, I guess I've never thought of it that way."

"You're spreading a whole lot of joy in spite of your disappointment. And if you ask me, that's pretty cool."

"Thanks," Holly replied, amazed that Nik was able to pivot her perspective with a simple observation.

"Now, I've really gotta run and find Frank. The mistletoe mission awaits!"

"Go get 'em. Save the party from the droopy—or already drenched—mistletoe."

With a determined nod, Nik headed toward the heart of the showroom. After a few steps, he turned back. "Whether in Bavarian Falls, or Chicago, or somewhere else, you're an artist, Holly. That's all there is to it." He walked away.

Holly uncrossed her arms and straightened her shoulders. Never would she have imagined that an ex-con's compliment would make her feel like a real artist.

CHAPTER THIRTEEN
Winter Blues

WITH HER COUNSELING APPOINTMENT SCHEDULED FOR the next day, Holly had to expedite her plan to help Lena before it was too late. Questioning her sanity for adding more to her already full plate with work, Christmas approaching, and trying to enjoy a smidgen of a social life, Holly resolved to do the hard thing of helping Miss Perfect in her time of need. Besides, Holly found satisfaction in spotting an inch of Wonder Woman's humanity showing.

After work, Holly pulled up to Music Keys. The window boxes housed pine boughs, white-capped pinecones, and realistic-looking holly berries. Leave it Lena to make time for intentional decorating in the midst of a demanding season.

Holly knocked before opening the Bavarian-styled door that led to the reception area.

"Come on in." Nik approached the ornate door.

"Elaine here yet? I came over as soon as I got out of work."

"She texted Lena and said she was running a few minutes late. Coffee?"

"Tea for me, thanks."

"Let me guess, chai?"

"How'd you know? Am I that predictable?"

"Truth? I noticed it on the counter at your house when the groceries were unpacked."

"You're quite the spy," Holly replied.

That or he was casing the joint. If the chai went missing with the TV, Nik was sunk.

"Oh good, you're here." Lena rounded the corner.

"Elaine's not far behind," Nik added.

"Come on back, Holly. I've got a spot set up for us to meet in my office."

"I'll bring your tea to you when it's ready. You can call me Barista Beckenbauer."

Lena offered what looked like a rehearsed smile and gestured for Holly to follow her.

Through a narrow door Holly entered the tidy workspace behind Lena. Mostly white walls were accented by a tiny bonsai tree and a large, framed picture of young Lena, in ballerina attire, looking quite serious. The room carried the slight scent of vanilla and pine.

Once settled at the small round table in Lena's office, the meeting began.

"Thanks again for offering to help. Late starts are not usually my style, but with the grant coming through at the last minute and our recording window being limited, it couldn't be avoided. So, what are your thoughts?"

"I contacted the local VFW to see if they'd like to participate. They loved the idea but couldn't commit because most of their volunteers are being utilized to set up for the annual craft show."

"This is what I was worried about—everyone's already at capacity. Please tell me you have more ideas. We can't stop now. The kids have been looking forward to recording for weeks." Lena tapped her fingers on the table as though letting out nervous energy.

Knock knock.

"A chai for you," Nik said as he set the steaming mug next to Holly. "And an almond soymilk steamer for you." He kissed Lena on the temple as he handed her the beverage. Holly couldn't help but notice that Nik's kissing ability appeared more tender and refined than Frank's.

"That was sweet, thank you." This time Lena offered him a genuine smile.

"I saw Elaine pull up. I'll let her in. Then I'm headed to shoot hoops with Frank and his buddies."

"Okay, have fun. We'll be solving the world's problems while you sweat," Lena said.

Nik paused in the doorway, looking back at Lena as if he didn't know how to take her statement. Holly wasn't sure either whether Lena had meant her words as passive aggressive, and she almost felt bad for him.

A knock on the door sped up his departure as Lena's finger tapping got louder. "Any more creative solutions for this complex problem?"

"I think Elaine's been working on a few angles, but I did have one more. What if we partnered with—"

"Sorry I'm late." Elaine barged in with a bottled water that displayed the Music Keys logo. Apparently, Barista Beckenbauer had filled her order as well.

"It's understandable. This town is on overdrive this time of year." With several swipes of her French-manicured nails, Lena closed a few apps on her phone.

"Nik asked me to give you this." Elaine handed Lena a *While You Were Out* slip. "He said it was from Chase's mom?"

Lena read the message aloud: "Chase has horse therapy today and will be twenty minutes late to rehearsal. So sorry. See you then."

"Horse therapy?" Elaine sat in the empty chair, scooting it closer to the table.

"It's wonderful—except when it conflicts with rehearsal.

Sorry, I shouldn't have said that out loud. It's truly amazing. Adoptive children, individuals with disabilities, and veterans have all benefited from it. The horses and instructors help them process trauma through intentional exercises that develop trust and confidence. The ranch is a big supporter of what we're doing. Horse therapy and music therapy both aid clients in getting unstuck and rising to their potential. The horses seem to understand what's going on even when the clients can't articulate it with words."

Could Holly switch her counseling appointment to the ranch instead? Horse therapy sounded much more appealing.

"So, ladies, any other ideas to move the needle forward?"

Elaine added her findings to the think tank, but after deliberation, none of their ideas were quite the right fit.

"I hate to cut this short." Lena glanced at her smartwatch. "But the clients will be arriving shortly for rehearsal. I need to step out, but if you're able to strategize a bit more, I'd really appreciate it."

"We can. Don't worry. We'll figure this out…somehow," Elaine insisted.

Lena was busy, but Holly couldn't help feeling as if they'd been brushed off.

"Great! I knew I could count on you two. As you can see, most of my time is accounted for."

Elaine shook her head. "I don't know how you do it all."

"When you really believe in something, you'll put in whatever time is needed to see it through," Lena stated matter-of-factly as she left her office.

After a few minutes, Holly suggested they relocate to the reception area of Music Keys. Lena's office was not sparking the creativity Holly needed to tap into. It was a lovely, in a minimalistic sort of way, but not stimulating enough to move the needle for Holly.

They armed themselves with a few chocolate mints from the glass jar near the front desk and sat down in the waiting area. Holly and Elaine put their heads together to come up with a workable idea to include military personnel in the grant project. It hadn't seemed like a difficult task at first, but they were coming up short and time was running out.

In the middle of their focused brainstorming session, a voice startled them. "Excuse me."

Just inside the front door, stood a middle-aged woman with a child hiding partially behind her.

"Hi, I'm Chase's mom, Rosalee, and I'm wondering if you could help me? I'm sure Lena's tied up with rehearsal, so I don't want to interrupt her. They should be taking a break pretty soon, so Chase can join them then, but he's having a hard time, and I'm wondering if one of you might sit with him? I hate to leave him like this, but my husband needs our spare set of keys, and Chase doesn't want to miss any more rehearsal."

Chase peeked out from behind his mother's back. She coaxed him further into the lobby area.

"No problem at all. I can do that," Holly volunteered.

"Oh, thank you. I don't usually leave Chase with strangers, I promise, but I .don't know what else to do."

Extending her hand, Holly introduced herself to Rosalee so they weren't strangers anymore.

"Besides, Chase and I bonded at Neumann's during a little field trip excitement there."

"Are you Chase's angel? The school filled me in on my escape artist's daring act of worship. They didn't know the name of the woman who found him. But it sounds like it was you? I'm so grateful."

An unexpected shyness came over Holly in the presence of Rosalee's shower of gratitude.

"In the flesh." Elaine pointed at Holly.

"As you can imagine," Rosalee said, "it's hard to send Chase off to school and to things like field trips and extracurricular activities. He's usually fine, but it's a leap of faith to trust that others are going to care for him like we do. We want him to be as independent as possible but learning when to let go and when to hold on feels like a physics equation—and math was never my strong suit."

"We'll definitely keep a close eye on him," Holly assured her.

"Does he like hot cocoa?" Elaine asked. "I saw some out front. My mom used to add as many marshmallows as my age—until a few years ago because it was getting a little out of hand."

"He's a cocoa fan for sure. Thank you. I'll be back as soon as I can."

Rosalee explained to Chase what was going on. He grinned when he heard about the cocoa, which Elaine had gone to find.

When he saw Holly, he said, "Ba-ba-baby Jee-jee-susss."

"I've never been called that before. But yes, that's where we met each other. You have a good memory. I'm Holly, remember? It's good to see you again."

Rosalee tiptoed out the front door with a small wave.

Holly led Chase to a chair and sat beside him. He looked toward the front door and then back at Holly. His grin was replaced by a bottom-lipped frown as he looked down at his Velcro sneakers.

"I hear you were at horse lessons." Holly tried to turn his

attention from his mother's absence.

Chase's downtrodden gaze seemed to perk ever so slightly.

"I'm not much of a rider, but they are beautiful, aren't they?"

Chase clutched something in his hand, and Holly leaned closer. A photograph of a reddish-brown horse.

"Who's that?"

Chase rubbed the photo as though he was petting the animal. He slowly turned it over, revealing the name: Solomon.

"Is Solomon the horse's name?"

Chase nodded.

"Is he your favorite?"

"Yup-uh."

"He looks kind."

"Sss-sick." Chase's lower lip turned downward as he searched Holly's face.

"Solomon is sick?"

Another nod.

"Is that why you're feeling sad?"

"Yup-uh."

"It's hard when those we love are sick, isn't it?" The irony was not lost on Holly. "You know what helps me when I'm feeling sad?"

Chase waited.

"I like to listen to jazz music. Not the sad and slow kind, but the upbeat, dance party kind. You like music, right?"

More nodding.

"What do you say we chase our blues away with a big band tune?" Holly helped Chase to his feet. She pulled out her phone and looked up one of the happiest songs she knew. She danced to the music, complete with shoulder sways and snaps on the off beat. Chase soon joined her, tapping his head and feet, still holding his beloved photo as Sinatra flew them to the moon.

The front door jingled while the dancing duo was in full swing.

"Hey, you two…nice moves." Nik shut the door and stomped off his snow-tipped boots, a few packages in one arm.

"F-f-for me?" Chase eyed the supposed gifts.

"Sorry, this is for my special lady."

"Ma-ma-miss Lena?" Chase thrust his tongue on the "L" as he answered.

"That's right, my man." Nik hung up his coat. "Lena still in rehearsal?"

"Yes, we're waiting until their break so Chase can join them." Holly tugged back and forth on her sweater, trying to cool off after elevating her heart rate.

"Good to see you again, bud." Nik extended a high five to Chase with his free hand before heading to the back office.

Holly admired Nik's knack for connecting with Chase. If she didn't know he was an ex-con, and if he wasn't attached to Lena, he'd be exactly the kind of guy Holly was looking for.

The last chords of the song rang out, cueing Holly to bow to Chase. He mimicked her final movement. Satisfied by their spontaneous dance party, Holly took a seat in the reception area and Chase settled on the chair next to her.

Elaine appeared with a large mug of cocoa—not too hot—and a candy dish full of marshmallows.

"How old are you, Chase?" she asked.

He handed the horse photograph to Holly and then held up both hands.

"Ten marshmallows coming right up."

Chase rubbed his hands together in anticipation, rocking

back and forth in his chair. His grin communicated Christmas-morning delight as he watched Elaine plop, plop, plop ten marshmallows into the festive mug.

Holly held onto Solomon as Chase enjoyed his drink, right down to the last drop. Soon the other clients took their break, and Chase joined them for rehearsal—cocoa mustache and all.

It was time to face the past. Not that Holly hadn't tried before, but if she was going to get unstuck, she needed to stop spinning her wheels, rehearsing the same hurt over and over.

Holly had gotten out of work early on Thursday to make it to her counseling appointment. She was thankful there wasn't such a stigma about seeing a therapist these days, but she also didn't feel like plastering it on a billboard, splattering it on social media, or telling her parents or coworkers.

Finding someone to fill in at work hadn't been easy. Thankfully, Betty Jo ended up helping out. Andy would probably need an ear detox afterwards from all her chatter, but at least he and Holly would have good material to laugh about together the next day.

An unassuming woman with salt-and-pepper hair and kind eyes greeted Holly as she entered the office.

"I'm Nina. It's nice to meet you. Feel free to have a seat."

Holly and Nina gelled quickly, which was good because Holly was ready for a deep dive. Well, she thought she was, until the ugly cry burst out and the snot started pouring, but by that point, it was too late to turn back.

Holly started by sharing what life was like before Dad's incident and how much had changed since he returned from his deployment. She talked about how Christmas triggered her grief. She mentioned her confession at Thanksgiving with her mom and how she had felt pushed aside as a kid because of her dad's issues, yet she felt guilty for feeling that way. And how even though she knew it hurt her mom to admit that, it felt freeing to no longer avoid the elephant in the room. The egg shells. The tip-toeing around landmines, which her family had become so proficient at. Holly brought up the failed start-up in the city, which led to her addressing her singleness and how she hoped it wasn't a permanent fixture. She admitted that it was hard to keep her hopes up, not merely in the guy department, but in general. A lot had gone wrong. She had spent so much time and energy wishing things were different. Her soul felt fatigued.

Nina listened intently, nodding, taking notes, and pausing to ask a few clarifying questions.

Holly had assured her that she was ready to deal with things.

"I don't usually recommend this in the first session, but I can tell you're determined. And Holly, you're strong." Nina paused. "What you've faced is not easy, but it's evident that you're resilient."

Determined. Strong. Resilient. These were not words that Holly would have used to describe herself, but hearing them from the counselor caused her to stand up on the inside.

"This might sound strange at first, but I want you to bury your dad."

Holly about came out of her chair, thoroughly shocked.

"I don't think I heard you right. Say that again?"

"I want you to bury the version of your dad that no longer exists. Picture yourself at his coffin. Remember the good memories before the crisis. Let yourself grieve what has been lost. Let yourself feel the letting go of that which you can't bring back."

"Whoa, this sounds really sad. I'm not sure I can do that."

"Your dad's aneurysm was really sad. Have you given yourself permission to feel the weight of that sadness?"

Later, Holly would designate The Winter Blues as Reason #13 on her list because Seasonal Depression sounded too dire, although it was probably more accurate. Holly was beginning to think her holiday funk wasn't simply a passing cloud of gray but a more permanent one.

"What if I get stuck there in that layer of grief?"

"There's another piece to this exercise. But its effectiveness is contingent on you seeing the first part through."

"Okay. What is it?"

"After you bury what will never be, you accept what is. You let your dad off the hook by burying your expectations and longing for him to return to who he was. And then you celebrate who he actually is, post-aneurysm. You find the good in his limitations and become acquainted with him in the here and now."

"Kind of like the Glad Game with a twist?" Holly asked.

"You could look at it that way."

"Actually, I think you might be on to something. Not gonna lie, the burial thing sounds a little hokey—no offense. But I think what's tripped me up and held me back for so long is the underlying frustration that things are not as they should be. No matter how much I wish or plead, or even try to distance myself from it all, I can't change what happened." Holly's hand started to shake as nervous energy coursed through her body. And she wasn't caffeinated.

"How does that make you feel?" Nina leaned forward as if waiting for Holly to answer.

"You know what—it makes me so mad! Why can't I have my dad back?" In the safe space, Holly let the heat of her suppressed emotions rise to the surface with lava-like intensity. She yelled, taken back by the force with which she shot out the words.

"That's good, Holly. Let it out."

"Why do I have to say good-bye? I'm just a little girl inside who wants her daddy to be the strong one for her again. I'm tired of being brave. I need him to help me believe that being back home after my failure to launch is not the final say on my worth."

Holly felt as if she'd been lugging around a gallon of paint for years, and her outburst had hurled it all into the air. They sat in silence as Holly's gut-wrenching honesty covered the office walls, dripping down slowly until it pooled on the floor at her feet.

Her heart pounded from the surge of adrenaline. She took in several stabilizing breaths and let them out slowly. While bright red anger had exploded out of her, it was a sad shade of winter blue that had been exposed.

"What we think is anger is often rooted in suppressed grief," Nina whispered.

Holly breathed deeply and more freely than she had in a long time.

She had finally turned the knob and let herself be found in the place where she was stuck. Everything wasn't fixed, but in the aftermath of Holly's unedited confession, the pent-up pain finally released from its sealed container, and an instantaneous peace filled the void.

CHAPTER FOURTEEN
Unsolicited Advice

THE DAY AFTER HER COUNSELING APPOINTMENT, Holly was tempted to take a mental health day instead of returning to work. She felt a strange blend of contentment and emotional depletion after her intense session. Relieved to have started the counseling process, she knew she had more work ahead of her—and not the ornament personalization kind but allowing a fresh perspective to be written on her heart and mind.

While she tried to resist the nap that was calling her name, she caught a glimpse of a very realistic-looking Santa wearing a T-shirt. Upon closer examination, it read, "If you want to sit in the chair, you've gotta grow the hair." Apparently, this Santa lookalike took the slogan literally. He sported the prettiest head of long, white hair Holly had ever seen. She thought she spotted a bicep tattoo that read, "Mrs. C.," but he wasn't close enough for her to confirm or deny.

As Holly returned to the ornament in front of her, another Santa lookalike walked in front of the counter. This Santa wore a Hawaiian shirt and shorts—in December. He looked like he ate more salads than cookies, and his hair was shorter. Maybe he didn't take his chair time quite as seriously as Santa #1? But the "Ho ho ho!" that he voluntarily offered on his way past Holly was the most authentic-sounding Santa voice she'd ever heard.

Soon after the trim, healthy Santa walked by, a third Santa-type moseyed her way decked out in sweatpants and an oversized red hoody with a larger-than-life button that read, "Mo cookies, mo presents. No cookies, no presents."

Good grief, Charlie Brown. Was this for real?

Holly rubbed her forehead. Had her time in Christmas Wonderland finally gotten to her? Or was her decision to face old wounds having residual effects? Were the Santas part of a hallucination?

To be fair, all three Santas had two things in common: white hair—whether real or wigged—and a jolly countenance about them. They seemed to be on a field trip. Maybe they were Frank's distant relatives or his neighbors from North Pole, Alaska?

Andy had been out running an errand for Leslie. When he returned, Frank was with him.

"I wanted to check on our supply of Christmas holly ornaments." Frank winked, as forthright as ever, even after their "frank" talk.

Was it a contrived pick-up line or a legitimate errand?

Frank's lingering at Station 8 confirmed the former. Holly decided to risk sounding like an idiot to get to the bottom of the mystery. "Either I've been putting too much time in, or I've lost it."

"Do tell." Frank leaned on the counter.

"I think I'm starting to see things that aren't there. No less than three Santas have crossed my path today. Doesn't Neumann's use one at a time?"

"I haven't seen more than one here today," Andy insisted with a mischievous grin.

"Spill it. What's going on?"

"It's the annual Kris Kringle Academy field trip," Frank explained.

"That sounds made up."

"I swear upon my hunting blind, it's the truth," Andy insisted. "The Kris Kringle Academy is only about an hour from here, as the crow flies."

"How did I miss that? I grew up near a training center for Santas and didn't even know it?"

"It's too late to enroll for this year. And I hear there's usually a waiting list." Frank waggled his eyebrows.

"Very funny."

"This is Betty Jo's favorite day of work," Andy added. "She highly anticipates the arrival of the Kris Kringle Academy students. She told me so yesterday. I have a hunch she wishes she'd been Mrs. Claus in another life."

"She'd be perfect for that," Holly concurred. "She could jingle the whole year through."

Frank's walkie talkie went off, summoning him to the warehouse to address a pressing issue. "Duty calls. See you kids around." He power-posed with one fist on his hip and the other extended into space, making a dramatic exit.

Holly shook her head at his over-the-top—mostly annoying, yet slightly amusing—departure.

"Where were you yesterday, anyway?" Andy asked. "It was a bit dicey here with your temporary replacement."

"I'll bet. Anything to report?"

"Are you avoiding the question?"

"That obvious?" Holly smiled.

"You tell me, I'll tell you," Andy reasoned.

"Are you bargaining with me?"

"I'd say it's an even trade."

"That depends on what you have."

"Ladies first. I insist."

"I'm going to counseling to face things I've been trying to run from."

"Cool. Me too. Several years in. Not fun, but necessary."

"We agree again. Now tell me something good," Holly urged.

"If you promise to keep it between us. Our store manager may have wanted to attend the same school as Mrs. Rasmussen."

"To be a gym teacher?"

"Not that. Kris Kringle Academy."

"Betty Jo wanted to be Santa? She'd have to stop waxing and plucking."

"Funny, but no. I did a little fact checking on the school's website and discovered that you can enroll to get trained as Santa *or* Mrs. Claus."

"That makes more sense."

"Yes to waxing and plucking continuing, please and thank you." Andy reached for his clipboard.

"I'm not so sure about Mrs. R. in that role, but I can totally picture Betty Jo as the quintessential Mrs. Claus."

"That's what I thought. It doesn't sound like the dream has died, either. I think it's alive and well."

"Why hasn't she pursued it?" Holly tried to ignore the lengthy list of custom orders hanging over her head, at least for a few more minutes.

"Not sure. Timing, maybe? No Mr. Claus? And can you imagine this place without her?"

"No way. She's part of the total package."

"No one sings the employee theme song with as much gusto as she does," Andy imitated the store manager's stance, clutching his hands together in front of his broad chest.

"And no one jingles quite like she does either."

"On the other hand, everyone deserves a shot at their dreams." Andy roughed up his bread before taming it down.

"Yeah, and she's missed out on a few already."

"What do you mean?"

"Just a hunch." Holly shrugged.

The conversation halted as Santa #4, clothed in a three-piece, reindeer-print suit topped with a fedora, asked for directions to the restroom.

"A little too much eggnog on the bus ride." He chuckled.

Andy pointed the way toward relief.

"How many Santas are here?" Holly asked after suited Santa was out of earshot.

"Hard to tell. Let's look it up."

Andy pulled out his phone and searched for the website as Holly looked on.

Nik strode up to the counter, "Hey guys, have you seen Frank? He's not answering my texts, and I need to finalize something with him for Lena."

Nik was so supportive of Lena. Holly wasn't sure Lena knew how lucky she was. Nik sure bent over backward for her, but he did it without cramping her style. Either that or he was buttering Lena up in an effort to scam her. But that was hard to picture now that Holly had gotten to know him better. Or had he tricked Holly too? Nik was still a mystery in many ways.

"He's over in the warehouse, but I imagine he'll be back soon. He's taken a special interest in the store's Christmas Holly." Andy snickered.

Holly rolled her eyes.

"If you're sticking around to wait, you want to do a little investigating with us?" Andy held up his phone.

"Sure, why not?" Nik moved closer to Holly and Andy, probably so he could see the screen better.

With a few clicks while bringing Nik up to speed, the coworkers found their answer on the Kris Kringle Academy's website.

"One hundred Santas. I've only spotted four so far. People who aren't from around here would never believe this is our real life. It's like we're living in a holiday cartoon special." Holly straightened her lopsided name tag.

"Or a Christmas novel turned movie," Andy said.

"That too. Although I hear they usually film those in Vancouver in the summer." Holly gestured toward the rafters, as if Canada was up there.

They returned to the website to mine for more material.

"One of the classes they offer is Santa sign language. I wonder what that entails." Holly's work apron came untied and nearly fell off. She struggled to retie it.

"Need some help with that?" Nik picked up one of the apron ties that Holly was reaching for behind her back and held it up for her.

"I can manage, thanks." Holly took the tie from him and finished the job.

"Santa sign language probably includes laying one finger aside of the nose with the pointer finger of the other hand beckoning children to come sit." Andy demonstrated.

Three-piece-suit Santa returned. "Couldn't help but catch that last part. You're right on the money." He laid a finger above his right nostril for emphasis.

"Santa, what's the weirdest request you've gotten for a present?" Andy asked as he and Holly exchanged knowing looks, Holly thinking back on Oliver's six-pack wish.

"There are the usual strange ones, like one little girl from North Carolina who asked for a dolphin and a rainbow. The rainbow was above my pay grade—the dolphin too, for that matter. As I recall, a dolphin poster and rainbow necklace may have found their way under her tree. Her brother asked for a golf cart. I'm not sure how much weight he thought the sleigh could take.

Pretty sure the little tikes don't factor in the total poundage of everyone's gifts when they make their requests."

Holly grinned at the image of Santa's sleigh dipping and tipping beneath the weight of a full-size golf cart.

"One boy, although his hands were fully functioning, asked for a fake hand and a bucket of dirt from Wyoming."

Santa tugged on the sleeve of his suit. "Then there's the one I'll never forget. A sweetie from Fort Hood climbed up on my lap. Her dad was deployed overseas. I prepared myself for her request, wondering if it'd be a letter from her daddy or to bring her daddy back home. Instead, she looked up at me with the sincerest expression and said, 'Santa, I'm only asking for one thing, so it shouldn't be hard to remember. World peace, please.' It seemed out of reach, but definitely worth asking for. And I've never forgotten it. It should be on the top of all our Christmas lists, don't you think?"

"A grown-up Christmas list of sorts," Andy said.

Holly covered her ears. "Not that song again. And don't get me started on 'Last Christmas' or 'All I Want for Christmas is You.' Gag."

"Where's your sense of romance, Holly girl?" Andy teased as he started humming the first few lines of the last song she'd mentioned.

"Romance to me is more like steadiness and tenderness versus hype and lavish displays of affection."

"Oh, come on. You mean to tell me you wouldn't get weak in the knees if a guy made a fool of himself for you?" Andy teased.

Santa inched closer, hand to his ear, a twinkle in his eye.

"I suppose an over-the-top moment or two would be okay, but I want a guy who gets me and who will get along with my family—or at least tolerate them—so holidays won't be tense. I also hope he's good-looking and a hard worker with a sense of humor. And this is very important—he has to be at least three inches taller than me."

"Sounds like an online dating service profile," Andy retrieved a pen from behind his ear.

"Don't act like you don't have one, too," Holly warned.

"Guilty as charged," Andy wrote something down on his checklist.

"I used to, but no need for it anymore." Nik smiled.

No way! Did Lena and Nik meet on a dating site? Holly couldn't imagine Lena doing that. Then again, she was always so busy. How else would she meet a bachelor from across the country? Holly made a mental note to investigate this theory with Elaine.

Santa leaned toward the single employees and cupped his mouth with his right hand. "If you can keep a secret, you're not the only ones." He winked.

"You have a dating profile?" Holly widened her eyes.

"Been looking for a new Mrs. Claus for a while now. The original took her last sleigh ride in the sky about a decade ago. But 2.0 has to be special—strong enough to keep up with the rigors of the season and tender enough to connect with all our children."

"You want children?" Holly picked up a paintbrush, she couldn't put her orders on hold any longer.

"At my age? Oh, no. Already have a handful back home and mini grands running around, too. I meant all the children at the shopping mall who come for a visit and a picture with us. She needs to be welcoming but not a pushover, since the line needs to keep moving so everyone has a turn. Takes a special lady to become Mrs. Claus. A real blend of grace and grit, laced with gentleness and blessed with wit. I'll know her when I see her."

"I bet you will," Nik said.

"And natural white hair is a plus. Although we learned in the Mrs. Claus breakout session that the right combination of at-home hair color can fix that. Oh, and there's one more piece of criteria that is of utmost importance." Santa adjusted his fedora. "It might seem nitpicky, but it's actually a big deal."

"What's that?" Andy egged.

"She has to look good in red."

"Of course she does. Comes with the territory." Andy held an even tone, but Holly knew him well enough by now to recognize he was teasing. "Santa, thanks for telling us what's on your grown-up Christmas list.".

"Your secret is safe with us. In fact, I'm kind of a professional secret keeper." Holly avoided a sideways glance at Nik, focusing on the order in front of her.

"If I can offer one piece of unsolicited advice, it's don't despise grand displays of love. Yet hold on to the everyday kind of love, too—his hand in yours, a listening ear when you're stressed, a shoulder to cry on when you're sad, and a smile that makes you feel like you're home, even when you're miles from it. Stick with the one who gets you and loves you as you are and with whom you can laugh and dream."

"Did you rehearse that?" Andy interrupted the sage wisdom of Santa #4.

"Thank you," Holly said. "I'll definitely keep that in mind."

"Me too," Nik added. His voice was thoughtful enough that Holly glanced up to see his serious face. What was he thinking?

Santas's unsolicited advice could serve nicely as Reason #14 on her naughty list. Except her coldness toward Christmas was melting ever so slightly in the presence of this kind soul. Maybe she could leave Santa out of it and just be mad about the unwelcome advice that well-meaning relatives doled out around the dinner table, especially in December.

With a nod, wink, and a bit more sign language, Santa #4 left to meet up with ninety-six of his bearded brothers who, according to Andy, were gathering outside for their annual Kris Kringle Academy group photo.

"A Mrs. Claus breakout session? Sure he didn't mean a Mrs. Claus make-out session?" Andy joked.

"You're terrible!"

"But that was fantastic. Wait until Ollie hears that I got face time with the big guy."

"You should've asked him for your own BB gun," Holly teased.

"Now you can see why I keep working here. It's never boring."

"That's for sure."

"I think we should recruit that Santa to fill in for Doc next year. That way there's no chance of emergency dental procedures calling him away," Nik suggested.

"Right on. My brief stint filling in for Doc was no picnic. I'm telling you, that red velvet suit does not breathe." Andy tugged on his red apron to demonstrate.

Nik laughed. "I'll bet! My elf leggings weren't the most comfortable, either."

"Holly-girl, you think you'll be back here next season? Then you could have more quality time with the likes of me and this cast of quirky characters."

"It's been real. Well, actually, more like make-believe, but you know what I mean. Here's the thing, though…I'm working through stuff, and I'm determined to see it through. And I'm saving up. After those things are taken care of, I'm planning on starting up again elsewhere, farther from Bavarian Falls."

"Say it ain't so. You're sure gonna be missed 'round these

parts, little lady," Andy twanged.

Nik pulled his phone out of his back pocket and scanned the screen.

Holly shifted her attention to Andy. "If you promise not to tell anyone about Santa's online dating profile or what I'm about to say…"

"Scout's honor." Andy saluted.

"Then I'll admit—only to you—that this place has grown on me."

"Ha! Knew it."

"Even Betty Jo's holiday radiance will be missed."

"And Frank's showmanship?" Andy pushed. "Talk about lavish displays of affection…that kid would be one to propose on a hot air balloon ride during the summer festival."

"You're on thin ice, bucko."

"Couldn't resist."

Nik shoved his phone into his back pocket. "Hey, guys, this has been fun. But that was Frank. I'm going to meet him now, and I'll be sure to fill him in on Santa's relationship advice." He smiled at Holly.

Holly was pretty sure Nik still thought she and Frank were a thing. She hoped Nik would not encourage Frank or offer unsolicited relationship advice regarding her. He didn't need any motivation to flirt more.

Once Nik was out of earshot, Holly turned to Andy. "Frank and I are just friends."

Betty Jo waved as she walked by, more chipper than ever.

At that, Holly and Andy turned to each other and exclaimed in unison, "Mrs. Claus!"

CHAPTER FIFTEEN
Scavenger Hunt

ONLY THREE DAYS UNTIL CHRISTMAS, AND Holly was doing some very last-minute shopping downtown after work, trying to find the perfect gift for her mom, who never seemed to need anything except for her daughter to meet her expectations. No pressure.

Bzzzt. Bzzzt.

Dare Holly hope that her Mom had started texting? She probably needed more baking items from the store.

Bzzzt. Bzzzt.

Holly set down a pine-scented candle at the gift shop on Main to read the message. She was surprised to see the sender was Frank.

Can u do me a favor?

What's up? Holly had no idea if Frank's request would be silly, serious, or flirtatious.

I'm supposed to unlock the showroom for a friend at 10.

After hours? Sounds mysterious.

Yes. I'm tied up.

Literally? Holly teased.

No. ;-) Tied up w/ big shipping ordeal in warehouse. Can u unlock showroom?

Sure.

U da best.

Where do I get the key?

Holly guessed a delayed or rush-order shipment was arriving after hours. But, if that were the case, why wouldn't Frank say so? Or ask someone else?

Promise you won't tell?

To. The. Grave. Holly repeated Betty Jo's mantra.
What?
Yes, I promise. Where is it?
In a secret compartment under Baby Jesus #1.
Dude, there are a lot of those babies on the property. Which one?
The one out front, under the store name and motto.
Chase's Jesus?
That's the one.
U owe me.
A carriage ride? ;-)
Ha! How about a hot cocoa voucher for Stocking Stuffers?
Done.

Holly concluded the conversation with a thumbs up emoji and pocketed her phone. Her mom had introduced her to the Nancy Drew books as a child, and now it seemed Holly had been invited to play a supporting role in *The Case of the Christmas Store Caper*—except the boss's grandson knew about the break-in. And it wasn't really a break-in, since Holly had been asked to unlock the door. But a girl could still pretend.

Holly left the store and hurried home. After stowing away her last-minute gifts, heating up leftover pot roast from their Sunday lunch, working on a painting for Claudia, freshening up, and tossing her pepper spray into her purse for good measure, Holly headed back to work. Cocoa instead of cash would be her prize, and maybe a glimpse of the mystery that was unfolding after hours at Neumann's.

Holly parked her Prius around the corner. If there was anything weird going on, she didn't want to get mixed up in it. Although,

Frank was a friend, and she was sure he wouldn't put her in danger.

Calm down. This isn't Chicago. It's the capital city of Christmas, remember?

She'd been cooped up a little too long in this Norman Rockwell scene. She made a mental note to schedule time in the city with Elaine as soon as Christmas was over.

Avoiding the temptation to treat this favor as a spy mission and sneak through the shadows, Holly opted for the run-as-fast-as-you-can approach as she sprinted over to Baby Jesus #1.

Sure enough, there was a doorbell-type contraption under the statue that released when pressed. Out dropped a key.

Holly's pulse quickened as she grabbed it and replaced the secret compartment. The nativity scene was lit up like a Christmas tree even when the store was closed, and she didn't want to be caught red-handed and confused as being involved in the Christmas store caper herself. It was almost ten, so she sprinted again to the west entrance as Frank had instructed her.

The wintry evening air in her nostrils and her shaking hands added to the drama as she fumbled to unlock the showroom door. Thankfully, the timed exterior and interior lights allowed her to make contact between key and keyhole, and she pushed open the door.

Inside, Holly was determined to warm up. As she did, she peered into the empty parking lot, anticipating the arrival of the mysterious guest.

Frank had failed to give further instructions past the request to unlock the door. Was she supposed to wait for someone to show up? Was she supposed to lock up afterward?

That was when she noticed the music. She had grown accustomed to tuning it out during work hours, but the cheery holiday tunes had been replaced by Vivaldi's "Winter" violin concertos. Had an employee forgotten to turn off the sound system? Maybe the cleaning crew had changed it and forgotten to shut it down? That seemed unlikely and negligent.

Tap into your sleuthing skills, Nancy.

Walking farther into the store, Holly spun slowly, looking up to where the music cascaded from. In slow motion, she started to notice what she had missed upon entering. Thousands of dainty white lights had been added above her, winding around the dimly light store.

She tentatively followed the strings of lights. As she passed through Station 10, she smiled, remembering Frank's clumsy encounter with the display there.

A spotlight from the rafters projected a ray of light onto a white envelope lying on the carpet. Holly stepped toward the envelope and saw that it read, "Open me first."

Holly glanced behind her. No movement. She inched closer. Was this for her?

Her hands had warmed but were now shaking in anticipation and healthy fear as she picked up the envelope. The lettering was more welcoming than menacing, more like an invitation than a ransom note. She opened it.

I realize this may be unexpected. You've been putting in a lot of hours, so I thought a scavenger hunt of sorts would be fun. Keep following the clues and see where it goes.

Love, Me.

P.S. Clue #2 is hanging with care, with holly on it. It's green like a pear.

Love? Oh dear. It couldn't be for her. Could it?

Was Frank trying to win her over, even though she had been careful not to lead him on?

The music continued to play, and Holly's heart continued to race, but her steps quieted to a tiptoe. The life-size nutcrackers seemed to stand at attention. The ornaments served as secret keepers as Holly meandered through the vast showroom.

The next envelope was located past the customization station. It was clearly positioned in a lime green stocking with a hand-stitched holly on the front of it.

I know we haven't known each other for very long, but it feels like forever. You bring light and beauty to those around you and to those who care about you. I think you have more than a clue that I deeply care for you.

Gulp.

Holly steadied herself, one hand on the wall, before continuing.

If I haven't scared you off yet, keep going. Clue #3 is all about dates. Go find the ones that open and close. And specifically look for Rudolph's nose.

P.S. I hope to go on many more dates with you.

Holly had been so caught up in the magical experience that her brain and heart hadn't synced until now.

Had Frank set her up—pretending that he was tied up in the warehouse? Hadn't she made it clear they were only friends with no promise of more?

Her stomach flip-flopped, yet she was determined to see the scavenger hunt through. She would face what was to come when she arrived at the final clue.

Envelope #3 was located at Station 5, near the Advent calendars. The huge Santa and his reindeer calendar stood out above the rest, with an envelope taped to the back.

We're a few days away from a special date on the calendar. It seemed fitting to surprise you with this before you were expecting a gift. This whole evening is to solidify that you are of utmost importance to me. And I hope you feel the same way, too.

Do you have time for a show? If so, enter the theater and sit at the seat with the bow.

Good King Wenceslas. What was going on?

Holly was tempted to text Elaine, but she couldn't do it. The intentionality and the drama of the whole thing couldn't be interrupted—even by an SOS text. Holly didn't feel as if she was endangered—at least not yet. But she paused before proceeding, long enough to wonder if the mastermind behind all this was in danger of heartbreak.

"Let's find out what's behind door number four," Holly whispered.

A string of white icicle lights was draped over a seat in the back row of the dark theater. A glittery, velvet bow signaled this was her assigned seat.

Holly sat down warily. She was the sole audience member from what she could tell. Vivaldi stopped. The string of lights dimmed. Now things were getting a little eerie. She slowly reached inside her purse to locate both her phone and pepper spray, if need be.

The screen in front of her came to life. During store hours, three different movies were shown here on rotation throughout the day: the history of the store, the life story of its founder,

Frank's great-grandpa, and the making of the Stille Nacht Sanctuary. During her training, Holly had seen them all. Which one would play now?

It wasn't any of them.

There on the ginormous screen was the man who was off limits to Holly for many reasons. His gorgeous eyes were seemingly fixed on hers as he spoke from his heart. "I realize this might be a bit of a shock to you—but don't worry, I didn't break in here. It was basically an inside job. As you can probably tell, this took work. But you're worth it. And I hope you think I am, too. This might seem like a grandiose way to tell you so, but I think this is what you want, too.

"It's a fresh start. A new definition to our relationship, if you're on board. And I hope you are. Because you're amazing. I wish you could see yourself like everyone else does. You don't have to have it all figured out. I don't have it all figured out, but...I guess what I'm saying is, will you take this next step with me?"

Holly wasn't sure she had breathed at all during the movie. She definitely had not moved a muscle except her mind was racing faster than a horse favored to win the Triple Crown.

She had half-expected to find Frank in the theater trying to seal the deal on the carriage ride. Never in a million years did she expect to see Nik projected in megapixels, professing his love for her.

Had he and Lena broken up? He sure didn't waste any time.

While she was trying to make sense of what had happened, the screen rose, and Nik's silhouette appeared behind it.

He dropped to his knee. "Will you marry me?"

Holly gasped.

From his chivalrous posture, Nik's eyes adjusted to the light change, and all of a sudden, he looked like a deer in the headlights.

"Holly? What are you doing here?!"

"What am *I* doing here? I should ask you the same thing."

"I guess you have a point there. You're usually here, and I'm hardly ever here. But Frank helped me put this plan together to propose."

"Frank was in on this?"

"Are you surprised?"

"Surprised that Frank was an accomplice or surprised by the proposal?"

"Oh! Oh, gosh! That wasn't for you. It was for Lena. What kind of guy do you think I am?"

His words broke the dam on the secret Holly had been keeping. "You're a criminal!" she blurted out. Nik stood.

"Since when has trying to love someone become a crime?" Nik shouted back.

"Your aunt told me you were released from Leavenworth. I've kept it to myself until now. But you already know anyway, so I guess it's still a secret, kind of. What do you have to say about that?" she challenged.

"About her confiding in you?" Nik moved closer.

"No, about Leavenworth," Holly clarified.

Nik shook his head. "What does that have to do with this?"

"Don't you think that affects a relationship with someone trying to run a nonprofit for kids?"

"I hoped it wouldn't." Nik glanced away, avoiding eye contact.

"Well, it's a big deal in my book."

"I'm sorry you feel that way, Holly."

She stood and marched down the aisle. "What did you do,

anyway? I guess it's not my business, but now that you've proposed, maybe it's more my business now than it's ever been."

"I was proposing to Lena, but you showed up in her place."

The sting of Nik's words created an emotional chasm between them, even as his steps toward her bridged the physical gap.

They locked gazes, and Holly tried to read the moment through the lens of their charged emotions.

"You really want to know, huh?"

"Yes."

"Everything I worked for was taken from me after a confrontation went south. I didn't know what hit me. I guess I should have read the writing on the wall, but I didn't see it coming until it was too late."

"What…a stray bullet? A drug bust gone bad? A heist?"

"What are you talking about? None of the above. I was working my way up in a major tourist corporation out west when—"

"I'm not sure I'd call Kansas out west, exactly."

"Kansas? No. I was working in Leavenworth, Washington, when one of the higher ups at the company called me into a meeting. Apparently, I hadn't been filling out part of our contracts correctly, and the company lost money because of it. But the guy who trained me never taught me how. Turns out he didn't have much integrity, but it was too late—the damage was done. They let me go. Released me from my job."

"Washington?"

"Yes, that's what I said. Leavenworth, Washington. The town that looks a lot like Bavarian Falls in all her themed glory."

Holly's jaw fell, her eyes as wide as her mother's fine china platter reserved for the main holiday dish. And she was beginning to feel like the Thanksgiving turkey.

"What did you think happened?"

Dumbfounded that she had been wrong about Nik the whole time, Holly managed to fumble over a few words. "I...I...gosh, this is going to sound awful. See, based on what your aunt said—about you being released from Leavenworth and it being difficult—I thought you had been a military criminal at Leavenworth, the U.S. Penitentiary in Kansas."

"What?" Nik whipped his head to the side. "Why on earth would you think that?"

Holly busily replayed the last six weeks in her mind—their interactions at church, Music Keys, the ride to her house, sitting around her kitchen table eating dessert, the concert, Thanksgiving Day in her driveway, working side by side on Black Friday, their conversation at the Christmas party, and now, this moment when he had proposed—accidentally—to her.

She rolled up the guarded armor around her exposed heart, trying to assemble any ounce of dignity she could muster after her outburst.

This straight-out-of-a-Christmas-rom-com proposal hadn't been for her. It was intended for Lena, his successful, beautiful girlfriend. The one who was not standing under a thousand sparkly lights with her favorite classical music sweeping overhead while her really good-looking, non-criminal boyfriend asked her to be his wife. Of course, it hadn't been for Holly—the stuck-in-her-childhood-bedroom, working-at-a-temp-job-in-her-thirties, plain old Holly.

When she started her Christmas list, she couldn't have dreamed Reason #15 would represent this nightmare of misunderstanding, appropriately called Scavenger Hunt. There, in the dimly lit theater, her pride had been hunted down.

Nik was only a few feet in front of her, still holding the small ring box. It was open, exposing a delicate engagement ring.

Holly tried not to stare at the diamond. And she couldn't bear to look into Nik's eyes, so she diverted her gaze to his right ear. That seemed safe enough. "I'm sorry, Nik. For everything."

His ear said nothing. Obviously.

But his lips started to speak…and then stopped.

There was nothing left to say.

The rest of the evening happened in fast forward. The ring was returned to Nik's pocket. Holly dashed out of the theater, passing each clue in reverse as she neared the exit. Once outside, the key was returned to Baby Jesus #1 since Nik had told her to lock up considering his plans were ruined. Her oversized emotions were packed away in a suitcase that wouldn't close entirely.

It was all a big mistake—Holly's wrong assumption about Nik's past and his accidental proposal to her. In hindsight, she should have simply unlocked the door and left. Curiosity has been known to kill the cat, but in this case, it led to an endearing proposal—meant for someone else.

After a few frantic texts with Frank, sharing the bullet points of what happened, Holly uncovered more evidence. She was supposed to unlock the door for Lena, who was coming to meet Nik at Neumann's. Nik's story to Lena was that he was having car trouble and needed her to come rescue him. The idea was that Lena would enter the store, complete the Scavenger Hunt, and become a fiancée by the end of the evening.

Apparently, Lena, like Frank, had gotten held up at work with a pressing issue of her own and couldn't get away to meet Nik. Maybe she had tried to text, but his phone was on airplane mode so it wouldn't make any noise while he hid behind the movie screen, waiting for her? Nik had no idea Holly would be the one sitting in the back of the theater—the unexpected recipient of his lavish display of affection.

Holly hurried to her concealed vehicle, trying to put emotional and physical distance between herself and Nik after the major mix-up. Holly slammed the driver's side door once she was safely tucked inside. Despite trying to think of anything else, she kept replaying the strange turn of events in her mind, drawn back like a magnet to a fridge. She wished someone like Nik would care enough about her to actually propose in such a thoughtful way. But the only guy she seemed to be able to attract was quirky and entirely devoted to staying put. Not that he was a bad guy, but Frank was not a solution to Holly's bigger life problem. She had reverted back to her twenties in nearly every way. She wanted a guy who would take her seriously, one she could dream with and confide in. She wanted someone who would help her move forward and one she could love with her whole heart.

How was she supposed to act normally around her parents after this debacle, and where in the world was she going to start the narrative with Elaine?

In her not-yet-warmed-up car, she chose to laugh instead of cry.

What a ride.

When Holly arrived at work the next day, she felt as if she was being watched—not from the security cameras, but from the thousands of white lights that served as witness to the previous night's bizarre experience. She felt as if everyone knew…but how could they? She had only told Elaine, and she was pretty sure Nik wasn't going to leak it to the local newspaper.

If he did, she could picture the headlines: *The Case of the Christmas Store Caper Solved by Local Sleuth*

Hometown Holly Accidentally Proposed to Days Before Her 31st Birthday

She Thought He was an Ex-con; He Thought She was His Girlfriend

With only a few days until Christmas, the procrastinators were on the prowl for the perfect gift—or any gift, really—for their loved ones. The customer flow had slowed down at Station 8, as people realized they'd probably missed their window to get their personalized orders back in time.

"You look different," Andy said. "Did you get your hair cut?"

"Nope." How could he tell something was up?

"Different makeup?"

"Same old, same old." Holly's face warmed as she tried harder to convince Andy nothing had changed.

"What's up with all the lights? You think an elf made a late-night visit?"

Warmer.

This was going to be a long morning. She'd better change the subject before Andy discovered she'd almost become a bride-to-be after hours at Neumann's.

"Do you have Oliver for Christmas?" She prayed he did. Otherwise, she'd feel like a jerk for bringing up a sore subject. She was desperate to divert the curious sleuth.

"Actually, I do. Bill is taking Tammy to meet his extended family down in Kentucky. They thought it'd be better if Oliver had a more low-key Christmas, and I agreed."

"I'm glad to hear that. About you and Oliver."

"Did you color your hair?" Andy insisted upon figuring out what had shifted.

"I'm pretty sure that's not a question you should ask a woman."

As if on cue, the guy whose proposal had epically bombed the night before approached the counter.

"Hi," Nik offered.

"Hey," Holly replied.

Andy announced an impromptu errand near Teresa's station.

As soon as he was gone, Nik started in. "So, look. Last night was really weird. I'm sorry you got brought into it. That had to be a shock."

"You proposing to me, or me finding out you're not really the criminal I had you pegged for?"

Nik scratched his head. "Just to make sure we're clear, I wasn't proposing to you, but to Lena…well, imaginary Lena, who was supposed to be there."

"Oh yeah, that's what I meant. And yup, loud and clear. I'm very aware that you were not proposing to me."

Holly couldn't help but feel a slight sting of rejection. It was as close as she had come to being the recipient of a marriage proposal, even though it hadn't been intended for her. She understood Nik wanting to clear the air, but the way that he was overemphasizing that she was not the object of his affection felt like being picked last in gym class.

He was watching her, and to be sure he couldn't read her thoughts, she turned things on him. "About the criminal thing…I'm truly sorry. The way your aunt said you were released from Leavenworth only meant one thing in my mind."

"You didn't automatically think of the charming village in the Pacific Northwest? My family vacationed there a lot when I was growing up. We moved around quite a bit when I was a kid, but Leavenworth was a constant. I guess that's what drew me to find a permanent job there—well, it was supposed to be permanent."

"The only association my family has with Leavenworth is my dad's experience transporting military prisoners in Kansas."

Frank walked up. "What did I miss, an inside joke?"

"More like an inside job." Nik laughed.

Holly joined him. It was a relief to know Nik wasn't living a double life.

Nik brought Frank up to speed on the rest of what went down when he sent Holly in his place to unlock the showroom. Holly couldn't help but analyze Frank's nonverbal reaction. Was that jealousy that flashed across his face or simply a general disbelief in what had transpired?

"That's wild, man. Sorry I wasn't able to do my part like we talked about."

"No worries," Nik assured Frank. "We sorted it out. Didn't we, Holly?"

"We did." Why did she feel that sting again?

"Thanks for letting me use the store, even though it turned out differently than we dreamed up."

Holly jolted. "We?"

"Oh, yeah. Frank and I plotted out the whole thing over chips and queso at the pub. I had swung by here to finish charting my course with Frank when you, Andy, and I had our encounter with wise old Santa."

"About last night...I've been thinking. Why didn't you leave the door unlocked, since you were already inside?" Holly asked.

"To fool-proof the plan." Frank shook his head. "Nik didn't want to accidentally propose to Betty Jo or anyone else, so I locked him in when I left work. That gave him time to set up the Scavenger Hunt without any accidental visitors. I was supposed to come back to unlock the west entrance so Lena could enter there and see the first clue. I was scheduled to arrive ten minutes before she did so I could get out of there before she suspected anything."

"But you sent me." Holly lowered her eyes.

"That I did."

Nik tapped the counter. "Hey, it's been real, guys, but I've gotta get over to the eatery. Lena's meeting me there. She insists they have the best chili in town. Time to fess up to the proposal fiasco before she reads about it in the paper." He winked at Holly.

Maybe the newspaper headline would read: *Holly Brigham Unlocks Love Only to Find Out It Wasn't Meant for Her.*

"Now that I have you all to myself," Frank teased, "you still going to be around at the end of January?"

"No offense, but I hope not."

"In case you are, what do ya say to joining me as a judge for the ice-sculpting contest?"

"That'd be fun, but like I said, I'll probably be gone by then."

"Bavarian Falls won't be the same without you. And Neumann's definitely won't look as spectacular in your absence."

"Aw, shucks. How will I go on without these frank conversations?" Holly laughed.

"I have no idea." With a wink of his own and a surprisingly coordinated pivot, Frank headed toward his office.

CHAPTER SIXTEEN
Extra Weight

HOLLY DECIDED AGAINST KARAOKE AT KLINGEMANN'S on Friday. She wasn't physically sick, which was the only thing that typically kept her away, but she was tired from the long days at work and the focus required to keep her brushstrokes steady and the names spelled correctly. Who knew there were so many ways to spell names like Hailey, Haley, Hayley, Haleigh, Haylee, Hallie, or Alicia, Alecia, Alesia, Aleesha, Alisha, Alicea. Holly had seen them all.

Even more than that, she didn't want to risk seeing Nik again after the mix-up. Or see him and Lena singing a power ballad love song while she ate humble pie. Although she couldn't quite imagine Nik and Lena gazing into each other's eyes and singing a power ballad together...that was more Frank's style.

Holly had filled Elaine in on everything that happened the night of the accidental engagement, so Elaine was understanding when Holly opted out of karaoke.

Holly slept in on Saturday, waking up from the weirdest dream about a bachelorette-style show where Betty Jo was trying to find a date for the work Christmas party. She had to choose from a room full of graduates from the Kris Kringle Academy. They tried to impress her with their belly laughs and reindeer handling skills, and they took turns performing a sign language piece set to their favorite Christmas song—kind of like the Happy Hands' Club from *Napoleon Dynamite*.

Holly decided she needed to lay off the late-night cookies and milk routine before bed. It was causing her to identify too closely with Santa. She resolved to probably join the gym again in the New Year. Her metabolism was bound to slow down the closer she got to forty. Plus, Christmas in the Midwest, followed by the long winter, was a recipe for packing on the pounds.

Reason #16: Extra Weight.

Holly climbed out of bed and stretched. Her binder from counseling was on her nightstand. She slid it into the drawer. The last thing she wanted was her mom seeing it and then having to talk to her about it.

Holly had an early afternoon meeting at Music Keys, after which she'd promised her mom she'd go with her to purchase the paint for the fellowship hall painting project at church. Mom wanted Holly's artistic ability handy to confirm she'd made the right selection.

It would've been more appealing to fill the time with mindless scrolling on her phone or to paint along with Bob Ross as she watched his old videos like she used to do at Grandma Bea's. But, as her birthday drew near, Holly felt an urgency to deal with her stuff. At the first counseling appointment, they'd surveyed a chunk of the iceberg, but there was more to address below the surface. She pulled out the exercise her counselor had suggested, about burying what was and accepting what is when it came to her dad.

Here goes nothing.

Holly's counselor had encouraged her to make the assignment her own and do what felt meaningful to her. With that in mind, Holly reached for her charcoal pencils and started sketching. Three separate images came to mind as she thought about the things she missed most about her dad.

The first was of her dancing with him before everything changed. Memories of attending a Daddy-Daughter dance together when she was Claudia's age filled her mind and poured onto the page. Her head was tilted back, and she was giggling. He looked down at her with a smile. Her feet were on his as they swayed to the music.

I miss this, Dad.

It wasn't just the dancing—it was more than that. The sketch represented a carefree moment before the heaviness fell.

The next sketch was of her mom playing the piano while her dad stood next to her, his trumpet to his lips. They were rehearsing for the Christmas cantata at church. Next to them, Holly was painting at her plastic easel. Gabe lay on the floor playing with his action figures and a wooden Nativity set, having an epic battle. This sketch was a snapshot of tradition and togetherness, of warmth and simplicity.

Holly's thoughts unwound like a diary entry as she drew. *I'm saying good-bye to this, too. Not forgetting it, but realizing this storybook image is not a part of our present reality. You're different, Dad. It's not your fault. And it's not ours, either. An awful thing happened, and in many ways, we're still removing the shrapnel. I'll constantly be frustrated and distant if I keep willing you to return to the way you were before. I want to accept you as you are now, instead of resenting what I no longer have.*

The last sketch was of a young bride, with a not-quite-as-messy-as-usual bun piled on top of her head. She stood at the back of the sanctuary at St. Schäfer's, a simple veil cascading down over her elegant, non-fussy wedding gown. Her strong dad stood with his hand on her back, whispering his best advice for the moment she had been dreaming about since she was a little girl. *I'm saying good-bye to what I planned on, Dad. Being married before I was thirty and you returning to your pre-aneurysm mind and body. Maybe I'll get married one day, and you'll be there to give me away. But it won't look like this. I want to have the courage to sketch a new image instead of fixating on the one I thought was guaranteed. I need to let us both off the hook. Sometimes, we can't make things happen, no matter how much we wish, hope, and pray for them.*

After the last bit of shading was complete, Holly lined up the sketches on her windowsill. She pretended she was at the Chicago Art Institute standing before a complex piece, evaluating each element and allowing herself to feel the artist's intention. Each stroke, each detail, each emotion. She let herself feel it all.

Her breathing quickened.

Her heart raced.

The flood of grief released out of Holly in silent sobs. She sank to her knees, her head on her comforter, her arms outstretched.

She didn't drown.

When her breathing returned to a steadier rhythm, she knew it was time for the next step.

With trembling hands, she ripped each sketch straight down the middle, signifying the breaking of her heart as she acknowledged what needed to be buried. It wasn't hope she was splitting, it was her bitterness, her expectations, and her presumed right to normalcy. As she tore the strips of paper, she could feel the tug and release on her heart.

She placed the papers in a shoebox and taped down the lid. There was too much snow on the ground to bury it now, so she put it away, on a shelf in the back of her closet. The act of closing the top of the box ushered in sharp tears—but they were cleansing tears. She had finally faced that which had held her down—not partially, but fully. Sure, there might be times when she had to address more. For now, though, she had done the hard work she'd been avoiding for years. The baggage had been unpacked and addressed, instead of being lugged around. Holly felt more settled than she had in a long time.

After showering and throwing on her comfy gray sweater and stretchy black jeans, Holly headed to the kitchen. Mom had left a note on the fridge in her near-perfect cursive.

Dear Holly.
At the North Star Elementary Craft Show. See you at 2 at the paint store. Walt is coming to pick up dad around 12:30. Can you make sure he's ready? Thanks!
Love you always, Mom

Holly had to smile. Leave it to her mom to write handwritten notes instead of texting on her phone. She groaned outwardly but secretly thought it was endearing. When Holly was in elementary school, her mom had sneaked notes into her lunchbox. She ended them with her signature "I love you to pieces," but in place of the word "pieces," she drew puzzle pieces. Over the years her mom had changed it to, "Love you always."

Holly devoured hummus, pita crackers, and carrots, trying to counter her bad habit of late-night sugary snacking. Afterward, she checked to see if her dad was ready to leave.

"Hey, Dad." She walked into the den as he was struggling to get his shoe on. "Need help?"

It was the first time seeing her dad post-counseling-exercise, and while the familiar heaviness threatened to resurface, she took a deep breath and reminded herself of what was true. Her dad had a brain injury. He had limitations, but he was alive and doing the best he could, given the circumstances.

She focused on helping him and then went and grabbed his

cane. He despised having to depend on it, but it helped steady him and prevented falls.

"Thank you for the help with the sha-shoes, not cane." He grinned.

That was where Gabe got it from.

"Walt should be here soon," Holly said. "But I wanted to say something."

Her dad waited.

"I'm sorry." She tried to think of a way to explain more, but she didn't know how to say it without hurting him or sounding weird.

Her dad seemed to understand all she was saying with her apology.

"Me too, Hol-ly."

And that was enough. A line in the sand between her past expectations and her new acceptance.

A loud *honk-honk* came from the driveway. Walt had arrived.

After her dad was on his way, she ran back into the house to get her notebook and purse for her meeting at Music Keys. As she passed the den on her way out the door, something caught her eye. She usually didn't pay much attention to it, but in that moment, her dad's trumpet, displayed on top of the built-in bookshelf, gleamed a little brighter than usual.

She thought back to the sketch of her family around the piano and Dad's confident stance as he let the notes soar to the festive tune.

That was it! The missing piece. Hallelujah, a divine download in the nick of time.

Holly grabbed the trumpet and dashed out the door.

What should have been a fifteen-minute drive took only ten.

At the meeting with Lena and Elaine, an out-of-breath Holly proudly set her dad's prized trumpet on the table in Lena's office.

"What's that?" Elaine popped a chocolate mint in her mouth.

"A trumpet, obviously…and a lovely one at that," Lena said. "No offense, Holly, but what does that have to do with the issue at hand?"

"Everything." Holly beamed.

The memory of her dad practicing the trumpet had reminded her that he used to play in a small band with Walt, the mayor, and Pastor Meyer. They had each served in the military in various capacities and used to play at churches, nursing homes, and local parades. After Dad's incident, the band disassembled and hadn't played together since.

"I haven't heard my dad play in years, but what if we could get the band back together and have them accompany the clients on one of the carols on the album like, 'Hark! The Herald Angels Sing'?"

"Hmmm. It's an interesting idea for sure. Do you think they'd do it? And pardon me for asking, but do they still have what it takes?" Lena placed her hands in her lap.

"I'm counting on it." Holly tried to hush any doubts.

"I think it's genius." Elaine slide a chocolate mint toward Holly.

"It's definitely intriguing. We don't have much time, though. Can you jumpstart this and report back?" Lena picked up her phone from the table and opened an app.

"You got it. In fact, my dad and Walt are together right now, so I'll go ask them. Elaine, can you ask the mayor? My mom and I are going to drop off paint at St. Schäfer's later today, so I'll talk to Pastor Meyer then."

"Great. Text me to let me know what you find out. Rehearsals will need to be scheduled for early next week. The singers' recording time is scheduled for a week from Saturday, so we need to record with the band by Friday. Time is of the essence."

"You got it, boss," Elaine replied.

"I hope this works out. Not only will it meet the grant requirement, but it'll be really special, too." Lena nodded at Holly.

"Yes, it will."

After all the emotional energy Holly had spent already, she hoped this idea was not one of wishful thinking. She prayed it might be part of new memories with her dad.

A half hour later, Holly received a text from Elaine:

The mayor is in! What'd u find out?

Shopping for paint w/ mom. I'll let you know as soon as I know.

Holly texted back rapidly while her mom examined two almost identical paint swatches.

Another text came through from Elaine:

Sounds good. BTW, guess who came to the inn last night?

Our favorite celebrity?

Nope. The power couple of Bavarian Falls.

Betty Jo and Santa Claus #4?

Holly's mom held up the swatches to the light before closing her eyes and opening them again. Then she set them down and backed up, as if trying to imagine how they would look from afar.

Nope. Guess again.

Nik and Lena?

Winner, winner, chicken dinner.

Andy gave them his reservation.

Things didn't go well.

Holly resisted the urge to type more.

Couldn't help but overhear their argument. Sounds like he's tried to be patient with Music Keys but feels pushed to the side.

Wow.

Holly walked toward her mother, hoping she could hurry the paint-scrutiny session along. She was about to tell her mother that no one else would notice the difference between the two paint colors when Elaine's next text came through.

Didn't sound like it was the first time they'd had this fight. Looked like Lena got a work-related call during dinner. She walked out and didn't come back for a long time.

Whoa.

Yeah, poor Nik sat there with his half-eaten meal.

For how long?

I tried not to spy on him, but being their server, it came with the territory. He was there for a while before she came back. It looked like he was asking her to stay, but she shook her head and left.

That's too bad.

Yeah, trouble in paradise. It's great what Lena's doing with Music Keys, but it might come with a bigger price than expected.

Think they'll work out? Holly was glad she was typing this out and not talking to Elaine, so she could keep her tone steady and nonchalant.

Time will tell. Talk later.

K, bye.

Holly slid her phone into her pocket. She wrangled her thoughts away from the overanalyzing zone, but she couldn't deny how her heart had leapt at the thought that Nik and Lena might not be a permanent fixture.

Holly and her mom had finally checked out of the paint store after *much* deliberation about which base paint brand was best. She'd not so patiently held off on sharing her idea until she had her mom's full attention. As they drove over to St. Schäfer's to give the paint to the pastor's wife, Holly took the plunge. She shared a condensed version of the sketch experience that had been encouraged by her counselor, omitting the first and last sketch and only telling her mom about the trumpet one. Holly went on to describe her idea about the military band reunion.

"You're in counseling, huh? How long?"

"Mom, I wasn't going to tell you…not yet. I've only had one appointment. Although it feels like five because it was so helpful." Holly anticipated a lecture or a series of pressing questions next, but her mom surprised her.

"I'm glad. That couldn't have been easy…the decision to go or the sketch exercise. I'm proud of you. Always." Mom made eye contact with Holly as if willing her words to express the full weight of her adoration.

Holly tried to let her protective wall down and receive her mom's words at a deeper level.

"Now about that band idea…"

Here we go. The caveat.

"Go ahead. Tell me what's wrong with it," Holly muttered.

"It's actually a wonderful idea. Your dad doesn't quite have the skills he used to, which is why he's never had the courage to initiate getting the band back together. He does practice on and off when no one is around but me, though. He says it reminds him of the good old days. Like I said, he's not as polished or quick with his instrument as before, but, Holly, I'm telling you, he's still got the basics. And the look on his face when he plays is a wonder to behold."

"I'm so glad to hear that."

They pulled up to St. Schäfer's and carried in the paint.

Holly set her can down on a pew. "While you and Mrs. Meyer duke it out over this, I'm going to go convince Pastor Meyer to join the ranks."

"Good luck!"

"Thanks." Holly squeezed her mom's hand.

After Holly explained the time-sensitive request, Pastor Meyer agreed.

"It's a busy time of year, but if your dad and the other guys are in, so am I. Better go practice my French horn. It's been a while. We can rehearse at my place. Ingrid can go shopping if the noise bothers her. I'm sure she won't mind—shopping is her spiritual gift." He chuckled.

"I can't thank you enough. Now I'm off to get Walt and Dad on board. See you tomorrow."

Holly left her mom working at the church while she drove to Walt's place. After several rings of the doorbell, there was no answer. Dad had a cell phone but wasn't swift to pick it up and was slow to talk, so she called Walt. He told her they were at the community center serving dinner.

Holly headed that way, anxious to get things underway and hopefully send a successful report to Elaine and Lena. It felt like her big moment to shine under the floodlights that seemed to follow Lena wherever she went. Holly's solution could save the grant and help Chase and the other clients finish the album project in time.

Holly walked into the crowded center. The aroma of comfort food swept over her. She scanned the rows of full tables for her dad and Walt. The room was abuzz with conversation. There in the middle of the action was Nik, laughing with an elderly couple as he wiped down the table next to them. Apparently, Dad and Walt weren't the only ones volunteering that day.

Walt and Dad roped Holly into helping for the last few minutes of the meal. Afterward, they all grabbed a bowl of broccoli cheese soup and sat down for a quick bite before leaving. Partway through Holly's appeal to get the band back together, Nik walked up.

"Mind if I crash the party?" he asked.

"Not at all." Walt motioned for him to sit. "Holly was telling us about her plan to save the grant at Music Keys."

He smiled. "It looks like I'm right on time."

Holly did her best to stay focused on laying out the plan in spite of Nik, Lena's boyfriend, who was a captive audience member.

"I don't know, I'm not s-s-s-oo good at playing any-anymore," her dad responded after hearing her grand scheme.

"Mom said you've still got it. And you and I both know she wouldn't say that if it weren't true."

"I think it's a great idea," Walt added.

"Me, too," Nik reached for the breadbasket in the middle of the table. "In fact, I may have played trumpet in the jazz band at college. I'd be happy to help you brush up, Carl, if you'd like."

"Is there anything you don't do?" Holly propped her chin with her palm, impressed by his breadth of skills and how he generously spent his time helping others.

Nik quirked a smile that made Holly feel like the only one in the room. She put a hand on the table to steady herself.

"I'm lousy at euchre and terrible at drawing." Nik laughed, electing a roll and buttering it.

"Not good at euchre? That's unacceptable, young man," Walt scolded.

"I'm not a fan of it either," Holly whispered. "But don't tell anyone…I don't want to be written out of the inheritance."

"I huh-huh-heard that."

"I think between us we can help you improve upon your weaknesses. I'll teach you to love euchre, and Holly can teach you how to draw the best stick people you've ever seen," Walt said.

"I appreciate the offer, but I think I'll stick with what I'm good at. Now, when can we schedule that tune-up, Carl? Lena's got an album to record." Nik bit into his roll.

"Yes, she does." Holly jumped up from the table. "Are you sure you have time, though?"

Good gracious, she sounded like her mother scolding her for overcommitting.

Nik chewed slowly, studying Holly for a moment, and she tried not to squirm under the examination.

Then he swallowed and grinned. "I think I can make time for this." He patted Carl's back.

Holly breathed a sigh of relief. "If you guys are able to work that out, I'll text Elaine and Lena with the good news. I've gotta go pick up Mom before she lets Mrs. Meyer talk her out of the paint color for the fellowship hall."

"Run along now." Walt shooed her away with both hands. "I'll bring your dad back after dinner."

Holly hauled her coat on. She headed out the double-doored exit. The warmth from the inside was left behind as she stepped into the cold outside. Snow crunched beneath her boots as she headed toward her car.

Nik ran up behind her. "Hey, can we talk for a second?" His coat was unzipped, and his white serving apron was still tied around his waist.

Holly stopped and turned around. "Sure. What's up?"

"Remember how I told you I was trying to figure out my next steps, and you said I was probably too busy for that because I was filling my days with all this volunteering?"

"I don't remember saying it like that exactly, but I think that was the gist." Holly shoved her ungloved hands inside her coat pockets.

"Here's the thing. You were right to ask me if I had time to help your dad. Ever since we talked about it at the party, I've been thinking about what you said. I've been trying to do everything and be everything for other people. I so want things to work out here and not turn out like they did in Leavenworth…" At the mention of that town, Nik smirked.

Holly lifted her arms halfway in surrender. "Don't worry, I know—the town, not the prison."

"Glad we got that cleared up. Like I was saying, I haven't taken the time to really sort things out after everything went down in Leavenworth. That's why I moved here—well, that and to help Aunt Claire and to be closer to Lena. In the process of meeting new friends and helping out around town, though, there hasn't really been time. Don't get me wrong. It's fulfilling to help people, but if I'm honest, I feel stuck in this pattern of overextending myself without really knowing what I want and…I don't know, you seemed like someone who would get it. Not because you don't know what you want. You seem the opposite of that, but you've mentioned feeling stuck here, and in a different way, I do, too."

"Have you talked to Lena about this?" Holly tilted her head

and returned her exposed hands back into her pockets.

Nik stared at his feet. "Yeah, so, we're not a thing anymore," he confessed.

Holly twitched as if she had been yanked from sleep. She tried to put forth her best euchre face, but again, she wasn't any good at it.

Why did this feel like good news? *Don't smile.*

"I'm sorry to hear that." She risked frost bite and laid a sympathetic hand on his arm, hoping it was an appropriate response.

"Thanks. Things have been tense for weeks, but I really care about her. After hearing Santa's advice about lavish displays of love, I thought the surprise proposal would be a good idea to help Lena and I take the next step forward, since she's been so preoccupied with Music Keys. I realize now that wasn't the way to try and patch things up. I believe in what Lena's doing and support her, and gosh, it's a blast working with those kids, but a relationship can't work if only one person is all in."

"That's really tough." Holly squeezed Nik's arm for a second before letting go. She tucked her hands inside the sleeves of her coat.

"Y'know, I hung in there. I picked up hobbies like volunteering at the shelter, dressing up as an elf, and attending concerts alone to try and give Lena space as she worked and worked and worked. Gradually, it became evident that this was more than a busy season. It's her typical mode of operation. The bottom line is that Lena is more committed to her career than to a romantic relationship for now, or maybe forever. Her words, not mine."

"Ouch." Holly resisted the urge to reach out again.

"Yeah." Nik shrugged. "I was surprised when it hit me, that what I thought was love for Lena was actually more care and admiration than it was commitment and affection."

Gulp.

"When did you realize that?" Holly managed, her voice wavering slightly.

The half grin again. *Lord, have mercy.*

"I'll have to tell you sometime, but I know you've gotta go. There's an album to record."

"Won't it be weird for you to keep helping Lena?"

"No. I mean, kind of, but I'm confident we will remain friends. In fact, we'll probably get along better this way. Besides, I'm not the type to leave a person hanging when they need assistance."

"Can I offer a piece of advice?" Holly reached for the hood of her coat and secured it on her head.

"Of course."

"If you spend all your time trying to be everything to other people, you'll never discover who you are on your own. Don't get me wrong. It's noble to help people, but I wonder if you're doing so much for everyone else in an effort to avoid finding out who you are apart from all that."

Nik stood in silence. The smile dropped from his face.

"It's like that Jana Bonparente song lyric that's helped me so much recently: The way to freedom is not out of reach. Turn the knob, let yourself be found."

Nik blew out sharply, his breath condensing an airy cloud between them. "I think you might be right," he mumbled, zipping up his jacket. "It feels strange, yet also kind of nice, to be on the receiving end of someone's kindness. It's usually the other way around."

"It's the least I can do, since you helped me see more clearly at the Christmas party." Holly's car keys jingled in her pocket as she bounced on her heels to warm up.

"After this album project is done, I'm going to pull back a bit and try to figure out things. Hold me to it?"

"Sure thing," Holly agreed.

They stood in silence for a few seconds. Nik kicked at a mound of snow as if he was debating something. Holly swallowed, not sure what she wanted to come next. She really did need to go, but—

"You know what I think?"

"What's that?" Holly curled her toes in her boots.

"I think what you offer this town and the people in it is pretty great. They're lucky to have you here—even if it's only temporary."

The warmth of the compliment heated her cheeks. Other people had said similar things, but it meant more coming from Nik. He retrieved gloves from his coat pocket. He offered them to Holly. She shook her head.

"Thanks for that."

"Of course, it's your decision, but you don't have to leave this town to be yourself. I believe there's more here for you than you realize." Nik put on the gloves.

"What do you mean?"

"Take Frank, for starters. He's a great guy who's obviously a big fan of yours." Nik's eyes danced.

"We're just friends. He wanted it to be more than that, but his early onset clinginess was too much. It made me feel like he wanted me to be his everything, and that felt suffocating."

"Wait, what? You said—"

"I wanted you to think I had a boyfriend. I don't know why...maybe because I get tired of people asking why I don't have one. I thought it'd be easier to pretend I did. Not that I need a guy to be complete or anything. I didn't expect to be single this long. More than likely it was because I believed you were a dangerous criminal roaming the streets of Bavarian Falls, and I might need a guard."

Nik breathed out a laugh. "Do you still feel that way?"

"I mean, you proposed to me the last time we were alone together, so I'm not sure I've let down my guard completely."

Nik laughed full and free, and Holly couldn't help laughing with him.

Standing outside together, volleying their observations about one another back and forth, was one of the most natural things in the world, like taking a breath or putting one foot in front of the other. Holly felt more herself than she had since moving back to Bavarian Falls.

"Hey, it's cold, and I know you have to go. But thanks for hearing me out and for helping me see how I've been using my good deeds as a distraction from figuring things out."

"That's what friends are for."

"I'm really glad we're friends, Holly." Nik squeezed her shoulder.

Even through the down of her coat, Holly felt a spark of exhilaration at his tenderness. Since he had stepped closer, she caught a faint whiff of his cedar and spice cologne.

He just broke up with Lena! Simmer down. Don't be the rebound girl—although Nik hardly seems like the rebound type.

Nik slid his hand off Holly's shoulder and down the upper part of her arm. Even though his glove and her coat served as a barrier between them, Holly felt tingly from his touch.

"You better get going." He nodded toward her car.

It took Holly a few moments to compute what he had said,

since she had been replaying snippets of their conversation. Suddenly, a gust of wind blew between them, interrupting the trance brought on by his cologne and her tingles.

"Right! I'm headed to the church now. See you later. Unless you volunteer at St. Schäfer's, too," Holly joked as she turned with a wave. She resisted the urge to turn back and see if he was watching her from the snow-covered sidewalk.

Holly drove to retrieve her mother from church with a smile on her lips. It had been quite a day. She'd ridden an emotional roller coaster, but as the day leveled out, she couldn't help but feel a sense of accomplishment—a breakthrough with the pain of the past, a pivotal conversation in the present, and now a promising way forward.

Holly was grateful that she was able to help Lena and her clients. In turn, she hoped this new development of the band assembling would fulfill the military personnel inclusion for the Music Keys grant and help her dad find his footing—discovering a purpose beyond occupying his recliner and watching sports on TV.

And she wasn't disappointed that she'd be seeing more of now-single Nik in the coming days.

CHAPTER SEVENTEEN
No Guarantee

HOLLY COULDN'T HAVE BEEN HAPPIER WITH the way things turned out. With Nik's help, her dad gained back a bit of confidence with his trumpet playing. It wasn't enough to win any contests, but it was sufficient for the task at hand. Upon Dad's insistence, Nik joined him and the old band members—the mayor on trombone, Pastor Meyer on French horn, and Walt on the tuba—to create a new band. Nik played the more complex descant on his trumpet while Dad offered steady undertones.

Nik's kindness and patience toward her father—not to mention his impressive musical talent—weren't making it easy for Holly to stay in the friend zone.

Holly and Elaine provided moral support and snacks for the band as they rehearsed each evening for almost a week straight, first at the parsonage, until Mrs. Meyer couldn't stand it anymore, then in the newly painted Ethereal White fellowship hall at St. Schäfer's. Holly wasn't sure that she or Elaine could take one more round of "Hark! The Herald Angels Sing." Elaine said it reminded her of her band camp days when she practiced the same sixteen measures all day long. Then the beats would plague her mind while she tried to sleep.

The brass quartet was now a quintet, with the addition of Nik. His skilled playing transformed the sound from mediocre to majestic. Even more so, Nik's encouragement transformed Holly's dad as he worked hard toward the common goal. What Carl Brigham lacked in skill, he made up for in heart. And Holly thought her heart might burst with joy because of it.

At their last rehearsal, Pastor Meyer insisted they take advantage of the outstanding acoustics in the church sanctuary.

While Elaine helped set up chairs and music stands on the platform at the front of the sanctuary, Holly made her way to the balcony with her phone camera. The sound of brass permeated the room. Holly marveled at how it had all come together in such a short time. She zoomed in on her dad, noting his concentration and newfound confidence.

It was there, midway through the song, that Holly remembered her prayer to the rafters over a month ago. *Help my dad experience freedom.*

And he was.

He would never be the same, but he was making the most of what he had, for the good of others.

It took strength, physically and emotionally, for her dad to play his trumpet again. He didn't know it, but this step of healing was initiated because Holly had let him go earlier that week. It cleared the path enough for her to see the man before her now. Her dad was broken. He wasn't perfect, he occasionally got angry, but he was her dad.

When the rehearsal ended, Nik offered to close up the church for Pastor Meyer, who was running late for a dinner party at the parsonage. Holly's father slowly closed his trumpet case and then looked from Holly to Nik. "Th-th-thanks for this." His few words and grateful expression spoke volumes. Then he added, "You two ma-make a good team."

It was a six-word sentence, but coming from her dad, it sounded like a blessing.

"I think you're right, Carl," Nik agreed.

Holly nodded her approval, hoping there would be more opportunities to team up with Nik.

"It's s-s-settled then." Dad tapped his cane as if adding a period to the end of his sentence.

Her dad might never be that pillar of support, whispering timely advice in her ear on her future wedding day. But he could still play the trumpet. And he loved his Holly in his own simple way. Somehow, that was enough.

Holly and her dad made their exit to the parking lot.

"Hey, Holly," Nik called out. "Do you know where the overhead light switch is for the dome? I can't find it anywhere."

The powerful domed light that illuminated St. Schäfer's altar area was the only light still on besides the exit signs. Holly joined Nik behind the massive altar, searching for the hidden light switch.

"Found it!" she sang.

"Oh yeah?" Nik rounded the corner to investigate.

Everything went dark.

"Nik!"

"I'm here." His hand cupped her elbow. "Sorry, making sure it was the right switch," he explained. "I'm going to turn it back on now."

"You are?" Holly whispered.

"Unless you don't want me to," Nik answered. His nearness in the dark sanctuary had her feeling all sorts of mixed up.

He gently rubbed the back of her upper arm. The electricity between them was evident, even though the light switch remained in the off position.

Holly closed her eyes in the pitch-black sanctuary as if it would help her see things more clearly. Or at least help her assess the situation outside of the super-charge that was making her feel weak in the knees.

Two words flashed through her mind as she tried to objectively survey the situation she found herself in. No guarantee.

Fitting words for Reason #17 on her list. There was no guarantee this was the right next step. No warranty against embarrassing misunderstandings or further heartbreak. No reason to believe there was a future beyond this flirty moment between two single adults who were trying to find their way in the dark.

Holly could feel Nik waiting, his breath near. She opened her eyes. "Here's the thing. I don't want to be Plan B. I want to be someone's one and only." Every ounce of restraint that Holly could muster allowed her to voice her hesitation.

Her offering of honesty hung in the air between them as they stood inches apart. His presence was palpable, even though she couldn't see him.

The wooden floor creaked as Nik took a step. A step closer. She felt the heat of his whisper near her ear. "Believe me, I understand where you're coming from."

"H-h-holly? You okay?" her dad called out.

"Yes, Dad. Give me a minute."

Holly had been so caught up in the moment with Nik that she'd forgotten her dad was waiting at the exit in the dark.

Nik turned the domed light back on. Holly's eyes—and heart—tried to adjust to the jolt. She felt exposed by her admission to Nik yet glad she had laid it out there. He would have to choose which direction he was headed.

"I promise you, this wasn't a setup. I didn't know where that switch was when I asked for your help. Thanks for helping me see the light." He offered a partial smile.

Holly couldn't help but smile back, wondering if he'd intended the double meaning.

Recording day arrived. Cars lined the street outside Music Keys.

Inside, jitters and a pipeline of energy coursed through the building. The singers, accompanied by their parents, filled the lobby. The military band had recorded their part of the album the day before, so the instrumental track was ready for the children to add their voices.

Holly, Shayla, and Nik were there for whatever Lena needed to help make the taxing process as smooth as possible. Elaine was sorry to miss it, but she hadn't been able to find anyone to cover her shift at the inn. Shayla was tasked with vocal warm-ups, Holly was on snack duty and client relations with the parents, and Nik was in charge of making sure the kids knew when it was their turn to record. Lena and the sound engineer would be stationed in the studio, overseeing the recording process.

Holly retrieved the morning refreshments from the kitchenette. When she was about to step into the hallway, a set of voices talking in hushed tones reached her ears.

"Thanks for being here today." It was Lena. "It know it's a bit uncomfortable for both of us, but you're so good with these kids, and it means a lot to me that you would put our differences aside to be here on the big day. You're a good guy, Nik. I'm sorry I hurt you."

"I'll be okay."

"We need to get started, but I wanted you to know that I thought I could manage a relationship and Music Keys, but it made me feel divided. Maybe my mom was right. She always wanted me to focus on one thing growing up, but I often got bored when I didn't have variety. I guess my strict upbringing is bearing its fruit, and I'm finally pleasing my mother."

"Lena, you don't have to explain."

"I want to. I mean, a husband and kids were part of her five-year plan for me. But that's not what I want. I'm sorry it was at your expense that I realized that focusing on this program and these kids is fulfilling enough for me. It goes against what people expect of me, but it's what I want."

"I know."

Holly felt conflicted as she eavesdropped. Part of her wanted to keep listening, and another part wanted to make sure the kids got their snacks before the recording started. And who was she kidding? She wanted to make sure Nik was okay. She cleared her throat as she walked out the door of the kitchenette.

Nik looked as though he was about to speak, but he stopped when he saw her.

"Holly, thank you so much for your help today. Let's get things started, shall we?" Lena's heels clicked down the hall.

"We shall." Nik said, heading after Lena.

Holly followed them. Once Nik reached the lobby, he walked over to Chase, offering a high five. "It's go time."

Chase responded, "O-o-oh yeah!"

After donuts and fruit had been devoured and the singers had been well hydrated, Lena gave the nervous bunch a pep talk. "This is an exciting day. You get to be a part of a real live recording session. Remember last week when we practiced using the studio microphone and how you need to be careful to not overemphasize your S's and P's?"

One little boy gave a quick nod. A little girl gave a thumbs up. Two more children nodded, and Chase responded with a "yup-uh." Most of the other singers showed signs of mild distress—fingers drumming or bodies rocking. Holly would have been concerned that the recording was doomed to failure, except she knew Lena wouldn't let it.

In fact, Lena stood at the far end of the room with her hands clasped in front of her with a radiant smile on her face. "You're going to do fine. Why don't we all take a deep breath? The kind that goes in through our nose and out through our toes. Ready?"

Holly joined in on the calming exercise.

"Miss Shayla is going to warm us up. Everybody stand, please." She turned to the young girl in the wheelchair who'd asked Nik to be her bodyguard against the paparazzi. "Julie, you sit tall. Good singing posture."

The clients stood to their feet, a picture of pride and anticipation.

"After our run-through, we'll head into the studio to start recording. Remember, I'll sing the verses, and then I'll cue you to join me on the chorus. Sing from the heart, my friends," Lena instructed.

Holly sat on a high stool off to the side. She leaned her head against the wall and listened.

After Shayla's piano introduction, Lena began singing the title song for the album, "Say Yes to Christmas." The song had been commissioned for the project and co-written by a local songwriter and a famous European songwriter.

The melody reverberated through the rehearsal room.

Snowdrifts cloud my view
Longing for something new
So off I go
My dreams in tow
Knocking on every door
Braving the winter storm
Empty hands
Buried plans

Frozen pine trees
Falling snow
Winds of change blow
through what's broken

How can I say yes to Christmas?
Starting over's not on my wish list
Twinkling star, traveled far
Through the midnight blue
Leading me back home, to you

Fire glow light the dark
Turning shadows into art
Show the way
Here I'll stay

Children singing
Melting hearts
This festive season
Draws us closer

What if I say yes to Christmas?
Starting with a brand new wish list
Twinkling star, traveled far
Bringing the good news
Leading me back home, to you

Uncertain of what comes next
But Christmas, I'm saying yes... to you.

    Lena's gentle vibrato held out the last note. Shayla effortlessly played the arpeggio that ended the song.

    Holly's hand rested above her heart.

    Since she had been tasked with the military personnel inclusion on the grant, Holly hadn't yet heard the clients sing. They were each exceptional in their own way. Tony's crooner flair, Julie's gusto, Chase's angelic voice, and the others worked in unison to fill in the sound. They were all in, sprinkled with talent and a whole lot of enthusiasm. It was a blueprint to enlarge any Grinch's heart.

Holly's chest rose and fell slowly.

The songwriters had read her mail. Lena and the clients had sung her story.

She was undone.

"Nailed it!" Tony shouted, which initiated a round of giggles from the clients.

"You most certainly did. Now let's go into the studio and do it again," Lena encouraged.

Holly would have to process her thoughts later. Duty called.

Throughout the rest of the morning and into the afternoon, the team worked together to help the kids persevere through the long day of recording. Holly had never been part of a professional recording experience before, and she was amazed at all that happened behind the scenes to produce a quality product.

The kids were troopers, fighting their nerves and learning—and re-learning—how close they needed to be to the microphone.

"Oh no!" Julie wiped her lips with the back of her hand. "I accidentally put my lips on the microphone. Does that mean I kissed it? I'm not supposed to kiss any boys yet. Daddy said so."

Clearly fighting laughter, Nik assured her that no, her lip smack on the wind guard had not counted as her first kiss and she had nothing to worry about. In five years or so, she could learn karate, at least from the waist up, so she could ward off any unwanted kisses.

He was so great with kids. Definitely an attractive quality in a guy. As if she needed any more convincing that Nik was great…and attractive.

Once recording started, each of the adult volunteers had their updated assignments. Shayla helped the kids with their vocal preparedness and tone quality. Holly served as the liaison between the lobby and studio as the students cycled in and out as needed, and Nik was resident peacekeeper, doing whatever was necessary to help the students feel comfortable, cared for, and heard. One of the kids asked incessant questions, yet Nik ever so patiently answered, redirected, and even turned it into a game. Lena ran the show with a color-coded spreadsheet, fancy-dancy stainless steel water bottle and phone in hand. She was all business yet not gruff. Holly wondered how Lena kept her emotions in check under the pressure of the album project.

Highly capable Lena still brought out Holly's insecurities, but not quite as much as before. In fact, Holly was glad she had said yes to helping with Music Keys, even though it would have been easier to say no.

At the end of the day, Nik walked Holly to her car and offered to scrape the snow off her windshield.

He slipped in the passenger's seat afterward while she warmed her car.

"You have a gift with kids," Holly said. "I was so impressed with the way you helped calm them and made them laugh."

"I enjoyed watching you mingle with the adults and steer them away from being stage parents. You're good at rallying people together for the greater good. I've seen you do it several times. First with the military band and then with the parents today, not to mention the patient way you deal with demanding customers at work."

"Thanks," Holly said, feeling a bit self-conscious.

"Like I said before, I think there's something here for you in Bavarian Falls. Not something you have to settle for, but something that you can't find anywhere else. I believe what you have to offer this town they can't live without, either."

Was Nik referring to a future between them, or was he strictly talking about work or volunteering?

"What do you mean?"

"You're obviously a talented artist, but I think it goes beyond the page. You're an artist in other ways, too…in the way you care about others and really see them. Gosh, I sound like a mushy greeting card. I should really stop catching parts of Aunt Claire's cheesy Christmas movies."

"Thank you." Holly laughed. "Sincerely."

"I gotta go. See you around, Brigham," Nik said as he exited her vehicle.

The way he called her by her last name was equal parts sports teammate greeting and adorably playful.

Tired feet and a full heart accompanied Holly on her drive home. A rousing rendition of "It's Beginning to Look a Lot Like Christmas" played through the speakers, and she didn't change the station.

Back at work on Monday, Holly prepared herself for a demanding day.

Upon Andy's arrival, she noticed a change in him. His furrowed brow from the last week had all but disappeared, and he was whistling while he worked.

"Christmas come early at your house?"

"Actually, it did."

"Did you and Oliver open presents this weekend?" Holly inspected the line of finished ornaments waiting to be picked up.

"Not yet, but something pretty amazing happened."

"What?"

He glanced around to make sure the employees and early

shoppers who had started filling the store didn't overhear whatever he was going to say.

"She said yes."

"Yeah, you told me that Tammy accepted Bill's proposal. Looks like you're feeling better about that?"

"Let me be more specific. The 'she' is Teresa, and she said yes to the house."

A squeal-escaped from Holly, crowned with air fist pumps.

"This is the best news!"

"Right?"

"Tell me more. How did it all go down?"

Andy explained how he had tried to keep his distance from Teresa so as not to scare her off more, but with it being prime gift-wrapping season and his two left thumbs getting in the way one too many times, he finally made his way over to her station.

"I told Teresa that I didn't want things to be weird between us, and I didn't want to risk losing her friendship, but I couldn't shake the house idea. Then she said my offer was incredibly kind and unexpected…different from anything she'd experienced before that she didn't know what to do with it—with how she was feeling or what was being offered. It was as if her prayers were being answered, like she and her kids could have breathing room. Teresa admitted to me that for the first time in a long time it seemed like stability wasn't a far-off land but within reach."

"Wow, that's poetic," Holly said.

Andy cleared his throat and lowered his voice. "I probably shouldn't have shared that last part." He placed the newest orders on top of Holly's clipboard.

"Oh, come on. You're getting to the good stuff. Don't stop now," Holly retrieved the information she needed from the order form.

"The good stuff? Do tell!" Betty Jo peered around the corner with a delighted grin.

"Come on over. I'll fill you both in at the same time." Andy motioned to the boisterous store manager.

Andy brought Betty Jo up to speed before recounting the rest of his conversation with Teresa. "I assured her that I didn't have ulterior motives and didn't want to complicate things, and that my offer for her to have the house still stood if she wanted it."

"What happened then?" Holly gathered brushes and paints to complete the first ornament of many.

"Teresa said she'd thought about it, talked with her kids, and thought about it more. As crazy as it still seemed, she decided to accept my offer."

Betty Jo's knee bends and arm flaps had increased in speed throughout his account, ending with her arms overhead in the victory symbol and a few slight hip shakes. The manager embodied joy from head to toe, and this moment was no exception. Once she had gathered herself, she pointed her finger right to Andy's nose. "And that's what Christmas is all about, Charlie Brown."

"The price was definitely right," Holly added.

Andy shrugged. "There you have it. You should feel lucky—I uttered more words in five minutes than I usually speak in a whole day."

"Lucky ducks for sure. Now I've gotta get back to managing this place." Betty Jo planted her hands on her hips and waddled toward the next station.

Andy and Holly hunkered down like Santa's elves on a tight deadline. While Holly's hands were busy adding her artistic finesse to each piece, she felt content. Hearing about Teresa's "yes" was the gumdrop on top of the gingerbread house. Teresa still struggled with health issues, Andy was still divorced, her dad was still disabled, her start-up had still flopped, and she was still single in her thirties—but that didn't mean she had to live a life of "no."

As she personalized a Nativity ornament, one particular line from a song in the Music Keys album stuck on repeat in her mind. It didn't let up until she paid attention to its persistent question.

What if I say yes to Christmas?

Andy's lavish gift to Teresa made the song lyrics come to life. He had put himself out there, setting himself up for rejection, forgoing his pride, to sacrifice for the good of his friend. He didn't force her to accept his offer. It was her choice as to whether she would say yes or not. She could walk away, misunderstanding his intention or discarding his grand display of care. Or she could willingly accept his offer to gift her a home with no strings attached. She didn't have to repay him. She simply had to accept that which had been freely offered.

Holly could walk away. Or she could say yes. Not yes to a house, but yes to finding home wherever her feet took her. whether back to Chicago or farther away. Possibly even, like Nik said, here in Bavarian Falls, where a little bit—or a whole bunch—of Christmas was present every day of the year.

For decades she had barely tolerated Christmas but not embraced it. It felt as if the holiday season had robbed her of so much, so her recompense had been to keep its joy at arm's length.

Holly knew that, barring a miracle, Dad's condition would not change, but a settled feeling took up residence within her frame now that she had stopped trying to outrun grief.

She felt good about saying yes to counseling, letting go of an unrealistic version of her dad, going to the concert with Frank, volunteering at Music Keys, encouraging Betty Jo, and helping Nik figure things out. Those weren't small things, but they weren't everything. She was still holding back in several ways. What would it look like—and what would it cost her—to say a wholehearted yes this Christmas? What would she lose if she did? What would she gain? It felt easier to keep her hopes low, anticipating disappointment instead of raising her expectations.

After more deliberation, Holly decided she was willing to say yes this Christmas. She wasn't signing up to be the next Miss Christmas Queen. It wasn't a go-tell-it-on-the-mountain yes—at least, not yet. It was a quiet yes, like when Mary pondered the mystery and majesty of the first Christmas in her heart all those years ago. Holly accepted the dare to open her heart and hands to what might come next. She didn't do this lightly or without trepidation. It felt a little bit like signing her name to a check but letting someone else fill out the amount with whatever they saw fit. It wasn't easy, but she knew it was right.

Saying yes was no guarantee that things would turn out like Holly wanted them to. Saying yes didn't make everything better, but it did change her perspective for the better.

Uncertain of what comes next. But Christmas, I'm saying yes...to you.

CHAPTER EIGHTEEN
The Yes of Christmas

"I'M AFRAID I HAVE BAD NEWS," Ms. Claire said. She stood in front of Holly and Leslie, who was filling in for Andy. He had taken the day off to spend time with Oliver while Tammy and Bill were in Kentucky.

"What's that?" Holly asked.

"I think what Holly meant to say was, 'I'm so sorry to hear that. How can I be of assistance to make things right?'" Leslie coached.

Thoroughly annoyed, Holly tried again, but in her own way, "Can you tell me more, please?"

"It's the ornament."

"The one for Nik and Lena?"

"That's the one. I know you worked diligently on it. But there's a problem."

Leslie's disapproval felt like a magnifying glass burning a hole through an oak leaf when the sun hit it just right.

"I'd be happy to make it right, Ms. Claire. Tell me what went wrong," Holly said.

Leslie attended to another customer.

"More than the ornament went wrong. Their whole relationships went poof! Up in smoke." Claire waved her hands. "Something about her career being more important than their relationship, and him thinking he loved her, but it was actually more care than romance."

"I see." Holly acted as if this was her first time hearing the news so she wouldn't complicate the conversation.

"I'm not going to need the Nik & Lena ornament anymore.

But I'm still paying for it, of course."

"You don't have to do that," Holly assured her.

"Well, I am. You worked so hard on it, and we had no way of knowing they'd break up before Christmas. Such a shame."

"I'll get the ornament." Holly returned with the work of art, holding its satin ribbon in one hand and cupping the air beneath it with the other.

Ms. Claire clasped her hands together then rested her chin on her fingertips. "Ooh, would you look at that? Stunning. Simply stunning. You have a supernatural gift with the paintbrush."

Holly spun the ornament around slowly, admiring the beauty of what she'd produced. She had spent extra time on this one.

"Teresa can wrap it for you if you'd like. You never know, maybe Nik and Lena will get back together." The thought made Holly's stomach ache, but she tried to keep her voice light so Ms. Claire didn't suspect Holly wasn't rooting for that at all.

Ms. Claire shook her head. "No, I don't think so. It seems final."

"What makes you say that?"

She lowered her voice, even though Leslie was preoccupied with a new customer. "Ever since Monday night, he's been different. He was out late, was supposed to be on a date with Lena. But he said she never showed."

"Really? What happened?" Holly fished to see if Nik had told his aunt about the proposal debacle.

"I'm not entirely sure, except he said there was a misunderstanding, and he was afraid that he'd hurt one of his friend's feelings because of it. He seemed worried about that, but not in the usual way. As though there was more to it than he was telling me."

Oh, there's more to it all right. Like the shiny ring he'd offered me in the dark movie theater—a stone's throw away from where we're standing now.

Holly didn't say that out loud, of course. "That's interesting."

"Word travels fast in small towns like ours. If he's not going to tell me, I'm sure someone will soon enough. Why don't you hold on to the ornament? Maybe you could use it as part of your art portfolio? I'd hate to see it thrown away, but I don't want it around the house for Nik to find."

"That's an idea." Holly stalled, not wanting to admit that, while the ornament was beautiful, she didn't want to include it in her portfolio.

"Thank you for your labor of love on this. Truly. I guess things don't always turn out like we expect."

"I know that's true."

"Elaine tells me you have a birthday coming up tomorrow?"

"That's true, too."

"On Christmas Eve, how wonderful. Any big plans?"

"I have the day off. Took a bit of finagling, but it worked out in the end."

"Oh good. I hope it's extra special. I'd say come to the inn, but it'll be a madhouse, and that's not exactly out of the ordinary for a townie like you, is it?"

Holly cringed at the term "townie." After the holiday rush, she needed to come up with a more concrete plan of escape, or her hometown was going to become her permanent residence instead of a temporary forwarding address. Yet Nik's observation about there being more here for her kept replaying in her mind, as much as she tried to downplay it.

"I might try to get out of town for a bit tomorrow. I think a change of scenery is just what the doctor ordered."

"Drive safe. There'll be a travel rush on the highway." Ms. Claire added, "And watch for deer."

She headed to the checkout with the receipt for the ornament she was paying for but leaving behind.

Holly placed the hand-painted Nik & Lena ornament in a white gift box and set it on a shelf in the supply room before returning to the counter.

Frank strolled up. "Thirty-one tomorrow. You old lady."

"Watch it, ya whippersnapper, you," Holly threatened with her best old-lady impersonation and pointing finger.

"I'm terrified," Frank ducked behind an artificial tree. A few seconds passed before he peeked out from behind it. "Any birthday plans?"

"Besides trying to compete with Christmas Eve services, holiday parties, family gatherings, and panicked, last-minute shoppers?"

"December birthdays are tricky, huh?" Frank strolled over to Holly.

"If you want people to forget how old you are or that it's even your birthday, it works out. If you want extra attention and a healthy fuss over you, then you're pretty much sunk," Holly admitted. She held up an ornament to the light, inspecting it from different angles.

"Aren't you a delight?"

"Just call me Turkish."

"What?"

"*Narnia. Edmund. White Witch.*"

"Are you feeling okay?" Frank tried to place the back of his hand on her forehead. Holly shooed his hand away.

"I'm fine." She sighed. "I was hoping for a different ending to this year. Or at least an alternate ending of sorts."

"I'm tracking with ya…like those Choose Your Own Adventure books where you control how things turn out—or at least change them?"

"Those are the ones." She scratched at a tiny dot of misplaced paint.

"If only life were like that," Frank mused.

"We definitely can't control how it all turns out, can we? Lots of twists and turns, ups and downs. But I'm learning that I can choose how I respond to that which I cannot control."

"You in counseling?" Holly returned the ornament to its holder.

"That obvious, huh?"

"Hey, I'm a fan. It helped me through Great Grandad's passing and a few other heartbreaks along the way."

Had she ever been the topic of conversation at Frank's appointments with her firm boundaries in response to his playful advances?

Before she could respond, he patted the counter. "Holly Noel, you know I think you're pretty great. I predict that soon, some guy is going to be the luckiest around, having you for his girlfriend."

Holly resisted the urge to blow off his compliment.

"Don't worry, you've made it clear it's not me," Frank said. "Think of what you're missing out on, though. You could have been mine—my hobby, Holly. Or should I say my Holly Hobby." He laughed.

"Um, Frank, for starters, aren't Holly Hobby dolls a little—or a lot—before your time? No offense, but you really need to work on your pickup lines. They're a little over the top."

"Why, that's my specialty." He gave an exaggerated bow. Upon rising, he added, "But in all seriousness, on the eve of your birthday, I think you should know how special you are."

Holly didn't know what to say.

Frank didn't let her silence mute his running commentary. "For you." He pulled an envelope from behind his back. On it was her first and middle name in fancy lettering. A realistic wreath of holly, with perfectly shaded berries, encircled her name.

Holly gasped. "Did you do that?"

"Ha! Not a chance. Leslie did it for me. She's been taking a hand lettering class online and needed the practice. I think she's trying to take over your job. Better watch out."

"Should I open it now? Or wait until tomorrow?" Holly turned the envelope over and studied the seal.

"Your call. Which reminds me, I've got to hop on a conference call. Peace out, my friend." And with that, thoughtful Frank morphed back into goofy Frank, flashing the peace sign as he darted off.

Holly was equal parts curious and apprehensive about the envelope's contents. Probably best not to open it at work. When her shift ended, she decided to walk over to the Stille Nacht Sanctuary before heading home. Feeling melancholy and contemplative on the eve of her birthday, she needed breathing room, a little sacred space to reflect.

December's blanket of white crunched beneath her fur-lined boots. As she neared her destination, her gaze followed the steeple to the inky sky.

Any chance You're gonna send that homing pigeon to show me what to do next?

Snow-laden pine trees welcomed Holly as she walked under the archway that led to the Stille Nacht Sanctuary. She passed by the wooden signs that held the first few lines of the historical carol.

Silent night, holy night.
All is calm, all is bright.

Before entering the domed chapel, Holly paused at the snowy white Nativity display. She studied it briefly, searching for answers in the faces and postures of the lead characters. Mary knelt before the crèche with open hands, but it was Joseph that drew Holly in. He stood, holding a lantern in one hand and a staff in the other. His attention was fixed on the child as he watched over Him with intention.

Holly's heart thawed in the night air. What if she stopped counting the reasons why she hated Christmas and started counting the positive aspects of the season? Following Joseph's gaze, she located what—or Who—deserved first place.

Reason #1: The Yes of Christmas.

She had other thoughts about what else to add to the list, like cocoa at Stocking Stuffers, the upcoming Christmas sing-along at Klingemann's, and her entertaining coworkers at the mile-long Christmas store.

A revelation hit her. She was no longer counting the pain of the past. She was focusing on the joys of the present.

Holly continued beyond the Nativity and walked up the short set of stairs which led to the serene chapel. She pushed open the heavy door, entered the hushed space, and sat down on a wooden pew. At her age, it was tempting to focus on all she didn't have or hadn't done. Instead, it was time to appreciate what she did have and had done.

She didn't have her notepad or charcoal pencils with her, but she started mentally sketching ideas about where she'd like to head in the New Year. Holly dared to hope. It felt thrilling and risky at the same time.

The door to the chapel opened, and a draft and a young family blew in. Two of the kids were shouting. Their mom shushed them. The dad cradled the youngest one in his arms, doing his best to wrangle the rambunctious crew.

No more silent night. Instead, Holly felt a renewed sense of purpose and vigor.

Twenty-four hours later, Holly was dolled up and ready for fun. She met Elaine and Shayla downtown for a last-minute birthday outing. Lena was supposed to be there too, but she canceled at the last minute, apologizing profusely for the change of plans. Was Lena's absence work or relationship-related?

The mission of the evening, as brainstormed by Elaine and approved by Holly, was to pretend they were tourists in their hometown. Elaine had gotten the idea from a book she read, in which the author stopped focusing on all that was lacking in the place she lived and instead started noticing its lovely attributes. Holly especially liked this idea in light of her epiphany in the chapel the night before, that she needed to set down her lack list and start making a lavish list. After all, it was a grown-up thing to do.

Arriving on Main Street with a hunger—literally and figuratively—the friends were armed with fully charged cell phones so they could take a bazillion pictures. The plan was to take on the crowds and get through as many of the most popular attractions in Bavarian Falls as they could until their money, time, or patience ran out. Club sandwiches at Edelweiss, a selfie in front of the Glockenspiel Clock, tortes at the Engel Haus for dessert, a few stops for souvenirs, and a walk on the covered bridge.

The laughter was frequent and the lightheartedness real as they pretended they were experiencing the wonder of Bavarian

Falls for the first time.

Holly selected a knickknack replica of the Glockenspiel Clock as her souvenir—only after she inspected it for evidence of rats. She picked up a second one for Gabe's stocking as a tribute to his endless childhood teasing.

The friends made it through most of their tourist list before calling it a night. It was a birthday to remember. One that hadn't passed like a blip, but had been seen, felt, and celebrated to the last tock on the clock.

Back at home, a few minutes before her birthday ended and Christmas began, Holly flopped onto her bed and reached for the envelope from Frank. After breaking the seal, she unfolded the handwritten note inside, and two tickets fell into her lap.

Dear Holly Noel:
Don't freak out! These aren't for us. They're for you. I'm sure you and Elaine will have fun using these, and you totally can—I'm not the boss of you. Might I suggest, though, that you wait to use these carriage ride tickets for when that special guy comes around—the lucky one you'll say "yes" to without hesitation? Again, do what you want. It's your special day. Happy Birthday!
Your Friend,
Frank (from the Falls)
P.S. These expire in a year.

Holly hoped that special guy was already in her life, and it was only a matter of timing.

The big hand on her oversized wall clock advanced, reminding her that she wasn't getting any younger.

CHAPTER NINETEEN
Ice Fest

For the first time since her seventh birthday, December 25 didn't break Holly's heart. She entered into the imperfect reality before her, not the polished version she had tried for decades to replicate.

Watching her niece, Claudia, open the artwork Holly had painted for her was a Christmas morning highlight.

"Ooh, it's so pretty. I love it, I love it, I love it!" Claudia hugged the framed treasure, to which Holly had added her signature, Holly Noel, in the right-hand corner.

"Is this one called Goldendoodle Topped with a Monogrammed Santa Hat in Front of a Massive Fireplace?" Gabe boasted a mischievous expression.

"You could say that," Holly said, amused with herself for capturing her niece's fondness for the breed while tapping into inspiration from Mrs. Rasmussen.

After Mom read the account of the first Christmas in the gospel of Luke, the all-day dinner preparations started for the traditional German feast. Holly had persuaded her mom to include Dad and Gabe in the meal prep. They were stationed at the kitchen table, peeling apples to go into the sausage stuffing.

Mom had gotten up early to get the turkey roasting, and she took it out of the oven to baste it again. Monica and Holly worked side by side prepping the red cabbage and potato dumplings.

Ding dong.

"Santa?" Claudia ran to the door.

"Santa already came, sweetie. I wonder who that could be?" Holly's mom wiped her hands on her festive apron before reaching for the doorknob.

"Hi, Anna. Merry Christmas!"

Nik stood on the front porch with a gift bag and a wide smile. He offered the gift to Mom. "From Aunt Claire. It's her famous *stollen*. She sends her love. She was going to drop it off herself, but I insisted. After all, I was familiar with the street where you live."

Holly, who had been watching the scene unfold, couldn't help but notice Nik's second reference to the Harry Connick, Jr. song and that he had turned his attention from her mom to her as he delivered his last sentence.

Their gazes met.

"Is he still taken?" Monica whispered in Holly's ear.

"Nope," she whispered back.

Her mother pulled the door open wider. "Do come in, Nik. We're prepping for our very Bavarian Christmas dinner, but we can take a break to visit."

"Thanks, but I need to finish my deliveries for Aunt Claire and then head over to the community center. It's my last day volunteering there."

Again Nik's gaze shifted back to Holly, a quiet knowing between them as he made good on his decision to pull back for a while to figure things out.

He lingered in the doorway.

"I'll walk you to your car." Holly joined him at the door.

She imagined her family's eyes following her every move as she grabbed her coat and headed for the door. Once outside, she closed it behind her.

"Merry Christmas, Holly."

"*Fröhliche Weihnachten*, Nik."

"I hope it was okay I stopped by. I know you've got plans with your family, but I wanted to talk."

"You did?"

"Yes." He paused, peering down Kühn's Way as if trying to make up his mind about what to say next. He turned to face her.

Holly tucked her flyaway hair behind her ear.

Nik took a step closer as if to shield her from the wind.

The intoxicating cedar and spice scent drew Holly closer.

She gazed up at Nik. "What was it you wanted to talk about?"

"Remember when I said there was a defining moment when I realized I admired Lena more than I felt drawn to her romantically?"

Holly nodded.

"This is kind of embarrassing to admit. But it was when I saw you, shocked and angry, standing there in the dark theater on the other end of my unsuccessful proposal."

"Really?"

"You were quite endearing with your hands on your hips, spewing your accusations about me being a prisoner and all."

Holly stared down at her boots.

"But it was like I could see a glimpse of what could be, if only I slowed down to really think about it, instead of filling my days with so much."

"You realized all that through my tirade?" A gust of wind swirled past them and Holly shivered.

"Well, not right then. But it was enough to cause me to second guess the direction I was heading."

"Where are you heading now?"

"Over to Walt's to drop off his stollen…but not before I ask you something first."

"What's that?" Holly shifted her weight from one foot to the other.

"Do you want to go to Ice Fest with me next month? I hear it's pretty amazing, and by then I think I'll have things sorted out and—"

"Like with a group of people or just us?" Holly resisted the urge to stare at her boots again. She looked up at Nik, instead.

His eyes twinkled. "I hear over a hundred thousand people are expected to attend this year, so we won't be alone. But, yeah, I meant just us."

Holly's heart thumped in her ears as she contemplated his ask.

"Holly, I promise I'm not the type of guy who moves from girl to girl. And I don't want to complicate things. But there's something drawing us closer. Don't you feel it?"

She didn't release her unedited thoughts that sounded an alarm. *From head to toe Nik, but you're fresh off a break-up with Lena. Are you going to decide one day that what you might be feeling for me is also more care than commitment, more admiration than affection?*

"I do."

Holly's internal dialogue chided her, *I do?* That sounded like a response to a wedding vow not a "do you think there's chemistry between us" question.

"It's settled, then? One month from now, you and me at Ice Fest."

Nik hadn't backed away, and his nearness made it hard for Holly to think straight. She tried to command her thoughts to get in line. "Is that the same night of the karaoke contest there?" Good. A concrete thought to anchor her before the butterflies in her stomach took flight.

"Could be. Are you going to enter?"

"I don't think so. I'll leave that to Frank and Elaine. One day

I do want to try my hand at ice sculpting." Holly momentarily broke eye contact with Nik, certain that if she stared into his eyes much longer, her knees would buckle and he'd be catching her again.

"You'd be amazing at that. I'd vote for you."

"I mean, I don't really know how to use those tools, and I'd have to practice, and I'm not sure I—"

Mid-sentence, as she was backpedaling from his compliment, Nik leaned closer and slowly pressed his warm lips to her forehead, kissing her gently.

Unlike Frank's clumsy temple kiss at the concert, Nik's tenderness melted Holly like a puddle on the driveway of her childhood home.

"Nik." Holly placed her hands on his chest, his blue ski jacket, soft beneath her fingers.

He studied her, resting his gloved hands on hers.

"Was that okay?"

Andy convinced Holly to work at Neumann's for another month. Holly figured it wouldn't hurt to earn a bit more money, since her bank account was not yet fully replenished after her failed start-up. It also bought her time to formulate a specific plan of action for whatever might come next. Nik's observation from the Christmas party kept replaying in her mind: "Whether in Bavarian Falls, Chicago, or somewhere else, you are an artist, Holly. That's all there is to it." For the first time, she considered that she might not have to leave her hometown to be herself.

True to his word, Nik stopped volunteering at so many places except for checking in with Chase from time to time at Music Keys and playing trumpet at St. Schäfer's. Pastor Meyer and Holly's dad had convinced Nik to join them as their reunited quartet played occasionally on Sunday mornings.

Holly and Nik spent time together in the weeks between Christmas and the end of January, usually in a group setting like at Klingemann's or Music Keys. They had agreed that, in light of Nik and Lena's recent breakup and their individual needs to sort through pretty major things, they would wait until their Ice Fest date to define their relationship.

Nik had shared that he was committed to figuring out who he was apart from what everyone else wanted or expected, and Holly was determined to outline her next steps with her art and upcoming move. After that, they'd see what happened.

After a month of Holly resisting the urge to text Nik every day, check in on what he was discovering, or make arrangements for a pre-date, Ice Fest finally arrived.

Holly took the time to curl her hair and attempt the smoky eye technique that Elaine had sent her a tutorial on. She reached for her dewy lip gloss and applied it, liberally.

Holly had suppressed her attraction to Nik, first because he was taken and then because she thought he was a criminal. Now that those barriers were removed, she could be honest about the way her heart beat faster whenever he was near. The truth was, the night of the romantic scavenger hunt and subsequent proposal, she had wanted it to be for her—not only because she wanted to be proposed to one day, but because Nik seemed to see right through any façade she tried to put up.

Holly didn't feel claustrophobic around Nik like she had with Frank. With Nik, there was room to dream and be herself and to be taken seriously.

After what felt like the longest month of waiting, Nik picked her up right on time.

As she situated herself in the passenger seat and they pulled away, Holly pretended not to notice her mom peering through the transparent living room curtains. "How are you, stranger? Haven't seen or heard from you in a week or so. That's not easy to do in this zip code. Did you go MIA?"

"You could say that, I guess," Nik said, not turning toward her.

"Why so mysterious?"

"I'm trying to sort things out, like we talked about."

"Are we taking this as we go, or is there a plan?"

"For the Ice Fest?"

"Sure. Where are we headed when we get there?" Holly didn't voice the questions she really wanted to ask such as, what's the plan for us, Nik? What's your next move? Where do we go from here?

"Why don't you pick, since you've been here before?" Nik said.

"Nice deflection. I'll play along. How about we head to the ice sculptures first and then to the snow carving section?"

"Sounds good to me," he agreed.

After they found a parking spot, they walked toward the sound of the festival in full swing. Holly linked her arm in Nik's, trying to ignore the fact that that he seemed distant. She had waited too long for this date for it to disappoint.

As they made their way to the ice exhibit area, Holly attempted small talk, but she had always been lousy at it. "Do you think it will be weird if Lena sees us here tonight?"

Nik stopped and faced her, her hand slipping from his arm. "I took her out for brunch the other day."

Mayday! Mayday! Nik must still have feelings for Lena. Were they getting back together? *Why did you untether your heart, Holly? You knew it was too good to be true.*

"You did?"

His serious face phased into a hint of a smile. "She got called into an emergency business meeting before brunch was over regarding the album and an interview in New York. But I wanted to make sure she was okay. I told her about our date. She seemed happy for us and said, 'I think you and Holly make a lot of sense.'"

Nik's broad smile replaced the subtle one he had originally offered. Holly released the breath she had been holding, filling the space between them.

"What do you think?" Nik asked, lightly grasping her elbow.

Holly searched his eyes, looking for clues as to what *he* was thinking. "I think Lena's right."

"I'm glad to hear that. Now, how 'bout that ice?" He rotated, letting go of her elbow and sliding his arm around her shoulder as they proceeded forward.

They took in the masterful ice carvings. Holly was mesmerized by the iridescent light that shone through the ice. Her favorite sculpture was a large, eight-point reindeer. Its crystal nose pointed to the night sky and its front right leg was poised as if it were getting ready to take a confident step into the unknown. That was how she felt, too.

The date was going well until they started watching the karaoke contest in the heated tent.

Frank and Elaine had decided to collaborate at Holly's insistence. They were up next, primed and ready to impress the crowd with a parody of "Ice Ice Baby," followed by a moving version of "Colder Weather" by the Zac Brown Band.

Right before they took the stage, Holly asked Nik, "What did you figure out this last month regarding your next steps?"

"You sure you want me to answer that now?" He glanced at the stage as Elaine and Frank waved to the crowd.

Pushing back the trepidation his words sparked, Holly stopped to cheer and offer a shrill whistle. "That's my girl!"

Frank, obviously hearing Holly, offered an Elvis-style hip thrust and finger guns in her direction.

"You got this, Frank!" Nik shouted, clapping above his head in approval.

Klaus started the iconic first beats of the song as Elaine and Frank bobbed to the music.

"Last week, I flew out for a job interview in Leavenworth," Nik said quietly into Holly's ear.

Wide-eyed, Holly turned to him, their faces inches apart. "You what?"

"Sorry, bad timing. I'll tell you more after this." He nodded toward the stage.

Holly felt torn. She wanted to watch her friends perform, but the bomb Nik had dropped demanded her attention.

"I think we need to talk now," she shouted over the booming music. The crowd was eating up Frank and Elaine's antics and adjusted lyrics to coincide with the Ice Fest.

"Okay." Nik rose, leading her out of the tent and into the brisk night air.

"Leavenworth?" Holly asked, trying to shove down the intensity of her emotions as they threatened to explode like the upcoming fireworks show.

"I didn't want to tell you because I didn't know if anything would come of it. Over this last month, though, I realized that I needed to try again at a different company instead of giving up on my goals. I'd been running from what's hard instead of facing it. And I didn't want to leave loose ends, ya know?"

"Oh, I know all about facing hard things." Holly proceeded to fill in Nik on everything about her dad—what she had lost and what she had found, the counseling experiment and everything.

"Wow, Holly. That had to be so hard, but I'm proud of you."

Supercharged by her feelings, she extinguished his pleasantry with an accusation. "You know what? I find it ironic that you basically told me to stay here in Bavarian Falls and figure out a way to be an artist here—that I didn't have to leave to find myself—and now you're doing exactly what I wanted to do for months."

"You wanted to find a job in Leavenworth?"

"No, but you know what I mean. It's like you left me behind and blocked me out of whatever you're doing next. I mean, I'm not even your girlfriend, but I thought we were close, Nik. Why wouldn't you tell me?"

"I didn't want to say anything in case the job didn't pan out."

"Well, did it?"

"I'm not sure yet—which is why I hadn't told you."

"And if it does? Then what?"

"Holly—"

She scowled. "I've never been good at masking my real feelings. They're written all over my face."

"It's a gorgeous face, by the way."

"There you go again, charming your way into my heart."

Whoops! I said that out loud, didn't I? How will I back track out of this one?

She crossed her arms and leaned toward him for emphasis. As she did, she nearly slipped on the icy surface. Nik reached for her, and she fell into him, his strong arms holding her close.

"Those guns again. Why do you have to have such nice, strong arms?" She half-laughed, half-cried.

They stood that way in silence for a moment, the lyrics from "Colder Weather" surging from inside the karaoke tent.

"Holly," Nik whispered into her hair, "I don't want to hurt you. But if I don't give Leavenworth another try, I'll always wonder. I don't want to live with regrets or keep making the same mistakes."

Holly willed herself to speak calmly, embarrassed by her explosive reaction earlier. "This decision affects more than just your future."

"I know. It's so unlike me to do this. But I need to figure things out so I can be a man who knows who he is, so I can better help those I care about."

"Maybe you've taken my advice to heart a little too much. I didn't know that you finding out who you really are—apart from being everything to everyone—would hurt so much."

Nik rubbed her back. "Holly, it's not a sure thing. I should hear in a week or so."

"Then what?" She bristled but didn't leave his embrace. "Are you going to tell me whether you get the job or not? Or are you going to keep that from me, too?"

Applause erupted from inside the tent as Frank and Elaine took a bow.

"Great, we missed it." Holly gestured toward the crowd.

Nik kept his attention on Holly, studying her. "We don't have to miss this."

He cupped her face in his hand. She let him for a moment before pulling his hand down and staring at the slick ground beneath them. "I don't know, Nik. I guess we'll have to see what happens next."

Holly hadn't known that her encouragement for Nik to figure things out might mean he'd move across the country. The possibility of him leaving mirrored the pain of her dad leaving all those years ago…and how completely different things were after he returned. She feared things would not be the same if or when Nik came back. After all, they hadn't really even defined their relationship.

Nik brought Holly in close for a hug. She wrapped her arms around him, tears stinging her face.

She resisted the urge to revert back to her lack list and tried to think of something to add to her lavish list. It wasn't easy. The hope of their future seemed to be slipping through her fingers. Perhaps she should add the comfort of Nik's arms around her, for now.

Was their relationship facing a dead end before it had even really begun?

Holly held Nik tighter—if only for a fleeting moment.

CHAPTER TWENTY
Heart Turn

One year later

FOR HOLLY NOEL BRIGHAM, TURNING THIRTY-ONE had ushered in major change, although a few things remained the same. On the night of her thirty-second birthday, she found herself back in her childhood room, this time as a passing visitor.

Above the bed was a framed picture of a painted horse. A gift from Chase. As she retrieved a pair of gold hoop earrings, she smiled at the snapshot she had placed under the glass top of her antique dresser—a photo of her standing outside the Music Keys building on her first day as a paid staff member.

After the successful release of the Christmas album the previous year, complete with "Say Yes to Christmas" and "Hark the Herald Angels" accompanied by the military band, Lena Albrecht was busier than ever. The story of Music Keys and the grant project had been picked up by a national morning television program. Lena, Shayla, Chase, and his mom had been flown out to New York City and interviewed. Afterward, the album sales skyrocketed, and Lena had job offers from all over the country to start branches of Music Keys in various locations. Lena was gone most of the time, flying from place to place, serving as CEO and consultant as more programs were started.

Lena appointed her accompanist, Shayla Johnson, as the director of Music Keys in Bavarian Falls so the program would continue to thrive in Lena's absence. Shayla was an excellent choice. She was in her element working with the clients and had a vision to expand the local nonprofit to reach clients who weren't as musically inclined. She had been impressed with Holly's commitment to the grant project and her innovation to include the military band, so she offered Holly a job.

Holly's seasonal job at Neumann's had ended, and even though she had grown to love the staff there, she was ready to use her art degree in a more challenging capacity. Not that hand-painting a zillion ornaments hadn't been challenging...and pretty fulfilling.

Holly was flattered when Shayla offered her a position. The only problem was that staying in Bavarian Falls had definitely not been on her vision board for the future. She wrestled over the decision, talked to her counselor about it, debated about it with Elaine, prayed about it, and ultimately decided to give it a chance for a year.

Saying yes to staying meant saying no to her dreams of trying the community art space again in the city, but no wealthy Mr. Darcy lookalike had yet shown up at her door offering to serve as benefactor.

Within a few months, Holly couldn't imagine not working at Music Keys. With Shayla's encouragement, she had designed a program called Heart Turn for young people and senior citizens to come together for basic art classes. Based on her own turn of heart through the sketches that helped her process her pain with her dad, the program turned the hearts of the old and young toward one another. Working on the album project had brought Holly and her dad closer, and now she helped different generations find a common bond through creating with one another. The young and old painted to music—everything from classical to jazz. At the end of each semester, Holly helped the clients turn their art into stationery, prints, buttons, and shirts to sell on the nonprofit's website to help fund the program.

It was fulfilling work that incorporated her art degree, her unique history, and the transformation that had taken place within her when she started living a yes life. It wasn't all rainbows and unicorns. Researching grants and coming up with creative ways to keep the program going was no cake walk. The pay made things tight, too. Thankfully, she had been able to afford a small apartment downtown above one of the local businesses. It was humorous that the once anti-Christmas girl's window overlooked the holiday lights and decorations the city of Bavarian Falls displayed 365 days a year.

Bzzzt. Bzzzt.

Are u almost ready, birthday girl? Elaine's text read.

Trying to hurry thru dinner w/ fam. Bro + crew are here too.

Tell them Hi. See you at 7?

C you then! ;-) Holly replied.

Per usual, Claudia kept the family entertained with her antics during dinner. Holly's mom held her dad's hand as the couple smiled wide, enjoying the few days with the whole family under one roof. Her mom's determination to hold her husband's hand through all the difficulty and uncertainty they had faced over the years was quite the legacy.

Holly thought back to several conversations she and her mom had had over the past year, about how good could still be found even when there are loose ends and tension, similar to what Holly had walked through in counseling regarding her dad. However, her mom had helped her to realize that she could live a yes life with an open heart, even when things were unknown and looked different than expected, as her mom had modeled for years. Her mom encouraged her not to give up on what might be growing between her and a special guy, even though it could be harder than she envisioned. Holly was an adult, but her mom still had lessons to teach her—not always with words, but by her example. Although they still had misfire conversations from time to time, over the past year, mother and daughter had grown in admiration and respect for one another.

After Holly's enormous homemade chocolate chip cookie cake had been devoured and the dishes cleared from the table, Gabe asked, "Anyone up for a round of euchre?"

"On my birthday?" Holly whined.

"Wait, you don't like it?"

"Not really."

The rest of the Brigham household gasped, clearly amazed that their blood relative had concealed her secret for so long.

"I don't even know how to process this info, sis." Gabe shook his head in mock disbelief.

"I'm sure you'll find a way." Holly closed the fridge door. "Dinner was delicious. Thank you, Mom. And the company was delightful." Auntie Holly stroked Claudia's cheek. "But now, as a thirty-two-year-old, I'm headed out for a night with my friends."

"Do you know who will be there?" Monica asked.

"Perhaps." Holly exited the room.

Holly rounded the corner to her former place of employment on 1225 Mistletoe Trail.

Neumann's closed early on Christmas Eve, but Frank had arranged to unlock the door—making sure not to ask Holly—so they could gather for an after-hours birthday celebration. No scavenger hunt this time, only hot cocoa, ornament decorating—Andy had insisted it would be fun—and a movie on the big screen.

She spotted the vehicles that belonged to Shayla, Frank, and

Elaine out front, and a few she didn't recognize. She headed inside, anticipating a fun evening with friends.

Jana Bonparente's Christmas album blasted from the sound system. Frank was sporting an ugly Christmas sweater replete with gaudiness, googly eyes, and tinsel. He stood next to Elaine, who had created a Pinterest-worthy mobile hot cocoa bar for the special occasion. Little buckets of crushed up mints, dark chocolate shavings, and sprinkles were ready to doctor up the drinks.

Shayla was deep in conversation with Teresa, and Andy was talking with a party guest who had traveled a great distance to be there. After a clumsy hug from Frank and an enthusiastic greeting from Elaine, Holly grabbed a steaming cup of cocoa and made her way over to Andy.

As Holly approached, Andy asked, "How's it going in Leavenworth?"

"You mean the village, not the slammer, right?" Nik said.

"Ha ha!" Holly responded dramatically.

"It's going well. Not what I thought I'd be doing but fulfilling in many ways."

"That's great, man. It takes courage to put yourself out there again. Especially after you've been hurt," Andy replied, which Holly knew came from a place of understanding.

Holly stopped in front of Nik. "It's good to have you back for the holidays."

"Thank you." Nik smiled at her.

"That cocoa looks great, Holly-girl. I'm gonna go get one." Andy walked away, leaving Holly and Nik alone.

"As I recall, I accidentally proposed to you a year ago around this time." Nik nodded toward the theater/

"Now that was a night to remember." Holly blew on her hot chocolate.

"Yes, it was." His voice had lowered.

Holly tried to take a sip of the steaming beverage but hesitated.

"Don't burn your tongue," Nik said as he brushed past her.

"Who's ready to paint ornaments?" Frank hollered over the music.

Teresa and Andy, with cocoa in hand, stood behind Station 8. It was all set up for the fun. Holly wandered over, Nik was a few steps ahead of her.

"Bring back memories?" Andy retrieved Holly's apron and nametag from behind his back.

"Where did you get those?" She took a careful sip of her coca and then placed her cup on the counter.

"Leslie was going to toss them, but I hid them from her in case you changed your mind and came back. I know it's going well with the art program thing, but I'm still holding onto hope that you'll return. Believe me, Leslie is not as fun to work with as you were."

Holly tied her apron and put on name tag for the ornament activity.

Nik helped Frank distribute fine-tip brushes and a variety of paint containers.

"I haven't seen Betty Jo around town in a while. How's she doing?" Holly asked Andy.

"She hasn't had much free time with the holiday rush. You haven't forgotten what that's like, have you?" Andy held up a stray clipboard and shook it at her.

"Oh, I remember all right. My feet are tired just thinking about it."

Teresa returned from the storeroom with several boxes of ornaments to choose from. She and her children had moved into Andy and Tammy's former house at the beginning of the year.

Her younger child was in one of Holly's art classes, so they interacted a bit, but Teresa wasn't one for many words. She seemed content, though. Holly was thankful for that.

The rest of the friends joined them at the counter, planning out how they were going to customize their individual ornaments.

"You have an unfair advantage, Holly," Shayla accused.

Nik came and stood next to Holly.

"She has put in her time in, that's for sure." Elaine grabbed an ornament.

"Hey, Andy and Frank have experience, too." Holly squeezed dollops of green paint and white paint onto the plastic palettes.

"I'll be the lone man out because my artistic expressions resemble the work of a toddler with a blindfold on," Nik admitted.

Holly nudged him. "I've seen your creative work before."

"Oh yeah? When?" Nik twisted open a small container of red paint and followed behind Holly, adding it to the palettes.

She stopped mid-squeeze and turned toward Nik, "An elaborate scavenger hunt with clever clues and tiny Christmas lights decoratively hung to set the mood. And let's not forget the way you encouraged my dad to offer his limited trumpet skills for the album project. That took creativity." Holly resumed her task.

"Maybe a few shots of creativity, but neither of those involved artistic painting." Nik finished the last palette.

"I'm going to draw a microphone on mine to signify all the good times we've had at Klingemann's," Elaine announced, dipping her paintbrush.

"I'll either attempt to paint a frankfurter, for obvious reasons, or a piece of decadent torte from the Engel Haus. To remind you of our date—I mean double date—I mean the outing with you and Elaine to the Jana Bonparente concert," Frank stammered.

"If it's not clear, we're making these for you, birthday girl, to hang on your tree," Andy held up an ornament and twisted it side to side. "That way you can feel our love each year on your birthday and throughout the Christmas season."

"You guys are the best."

"Uh-oh. This one is already painted on." Teresa held it up to get a better look.

"Nik & Lena?" Shayla read aloud.

"Where'd that come from?" a flushed Nik asked, shoving his hands in his back pockets.

Teresa quickly returned the ornament to the box.

"You were never supposed to see that." Holly reached for Nik's forearm. "Well, not never. After you and Lena broke up, though, it was no longer applicable." She went on to explain how his Aunt Claire had saved up for and commissioned the piece, and how Holly had meant to dispose of it but had forgotten. "I'm sorry."

"It's okay. That was another time. It jolted me, that's all. I'm good. Now, what are you going to paint, Monet?" Nik joined Holly at an open spot at the counter.

"Hmm, I was thinking of a door with a knob that has a heart on it."

"Interesting choice. Tell me more."

"Last year I metaphorically turned the knob to open a door that had been closed. It was my way of saying yes to Christmas and a whole lot more." Holly swiped her paintbrush on a scrap piece of paper, removing the excess from her brush.

"Like the song from the album?"

"Which one, Jana's or the Music Keys one?" She positioned her brush above the ornament.

"Either?"

"Both, really."

"You are definitely the creative type." Nik dipped his brush in white paint.

"Why, thank you. What are you going to attempt?" she teased.

"You'll have to wait and see," Nik replied, shielding the red ornament in front of him.

The hum of conversation among Holly and her friends was layered with laughter, teasing, and catching up as they worked to complete their works of art, side by side.

As the ornaments were drying, the party of seven moved into the dimly lit theater. Déjà vu hit Holly as she walked in.

"Shall I stand behind the screen again, declaring my intentions?" Nik whispered from behind her, his breath on her neck.

Holly turned around. "Well, Lena's not here, so…"

"That's history." He frowned.

"I'm sorry, I didn't mean to—"

A bellowing voice boomed from the projector booth, "Hey guys, keep it down, the movie's about to start." Frank and his timing again.

"What are we watching?" Shayla asked as the lights went out.

"If I had my way, it would have been *Pepper*'s Mint Twist or another rom com, but we let the birthday girl decide," Elaine took a seat and propped her feet up on the seat in front of her.

"What did ya pick?" Andy shuffled down the row in front of Elaine.

"The original Grinch," Holly announced with a wave of her hand.

"Well played." Shayla put her stamp of approval on her choice.

"He used to be my spirit animal, until my heart grew. I still hold affection for the green guy," Holly said.

"True story." Elaine smiled at Holly.

Frank nearly did the splits trying to walk over two sets of chairs to sit between Elaine and Shayla. Andy was a few seats down in the row in front of them, with several chairs between him and Teresa. Holly sat down in the back row behind Elaine.

"Can I sit here?" Nik pointed to the empty seat on the other side of Holly.

"Sure." Holly's pulse quickened.

Over the past year, she and Nik had texted and video chatted once in a while, but they'd intentionally delayed defining their relationship beyond friendship until they had time to find their footing independently. It hadn't been easy, but they'd felt like it was the adult thing to do—to have their eyes wide open and get to know each other better before committing to more.

About the time that the Grinch was stealing the toys out of homes, Nik turned toward Holly. "Can we talk for a sec?"

"Here?"

"No, out there." He nodded toward the exit.

"Um, sure."

"Shh! I love this part," Frank said.

"We'll be right back," Holly whispered to Elaine as she followed Nik out of the theater and into the showroom.

Once they were in the shopping area, Nik, who was walking ahead of her, reached a hand behind his back, offering it for Holly to take if she wanted to.

She did.

He led her over near Station 8, where the mess of art supplies was strewn about. When they arrived, he turned toward her, not letting go of her hand, but rotating his so they were still touching.

"I think it was right about here that you found clue #2 in the proposal gone wrong."

"I think you're right," Holly agreed.

"Here's what I'm wondering. Do you have a clue how I feel about you?" Nik's gaze moved from their hands to her wide, brown eyes.

"I think I need more information to answer your question." Holly tried to keep her tone even.

"Hang on." Nik let go of her hand to grab something off the table.

What was happening? She pinched her arm to make sure it was real.

"For you." Nik returned with his hand under a freshly painted ornament.

The words Nik & Holly were written in glittery white on the red ornament. The names looked like a toddler had painted them while wearing a blindfold.

"I don't know what to say." Holly laughed. "It's a work of art for sure."

He set the ornament on the counter. Holly admired its sentiments for a moment.

"Holly." The way Nik said her name felt like an embrace.

Her shy gaze met his.

"Say yes?"

Gulp.

"What am I saying yes to exactly?" She volleyed the ball back into his court.

Nik paused before saying, "Yes to us figuring out what's next. Yes to more of this." He held up their intertwined fingers.

Holly swallowed hard.

He glanced at her nametag before looking deep into her eyes. "Holly Noel, I can't be your everything, but I'd like to be your one and only."

A lump formed in Holly's throat. She swallowed before answering, "I'd like that very much, Nik Beckenbauer."

"Really?"

"Yes!"

"That's the best news I've heard all year." He beamed, wrapping his arms around her and lifting her off the ground. He spun her around slowly as her feet dangled in the air.

"I know this long-distance thing won't be easy, but we'll figure it out—together."

"Together. I like the sound of that." Holly smiled as a stray tear escaped down her cheek.

"Happy thirty-second birthday to you." Nik brushed her cheek gently before moving his lips to her forehead. This time he held the kiss for a while.

When he pulled back, Holly could still feel the tenderness he had left behind.

He pulled her in for an all-encompassing hug. They stayed that way for a few moments as time seemed to stand still.

"What now?" he asked.

Holly leaned back so she could look at her one and only.

"I was hoping for a kiss on the lips and a carriage ride. We have to hurry, though, because they're about to expire."

"Your lips?"

"No, the carriage ride tickets."

Holly texted Elaine while Nik grabbed their coats.

Sorry to bail, but my birthday wish is coming true! I'm changing my relationship status. I'll tell u more tomorrow. But here's a clue for you...I found love in Bavarian Falls, by way of Leavenworth.

Hand in hand, they left Neumann's, stopping in front of Baby Jesus #1 where Chase had been found.

Snow crunched beneath their feet, but no snowflakes fell from the sky. There were, however, sparks present as Nik turned to face her. He placed one hand on the small of Holly's back and the other at the base of her neck, drawing her closer. One of her hands slid around his waist and the other instinctively reached over his shoulder. Their lips met, locked…and lingered.

Holly's heart pounded as she and Nik eventually—reluctantly—parted after their gentle yet electrifying kiss.

With a wink, Nik offered his arm to the birthday girl. Despite the chilly temperature, Holly was warmed from the inside out.

They made their way across the parking lot. "If you decide to paint backdrop scenery for our love story, make it Bavarian. Whether from across the country or in the same town, it seems to work for us, doesn't it?" Nic said.

"Mind if I add mistletoe into the scenery?"

"Only if Holly's there, too." Nik turned to kiss his one and only again, aligning his lips with hers and pressing in. She readily responded as he wrapped her up tight in his arms. Their winter coats meshed together. Time froze as their kiss, longer and more intense than before, sent fiery sparks up Holly's neck. They melted into one another.

Cue the idyllic snowflakes.

The next item on her new list would be: Kissing her boyfriend under the stars.

When they reached his car, breathless—more from their full-on lip lock than the frigid air—Nik opened the car door for Holly, executing the chivalrous gesture with care and respect. It did not annoy Holly in the slightest.

As she buckled in and Nik walked around to the driver's side, she had a moment to collect her thoughts. Hopefully their

Bavarian backdrop wouldn't have to stretch 2,167.3 miles—she had Googled the distance between Bavarian Falls and Leavenworth—apart for very long. Time would tell.

For now, she was determined to enjoy each moment with this man by her side.

Nik pulled out of the parking lot. She removed her gloves, and he reached for her hand, gently stroking her fingers with his thumb. Nik's touch felt familiar yet thrilling. She welcomed the tingles that started at the tip of her toes and surged through her body.

Soon they were driving past the Stille Nacht Sanctuary and toward downtown Bavarian Falls for a Christmas Eve carriage ride.

Holly couldn't believe this was her actual life.

AUTHOR NOTE

Dear Reader:

While this story has a happy ending, book #1 of the Very Bavarian series was birthed out of a big disappointment—kind of like what Holly felt about her failed creative endeavor, huh?

These are the main reasons I tried my hand at fiction:

Reason #1: I pitched a non-fiction book idea that got rejected by many publishers. I was disappointed and discouraged.

Reason #2: I read a few of my friend's rom-com novels, which gave me the courage to try writing fiction.

Reason #3: While vacationing one summer, my family and I visited a giant Christmas store that provided instant inspiration for a story like this.

Instead of letting Reason #1 deter me with its closed door, I went around the back and found an open window and climbed into the joy-filled space of inspirational fiction.

I grinned as I wrote about the quirky cast of characters in Bavarian Falls and shed a few tears too. I had ideas about where I wanted this story to go…some of them ended up in the book and others didn't. I know it sounds weird, but I felt like more of a quiet observer than a director with a megaphone as I wrote. Like I was peering out from behind a tree—in a curious, non-creepy way—to see how the characters would choose to interact with each other as their story lines unfolded.

About three-fourths of the way through the writing process, I wondered if Holly was going to pick another man. One of my teen sons is still pulling for #teamfrank.

I've always been an audacious dreamer, even though I live in small town USA. As I wrote this book, I wanted it to be a movie or musical one day. I could picture it! You can imagine my surprise when I got an e-mail from a businesswoman, a cheesemaker in Ohio, who happened to find the novel online and wanted to produce the audiobook. At first, I thought it was spam.

This woman ended up producing a musical style soundtrack to go along with the story as well. Did I mention she writes Christmas music and has charted on the Top 40 in Germany? The cheesemaker also opened the door so I could co-write "Say Yes to Christmas" with Christopher Eaton, the songwriter who wrote one of my favorite Christmas songs, "Breath of Heaven." You can't make this stuff up, even though it sounds like fiction.

Fast forward and I received another e-mail. This time it was Carlos from California. He worked for a film company who read *A Very Bavarian Christmas* over the holidays, and they wanted to purchase the movie rights. Again, I thought it was spam.

Upon further examination, I realized it was a legit offer.

I can't promise that all of a sudden you'll get an e-mail from a cheesemaker in Ohio who believes in your creative project or that a film company will reach out who happened to find your story online because they wanted to film a German-style Christmas movie. But, from an audacious dreamer from small-town USA, I can promise you this: God knows your address.

Anything is possible! Even when you are staring down a closed door and people think your latest dream is nothing but wishful thinking or grasping at the wind…like a failed community art space in the city.

It is my hope that, like me and like Holly, you will choose to find an open window around the back when life has slammed doors shut. That you'd have the courage to make a lavish list instead of a lack list and see the possibilities instead of the limitations, the opportunities instead of the obstacles.

The Very Bavarian series is proof that life's disappointments can lead to surprising breakthroughs. And audacious dreams can come true.

The first step is saying Yes!

With Joy,

Katie

Psalm 126:3

I'd love to connect with you. Be sure to subscribe to my website in order to receive my monthly Good News-letter. You can also find me on Instagram and Facebook.

Connect with Katie at:
katiemreid.com
Instagram @katie_m_reid
Facebook Katie M. Reid
Listen to the Martha + Mary Show podcast

P.S. In the following pages, enjoy a sneak peek of the sequel, *A Very Bavarian Summer,* as Holly's dating adventures continue…and don't go as planned. The full novel releases July 2025.

A VERY BAVARIAN SUMMER

~ SNEAK PEEK ~

CHAPTER ONE
What's Your Next Move?

THE DISTANCE BETWEEN HOLLY AND HER boyfriend was 2,167.3 miles. Almost a three-day drive by car, over five hours—and hundreds of dollars—by plane, or a few seconds by video chat. Although Holly couldn't smell Nik's cedar spice cologne through cyberspace, the latter option of connecting with her boyfriend was better than nothing—yet still not ideal.

It had never been clearer than it was at this precise moment that Bavarian Falls, where Holly Noel Brigham currently resided, was nowhere near Leavenworth—the quaint town in Washington state, not the military prison in Kansas, although that's another story—where her boyfriend lived. Although both towns were German-themed, with charming storefronts that almost looked as if they were clothed in dirndls and lederhosen, it felt as if an ocean lay between them.

At thirty-two years of age, Holly had experienced her share of unfair. Her beloved Dad suffering from an aneurysm when she was young and never being the same, a failed community art space in the city that resulted in a move back home, to being single longer than she planned. But now, five-ish months into a long-distance relationship with her oh-so-handsome boyfriend, Nik Beckenbauer, the distance between them felt unfair. Holly had waited a long time to be wrapped in the arms of the one she adored and who adored her, and now those strong arms were out of reach. Nik's steely-blue eyes had a way of seeing right into her soul—in a good and not creepy way—yet the pixelated phone screen didn't offer the same effect.

Holly couldn't imagine what it was like, back in the day, when all you could do was send a postcard to your long-distance beau and hope it made it to him and he'd write back soon. Or if you had to limit your words to the space on a telegram, like Rolf and Liesl in "Sound of Music."

> 04 JUNE
> DEAR NIK - (STOP) -
> IF I STRIKE GOLD, I'LL HITCH A RIDE ON THE 1ST WAGON TO LEAVENWORTH - (STOP) -
> I MISS YOU TERRIBLY - (STOP)-
> YOUR ONE AND ONLY,
> HOLLY
> - (FULL STOP) -11:45AM

At least Holly's updates and playful sentiments could be received within seconds by text, which was usually a positive thing, unless of course she didn't check auto-correct and hit send too soon and "Hey, whatcha up to, hot stuff?" actually read, "Hey, watch out, too hostile!" *Big difference.* With the swoosh of a quick text message, Holly could accidentally start a fight with her boyfriend when she intended to flirt. Ah, the perils of twenty-first-century dating.

The catchy tune from the beach scene of the second "Top Gun" movie blasted from Holly's phone.

She picked it up, swiveling in her desk chair. "Talk to me, Goose."

"Gosh, I miss you, Hol." Nik's warm baritone voice made her feel at home, despite the distance.

"The feeling is mutual." Holly pressed the cellphone harder to her ear, imagining Nik settling into his desk chair as he surveyed the snow-capped mountains from his office cubicle. While Bavarian Falls could easily win a prize for most Christmas spirit, it could not boast the panoramic views surrounding Leavenworth. Holly hoped to see its stunning peaks in person instead of vicariously, like last week when Nik briefly video chatted before his work day started. According to Nik, the postcard-like setting through his office window showcased the beginning of the Stuart range of the Washington Cascade mountains.

Outside Holly's office window, a crowd was lined up to sample bits of hazelnut fudge from the shop next door. Aroma of said fudge wafted through the air like Bavarian Falls' signature perfume. While Leavenworth enjoyed fresh mountain air, Bavarian Falls produced a sweet and savory aroma all year round.

When Holly and Nik were trying to figure out who would visit whom and when this summer, Bavarian Falls was the winner, winner chicken dinner. Nik had a few weeks of paid vacation time built up, and he could also see his Aunt Claire while he was in town. Not to mention it would be fun to visit a few of the landmarks that marked the beginning of Nik and Holly's unexpected love story.

"Hang on," Nik said. It sounded as though he muffled the receiver as he offered a garbled, "Just a sec…yes, it's her…I can in a bit. No, that hasn't been disclosed yet. Give me five?" When he spoke again, the words were clearer. "Sorry about that. Where were we?"

"Professing how much we miss each other." Holly smiled. "This place is not the same without you. Chase asked about you the other day when he was at Music Keys for choir practice. He's afraid you'll never come back."

"Aw, I miss that kid. Can you give him our secret handshake when you see him next?"

"I'll do my best to remember it. Hey, speaking of you visiting. Did HR get back with you about your vacation request?"

"Yeah, about that…"

The minimal background noise on Nik's end crescendoed as the work day was soon to begin for him. Holly slid her thumb up the side of her phone to increase the volume so as to not miss a syllable of Nik's response. She tried to keep her breathing steady and light. Her pulse quickened in anticipation of seeing him in the not-so-distant future. She was more than a little eager to plant a big 'ole kiss on Nik and finally enjoy quality time and close proximity again.

"I want to be there, but work is not making things easy. With this new account and tourist season upon us, I'm not sure it's going to fly for me to leave as planned. I'm working on it, but I don't…"

Nik's soothing voice flew the coop, the scratch and screech of an album halting on a record player replaced it. "Wait, what? Surely, you're joking?"

Holly paused for the punchline. None came. A few minutes later, she hit the red "X" to end her call with Nik, so he wouldn't be late for his meeting. He was on Pacific time and she on Eastern, the three-hour difference making it tricky to chat during the work week. The end of their phone conversation had been an awkward dance as Holly had tried to downplay her disappointment that Nik hadn't yet solidified his plans for his much-anticipated visit to Bavarian Falls.

Holly knew relationships took work and time. Having a disabled father and a well-meaning but opinionated mother had taught her that. She was thankful she had moved toward healing with her parents and not given up when it felt like too much to face. Yet she hadn't expected that she and Nik would be out of sync. It threw her off, like a skip in a record during a favorite part of the song. The thousands of miles between them were proving to be more challenging than expected.

Holly took a swig of water and then let the rest of it dribble into the viney succulent on her desk. A clothesline hung against the brick wall of her quaint office space at the Music Keys building. Clothespins held works of art from her students, like proud parents displaying their children's most recent creations. Holly wished Nik was here to see firsthand how the Heart Turn program was flourishing from its modest roots. She had tried her best to describe it to him over the phone and show it through the screen, but that didn't do it justice. He needed to experience it up close and personal.

Holly pushed open the ornate, wooden door at Music Keys, the non-profit that helped individuals with disabilities unlock their potential through music therapy, and headed to her Prius parked on the street—the one with the dented bumper. The humidity coating the June afternoon made Holly feel as if she'd stepped into a sauna as she clocked out for her lunch break. She pulled at her athletic shirt with the colorful heart screen-printed on it—designed by one of her clients. Her thick, brunette hair was piled on top of her head in an effort to relieve her neck of the heat.

It had been almost a year and a half since Holly founded Heart Turn, a program that brought students and senior citizens together for art classes—overseen by Music Keys and housed in their building. What began as heartbreak due to her reluctant return to her hometown, morphed into a fulfilling outlet for her passion for art, children, and making a difference. Thankfully, the job paid enough to cover her bills and leave a little room for fun.

Even in summer, Bavarian Falls was outfitted with Christmas decorations. Velvety red ribbons hugged the historic lamp posts that lined Main Street. The downtown fir trees were still adorned with ornaments, but sea shells, sand dollars, and burlap ribbons had temporarily evicted Santas and snowmen. Instrumental versions of classic holiday carols rang through the thick air as tourists, dressed in way less than was typical in the colder months, licked drippy ice cream in freshly baked waffle cones from Sugar Shock.

Holly wiped the sweat beading on her forehead with the back of her hand, willing the AC in her vehicle to cool her off faster. She was running late for a lunch date with a friend who had a way of lifting her spirits. As she snaked through the noon traffic of her small yet crowded hometown, Harry Connick, Jr. crooned from the radio. She and Nik shared an affection for his music. Holly sighed, hoping she and Nik could talk again later and figure things out after he finished work.

Holly pulled into the mammoth parking lot at Neumann's, the mile-long Christmas store—her place of employment before Heart Turn where she'd clocked umpteen hours hand-painting custom ornaments during the holiday season. When she passed Station 8, where she had spent most of her time, her previous co-worker and good friend, Andy, waved as she rushed past. Holly mouthed to him, "Betty Jo awaits!"

"Go get 'em Holly-girl." He offered a head nod and bearded grin.

The tantalizing aromas of freshly baked German pretzels,

steaming sauerkraut, and almond stollen flooded Holly's senses as she neared Stocking Stuffers' Eatery. The hubbub of the café located inside Neumann's was a mix of lively conversation, a peppy version of "Sleigh Ride" and an announcement over the loudspeaker, "Leslie, please report to Section 16 for a Code Icicle." Holly smirked, knowing that no-nonsense Leslie from customer service would not be happy with this announcement. A Code Icicle usually meant that a glass ornament or two or twenty had broken and needed to be cleaned up in order to keep everybody safe. Usually the culprits were adorable toddlers who ignored their parents' warnings not to touch the sparkly glass ornaments within reach.

Holly spotted Ms. Betty Jo Wilson, the store manager, nestled in a booth. She was enjoying what looked like the café's frozen cocoa, complete with whipped cream and a cherry on top.

"Holly No-el! Yoo-hoo, over here!" Betty Jo took a quick sip of her sweet treat before standing to envelop Holly.

"Hi there, good to see you too," Holly said.

Betty Jo rocked her side to side in a grandmotherly embrace.

After they situated themselves in the booth, Holly noticed remains of whipped cream clinging to Betty Jo's upper lip as she grinned widely. Holly wished Andy was there to witness her fluffy white mustache. They always thought Betty Jo would make the perfect Mrs. Claus—although at present she could give Santa a run for his money with her jolly enthusiasm and edible facial hair.

"Do tell, Holly dear. How is your man?" Betty Jo offered her infamous snort laugh. "He sure is dreamy, isn't he?"

Holly nodded. "My mom once pointed out, rather awkwardly, that he's not hard on the eyes. And I can't argue with her assessment."

"Oh, but he's so much more than his good looks. The way he cares for others is equally attractive. He's thoughtful and a hard worker to boot. And the way he looks at you. My oh my, that one is a keeper."

"You've got that right. Although, I'm starting to think his job might never sign off on his long-overdue vacation days. We were supposed to see each other in a few weeks, but HR isn't cooperating."

"That is tough to be so far away."

Betty Jo's offering of comfort carried weight, hemmed with a tinge of regret, based on a past confession during last year's staff Christmas party.

"I hope you get to see each other soon." Betty Jo patted Holly's hand across the tabletop, her creamy skin contrasting Holly's sun-kissed tan.

"Me too." Holly lifted her gaze from her hands to the manager's kind eyes.

"In situations like this, my mother often quoted Friedrich Heinrich Wilhelm Körte," Betty Jo said.

"That's a mouthful. Reminds me of a children's book my mom used to read to us. The child's name had more letters than I could count. Hey, speaking of, remember that crazy custom ornament order Andy received when I worked here?"

"Which one?" Betty Jo chortled.

"That long one. I'll never forget it. The customer wanted 'Matilda Jenaye Gertrude Perry-Harrison' hand-painted on an ornament for her goddaughter."

"Oh my, now that's ambitious." Betty Jo raised her penciled-in eyebrows. "Now, as I was saying, my *Mutter*, in her thick German accent, would point her finger right down her nose in my direction, look me square in the eyes—usually because I was getting lazy with practicing my violin or trying to avoid washing the dishes after supper—and she would say, '*Anfangen ist leicht, beharren eine Kunst.*' Basically it shut me right up. How could I argue with that?" Betty Jo snorted again.

"It's embarrassing to admit, but my German is not exactly top-notch. What was she saying…in English, please?"

Betty Jo winked, pointing her finger down her nose and looking deep into Holly's brown eyes. "To begin is easy, to persist is an art."

Holly let the profound statement sink in. As an artist, she knew this to be true. During her schooling, at work, and even in her spare time, she did not rush her art. It required dedication, along with confronting the voice in her head that called her an imposter and tempted her to call it quits *about every twenty-eight days.*

"Wow, I don't think I'll be forgetting that any time soon."

"Holly, you and Nik go together like peanut butter and jelly."

"We're not that boring and predictable, are we?"

"You're right, I stand corrected. You two are more like corn beef and sauerkraut. You make sense. But it seems you're at the stage and circumstance in your relationship where you need to fight for one another instead of fighting each other. *Persist*, Holly dear."

"How'd you get to be so smart?"

Betty Jo presented her German mother's scowl and finger pointing again as she answered, "*Mutter* knows best!"

"Nik and I are committed to this long-distance relationship, but it certainly is no picnic. It'd sure be nice if we were together, having a romantic picnic in the park, sitting by the river on a gingham blanket with a wicker basket full of Spundekäs cheese, soft pretzels, and juicy strawberries from the Farmer's Market, paired with a glass of Riesling. We could watch the riverboat go by, or maybe hit up Klingemann's Tavern for karaoke, or even splurge and go for a sunset carriage ride through historic downtown."

"Now, that does sound nice and it's making my belly rumble. What'll it be, Holly? Get whatever your heart desires—my treat."

Holly enjoyed the casual conversation over fruit salad and Schnitzel. Nearing the end of the meal, Betty Jo's demeanor changed slightly as she leaned in and lowered her melodic voice half an octave.

"I probably shouldn't disclose it here," her eyes darted to and fro as if searching for a lurker nearby, "but I want to run something by you. It's only an idea, but I can't shake it, and I fondly recall how you, Frank, and I helped Andy make an important decision around one of these tables awhile back, so it feels right."

Betty Jo took a deep breath, puffing out her well-endowed chest as if revving up to blow out sixty-ish candles on an invisible birthday cake."

"What is it, Betty Jo? You can trust me."

"To the grave, right? You won't utter a word of this to anyone? Except Nik, of course, as long as he doesn't spill the beans from across the country."

Holly shook her head. "He wouldn't."

"I'm, oh, it feels so bold to even whisper this, but I'm thinking of…retiring from Neumann's." Betty Jo released her breath with force.

Holly's eyes widened. Although Betty Jo wasn't getting any younger, she was as much a part of Neumann's as Baby Jesus #1, the life-sized ceramic figurine right outside the entrance that held the key to unlock the storehouse. Both were iconic centerpieces that represented the values the mile-long Christmas store held dear. Both had put in decades upon decades of faithful service to the millions of customers that visited Neumann's each year.

"Really? Is everything okay? Is Frank driving you crazy?" Holly asked.

"Oh no, I'm fine, really. And don't worry, Frank has nothing to do with it. You know, I think Nik is wonderful and all, but when you first started working here, I would have placed my bets on you and Frank. Of course, I'm not the gambling type. He was quite smitten with you though. Imagine you ending up with the boss's grandson. You might still be working here if that was the case." Betty Jo snorted again.

"I see what you're up to. You're trying to divert my attention away from the zinger you just dropped. Please tell me, what brought on this thought process of..." Holly leaned in and whispered the final word, "retirement?"

"It may sound silly, but I'm confiding in you because, truth be told, you inspire me, like when you didn't give up on your dreams when everything went belly up with your community art space in the city. I know it wasn't easy for you to regroup and move back home, but you stuck it out and started Heart Turn—which would have never happened had everything gone according to plan. It's like you made frothy frozen cocoa out of that which was bittersweet and out of season. Speaking of..."

On cue, Betty Jo sucked the last drop out of her fountain glass, making a loud slurping noise. She grabbed her napkin to dab her lips. *No more mustache.*

"As I was saying, even though I adore this place, I don't want to kick the bucket before I check a very important item off of my bucket list. I've stayed put and comfy for most of my adult life, even missed out on a chance for love because of it, but the time has come to stop procrastinating and take the plunge."

"The suspense is killing me. Where are you plunging?" Holly hit the table.

Before her former manager could respond, a familiar voice interrupted the pair. "Never fear, Frank is here! I got you, Betty Jo. I'll handle the plunging while you finish lunch with my favorite Holly."

The voice belonged to the boss's quirky grandson.

"Not that kind of plunging." Holly clarified, eyeing Betty Jo, who was now the shade of Rudolph's nose. Her coloring was less likely a result of the misunderstanding about plunging toilets and more likely because the boss's grandson might have overheard the news about her possible retirement—assuming he didn't already know, which was a reasonable deduction, given Betty Jo's blotchy neck and the way she was fidgeting with her brass name tag.

"So, you're saying my ninja-plunging skills are not actually needed?" Frank demonstrated a karate chop move.

"Ding, ding," Holly said.

"Carry on then, ladies. I'll take my five-star services elsewhere." He aimed a playful finger gun at Holly and tipped an imaginary hat to Betty Jo upon his exit.

Classic Frank: over-the-top, thoughtful, and moderately obnoxious.

"That was close! What do you think, Holly? Could this place get along without me?"

"It definitely wouldn't be the same. I'm happy you want to try something new, though. And what is this new thing exactly?"

"It's not set in stone. I'm still waiting to see if a spot opens up, but I applied to attend the top-rated Kris Kringle Academy. Their next class is in July, naturally, you know, Christmas in July and all. But you may be looking at the new Mrs. Claus of Bavarian Falls!"

"That's fantastic. You're made for that role." Holly couldn't wait for Andy to discover that their hopes and dreams for Betty Jo were coming true.

"You think so? My grand plan was to get trained as the best Mrs. C I can be and then approach Mr. Neumann to see if I can use my training right here in the store—come the day after Thanksgiving, of course. That way I'm not totally leaving this smorgasbord of Christmas cheer, only spreading my wings a bit."

"I think it's perfect. When should you hear?"

"Any day now. And don't you worry, Holly dear, you will be the first to know."

After her eventful lunch with Betty Jo, Holly finished her shift at Heart Turn and met her best friend, Elaine, at the park on Main.

They tried to fit in exercise a few times a week when the summer tourists were inside enjoying the local cuisine from Edelweiss Inn or Engel Haus. The friends circled the historic park as they caught up on what had transpired since their last walk.

Holly recounted her and Nik's tense phone call from earlier.

"Girl, you've got to figure things out. You and Nik are made for each other. So whatcha gonna do to smooth things over?" Elaine adjusted her crimpy ponytail on the top of her head.

"Smooth things over? He's the one who seems too busy for me. Oh brother, do I sound like a possessive girlfriend? That's the worst."

"I cannot confirm or deny your claim." Elaine shrugged.

"I'm so determined to prove others wrong, that long-distance relationships can work. But right now, it stinks. I think I'm whining. Gosh, I like Nik so much and was looking forward to face-to-face time."

"Ha! I think you mean mouth to mouth." Elaine laughed.

"That too." Holly's face warmed.

"What's the game plan, boss? You're creative…paint an alternative."

"If you say the word *pivot* next, I'm going to scream. What once was a beautiful word has been hijacked."

"I can't argue with that, Brigham. But seriously, what now?"

They rounded the corner and passed the stately fountain filled with coins from secret wishes tossed into the crystal-clear water.

"I'm not sure. Any ideas? You watch so many of those rom-com movies all year round. Surely, there's an idea about how to fix this in one of those shows?"

"You've got a point. Hmm, let me see. What about stealing an idea from *Lottie Wins the Lottery*? You buy a five-dollar lottery ticket, win the jackpot, and use your earnings to relocate Nik's entire office building to Bavarian Falls?"

"That's what they did? The heroine moved her man's place of business to her hometown, so they didn't have to live and work apart?"

"No, that's not exactly what happened. But it could work."

"Elaine, I'm losing faith in your abilities."

"Wait, I've got it! In *A Fixin' Kind of Love*, the main character, Everleigh Rae, and her high school boyfriend, Cash, have a shotgun wedding, followed by a set of twins and a handful of a third child in rapid succession. Between working two jobs to keep them afloat and taking care of a fixer-upper farmhouse they inherited, they have to grow up fast. Everleigh and Cash are like ships passing in the night as they attempt to manage it all. When their kids are finally grown and they've survived bankruptcy, they finally finish the farmhouse, transforming it into a B & B. But they realize they don't really know each other anymore. They have operated in survival mode for so long they haven't stayed emotionally connected through the crazy of it all."

"Wait, what are you saying? That Nik and I are drifting apart?"

"Hold on. I was getting to the good part. Cash and Everleigh are on the brink of divorce until their elderly neighbor, Ms. Ida Devine, gives them an idea about how to reconnect. When she was a young bride, her husband was drafted for war. They wrote letters to one another to stay connected, taking turns asking questions and responding back with the answers. Then Ms. Ida wrote out, in near-perfect cursive, the same twenty questions that she and her now deceased husband asked one another. She cut them into thin strips, dropped them into a decorated Mason jar, and presented it to the struggling owners of the B & B. She added a label to the jar that read, 'Twenty Questions IOU'. She instructed Cash and Everleigh Rae to pull out a few questions a week and take turns answering them. After a few months, the couple connected emotionally and physically because surprise—they had a bonus baby on the way and rediscovered why they fell in love in the first place."

"What in the world, Elaine?"

"I realize it's farfetched, but ya have to admit it's endearing, right?"

"No, not that—I mean, yes, far-fetched, aren't they all? But it makes no sense."

"What doesn't? Cash and Everleigh Rae and their restored home as the backdrop for their restored love? It's priceless."

"No, no, that's fine. I'm talking about what Ida put on the mason jar, 'Twenty Questions IOU?' That doesn't make sense."

Elaine offered a friendly wave to a passerby.

After the Midwest pleasantries were taken care of, Holly said, "Let me guess, IOU was an acronym for Interesting, Outlandish, and Unique, as in, don't offer any boring answers to my questions, Cash, because we need to spice things up before our love grows cold and our money runs out?"

Elaine remained silent as Holly's agitation grew. She was convinced one of Elaine's hobbies was withholding information so that Holly looked the fool as she tried to figure things out.

"You don't pay somebody back with a question, you pay them back with a good old-fashioned answer. So why did Ms. Ida call the whole questions game 'Twenty Questions IOU?' Give me an answer or else doesn't sound romantic. That's all I'm saying. If I'm going to buy into this, I need more info, pronto."

Elaine chuckled. "What you're saying is I owe you an answer?"

Holly rolled her eyes. "You don't owe me a question, that's for sure."

"IOU stands for an Investment Opportunity in Us. Twenty Questions to deposit wealth into the relationship. That's what it was all about," Elaine said, a tad smugly.

"Why didn't you say so in the first place?"

The two friends rounded their third lap around the park.

"You know, that's actually really beautiful," Holly said, her steady, reflective voice in stark contrast to her frantic interrogation a few moments prior.

"Isn't it? It's not an 'I have to,' like I owe you this. It's an opportunity. It's an 'I get to,' because I believe what we have is worth investing in."

Holly was surprised by her friend's profound observation. "That's one of the most romantic things you've ever said."

"I guess the rom-com marathons are paying off."

"Apparently."

"I need a pit stop before the next lap." Elaine entered the Bavarian-themed bathroom facilities.

Holly drew near the fountain. The copper and silver coins reflected through the water as they caught the floodlights and appeared to dance. She dipped her sweaty palm into the cool, aquamarine water and delicately traced an invisible figure eight under the surface. Like a watercolorist softening the saturation of paint before putting brush to paper, a thought crystalized in her mind. "If you want the interest to keep growing, continue to feed the investment."

Holly smiled, equal parts surprised and satisfied by the fountain-side revelation. "Thank you," she whispered as she plunged her hand deeper to retrieve one of the coins.

"I know money is tight, but really, Holly? Stealing from the fountain?" Elaine had returned.

"No one will miss it. Besides, it's going to help me remember something." Holly slipped the coin into her pocket.

"Hey, while I was in the bathroom, I remembered another thing about *A Fixin' Kind of Love*. But, shoot, I forgot again."

They left the fountain area and headed around the park loop for their final lap.

"How on earth you recalled all those details from the movie in the first place is beyond me. Don't they all run together? I usually fall asleep after the first fifteen minutes when you force me to watch them. I do think you might be onto something, though."

"You're going to open a B & B?"

"Ha, no. But I think the twenty questions thing might help.

I mean, it won't help Nik get here faster, but I think it might help us feel closer than five states away."

"See, my marathon movie watching isn't all bad," Elaine teased. "Now, let's try to find it on-demand, so we can write down those questions."

"Would you look at the time?" Holly said. "How about you do that. Then text me your findings and I'll type them up—maybe even add a fun illustration to them and give it a shot."

"Oh no, you're twisting my arm. I *have* to go do something I enjoy," mocked Elaine.

"Thanks for being a good sport and for putting up with me."

"No prob, friend. You and Nik are worth it."

"What about you? Anything to declare in the guy department?"

"Hmm, not sure how to answer that." Conveniently, Elaine's watch beeped several times. "Gotta go!"

"Where are you headed?" asked Holly, wanting Elaine to 'spill the tea' about any romantic developments that might be percolating beneath the surface of her easy-going exterior.

"Frank and I are going to shoot hoops at the community center tonight." She checked her watch.

"Oh, really?" Holly's voice lifted as she raised her eyebrows.

"Brigham, don't push it. Hey, I remembered what the first question was that Everleigh drew out of Ida's jar.

"Oh yeah, what was it?"

"What's your next move?"

"Next move? I've finally come to terms with living here in Bavarian Falls for a bit, not planning to move anytime soon, thank you very much."

"No, I'm not asking you. I'm telling you that was the question, 'What's your next move?'"

"That's a weird one. What did it mean? Did Cash and Everleigh play chess as a hobby?"

"I think it was meant to help them get on the same page. Like, where are you headed so I can decide if it's where I want to go too?"

"Sounds risky," Holly blew her bangs off her forehead. "What if they weren't headed in the same direction?"

"Love is risky, my friend. Now, it's been real, but I'm going to be late for the pick-up game if I don't leave soon." Elaine bent down to tighten her shoelace.

"Your next move is on the b-ball court?"

"You could say that. And you?"

"I'm going to wait to see if Nik calls back. Hopefully, he'll be game for the Twenty Questions thing you suggested—I mean, it's worth a shot, right? Hopefully, it won't seem too cheesy, or annoy him, or, worse, drive him away."

"If he gets any farther away, he'll land in the Pacific."

As Elaine jogged from view, Holly prayed that Nik's next move would be an airline ticket to Bavarian Falls.

Book Club Questions for
A Very Bavarian Christmas

1. Have you ever worked at a job you didn't like? Was there a silver lining in working there?

2. Kühn means "bold" or "brave" in German. When were you brave recently?

3. When you are around someone like Lena, how do you avoid falling into the comparison trap?

4. Have you or a loved one experienced a health crisis or disability? How has that impacted you?

5. Is there a part of your heart that you are holding back from God? Why do you think that is?

6. What words of comfort would you offer young Holly after her dad's angry words?

7. What is a challenging situation you've had to face from your past? What or who helped you overcome it? Did you learn anything?

8. What is an activity or tradition that you're definitely saying yes to this holiday season?

9. Holly is no longer counting the pain of the past but focusing on

the joys of the present. What are some joys in your life right now? How have you dealt with pain from your past and what helped you the most in overcoming that pain?

10. Do you like to be in the know and have all the information ahead of time or do you tend to go with the flow and take life as it comes? Do you feel there's a right or wrong way to deal with those situations?

11. What might a "yes life" look like in regards to your future, your faith, and your relationships?

Acknowledgments

Adam: Thanks for being my one and only, and for your help with "kiss research." I know it was quite a burden—ha! Thank you for being the kind of guy who holds the door open and also makes room for my dreams.

Brooke, Kale, Banner, Isaiah, and Lark: Thanks for waiting in line for hours at the Santa House. You are five of my favorite gifts from God. I love you more than you know.

Dad and Mom: Thank you for introducing me to the charming town of Leavenworth and for endless encouragement.

Brian: Thanks for modeling Chase's mannerisms and his heart of gold. I love yew.

Mary: *Vielen Dank* (many thanks!) for your willingness to proofread and for your German language insights.

Laura and Jake: Still laughing about our rom-com movie brainstorming sesh.

Jody and Hailey: Thank you for your listening ears, excitement, and feedback.

Austin: Your line made it into the book. ;-)

Martha: Grateful for the inspiration you provided to help Holly heal.

Riley: Thanks for telling your mama about your vision, "This is going to be big!"

Holly Noel: Where would this story be without you? Thanks for being my Christmas-loving friend. You're the real deal.

Dave Schroeder: Thank you for opening the door to more for Bavarian Falls and for your encouragement to keep writing rom coms.

Jenaye Merida: Honored to be represented by WTA Media.

You are a dynamic literary agent and a good sport with this out-of-the box "I have another idea" author.

Miralee and the Mountain Brook Ink Team: Overflowing with gratitude for your belief in this series and your willingness to make it shine. Sara: Thank you for elevating this story with your proofreading pixie dust.

Lisa: Thanks for believing in Bavaria big time. Thank you for the music.

Jillian: Thank you for bringing life to this story with your singing and speaking voice.

Christopher Eaton: A dream come true to co-write "Say Yes to Christmas" with you.

Harry Connick, Jr.: Grateful your music is part of this love story.

Chevonne & ACI: Thank you for acquiring the movie rights and for seeing this story's potential for the screen.

Jami, Melinda, Janyre, and Kate: Thank you for your investment of time and talent in this project in its initial form. Your fingerprints made it better.

Jen Bleakley: Forever grateful you introduced me to the Santas, their school, and the "hair and chair" line. Still laughing.

Jenn H. and Nicole H.: You live a yes life. Inspired by your examples.

Lee: Please tell me it's better than the Christmas chick flick we saw. :-)

Dawn: Grateful you recognized the bigger vision right away.

Prayer Team and Erin, Amber, Becky: Thanks for your support, cheers, and accountability.

Mike, Kate, and Frannie: Your faithful example sings within these pages.

Amy Durfee: Thanks for lending me your German skills. And, Dani, thanks for loving this book over and over.

Amber, Bethany, Crystal, Jenn, Kate, Lisa-Jo, Mary: Deepest thanks for your investment of time and your gracious endorsements.

Team Holly: Beyond grateful for your enthusiasm in spreading the word and making this season bright.

Jesus: Thank You for saying "yes" to Christmas and "yes" to the Cross. Thank You for this story and the songs. Thank You for EVERYTHING!